NANCY DREW

girl detective®

W9-CMA-018

PAPERCUTZ

NANCY DREW GRAPHIC NOVELS AVAILABLE FROM PAPERCUTZ

NEW STORY! FULL-COLOR GRAPHIC NOVEL
NANCY DREW
girl detective
#1
BASED ON THE SERIES BY CAROLYN KEENE
Stefan PETRUCHA • Vaughn ROSS
PAPERCUTZ

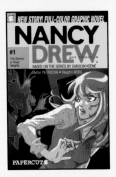

Graphic Novel #1
"The Demon of River Heights"

NEW STORY! FULL-COLOR GRAPHIC NOVEL
NANCY DREW
girl detective
#2
BASED ON THE SERIES BY CAROLYN KEENE
Stefan PETRUCHA
Sho MURASE
PAPERCUTZ

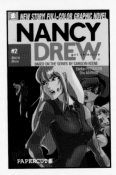

Graphic Novel #2
"Writ In Stone"

NEW STORY! FULL-COLOR GRAPHIC NOVEL
NANCY DREW
girl detective
#3
BASED ON THE SERIES BY CAROLYN KEENE
Stefan PETRUCHA
Sho MURASE
PAPERCUTZ

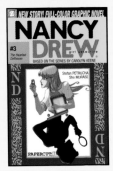

Graphic Novel #3
"The Haunted Dollhouse"

NEW STORY! FULL-COLOR GRAPHIC NOVEL
NANCY DREW
girl detective
#4
BASED ON THE SERIES BY CAROLYN KEENE
Stefan PETRUCHA • Sho MURASE
PAPERCUTZ

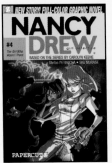

Graphic Novel #4
"The Girl Who Wasn't There"

NEW STORY! FULL-COLOR GRAPHIC NOVEL
NANCY DREW
girl detective
#5
BASED ON THE SERIES BY CAROLYN KEENE
Stefan PETRUCHA
Vaughn ROSS
PAPERCUTZ

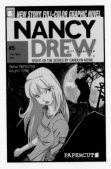

Graphic Novel #5
"The Fake Heir"

NEW STORY! FULL-COLOR GRAPHIC NOVEL
NANCY DREW
girl detective
#6
BASED ON THE SERIES BY CAROLYN KEENE
Stefan PETRUCHA
Sho MURASE
PAPERCUTZ

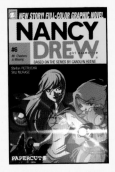

Graphic Novel #6
"Mr. Cheeters Is Missing"

NEW STORY! FULL-COLOR GRAPHIC NOVEL
NANCY DREW
girl detective
#7
BASED ON THE SERIES BY CAROLYN KEENE
Stefan PETRUCHA
Vaughn ROSS
PAPERCUTZ

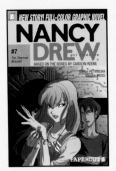

Graphic Novel #7
"The Charmed Bracelet"

NEW STORY! FULL-COLOR GRAPHIC NOVEL
NANCY DREW
girl detective
#8
BASED ON THE SERIES BY CAROLYN KEENE
Stefan PETRUCHA
Sho MURASE
PAPERCUTZ

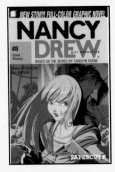

Graphic Novel #8
"Global Warning"

NEW STORY! FULL-COLOR GRAPHIC NOVEL
NANCY DREW
girl detective
#9
BASED ON THE SERIES BY CAROLYN KEENE
Stefan PETRUCHA
Sho MURASE
PAPERCUTZ

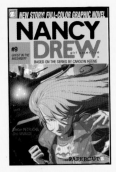

Coming in May
Graphic Novel #9
"Ghost In The Machinery"

$7.95 each in paperback, $12.95 each in hardcover. Please add $3.00 for postage and handling for the first book, add $1.00 for each additional book. Send to:

Papercutz, 40 Exchange Place, Suite 1308 New York, NY 10005 • www.papercutz.com

3 1526 03213671 2

NANCY DREW

#8 girl detective ®

Global Warning

STEFAN PETRUCHA • Writer

SHO MURASE • Artist

with 3D CG elements by CAROLOS JOSE GUZMAN

Based on the series by

CAROLYN KEENE

HARFORD COUNTY
PUBLIC LIBRARY
100 E. Pennsylvania Avenue
Bel Air, MD 21014

PAPERCUT**Z**

New York

Global Warning
STEFAN PETRUCHA – Writer
SHO MURASE – Artist
with 3D CG elements and color by CARLOS JOSE GUZMAN
BRYAN SENKA – Letterer
JIM SALICRUP
Editor-in-Chief

ISBN 10: 1-59707-051-3 paperback edition
ISBN 13: 978-1-59707-051-5 paperback edition
ISBN 10: 1-59707-052-1 hardcover edition
ISBN 13: 978-1-59707-052-2 hardcover edition

Copyright © 2006 by Simon & Schuster, Inc. Published by
arrangement with Aladdin Paperbacks, an imprint of
Simon & Schuster Children's Publishing Division.
Nancy Drew is a trademark of Simon & Schuster, Inc.
All rights reserved.

Printed in China.
Distributed by Holtzbrinck Publishers.

10 9 8 7 6 5 4 3 2 1

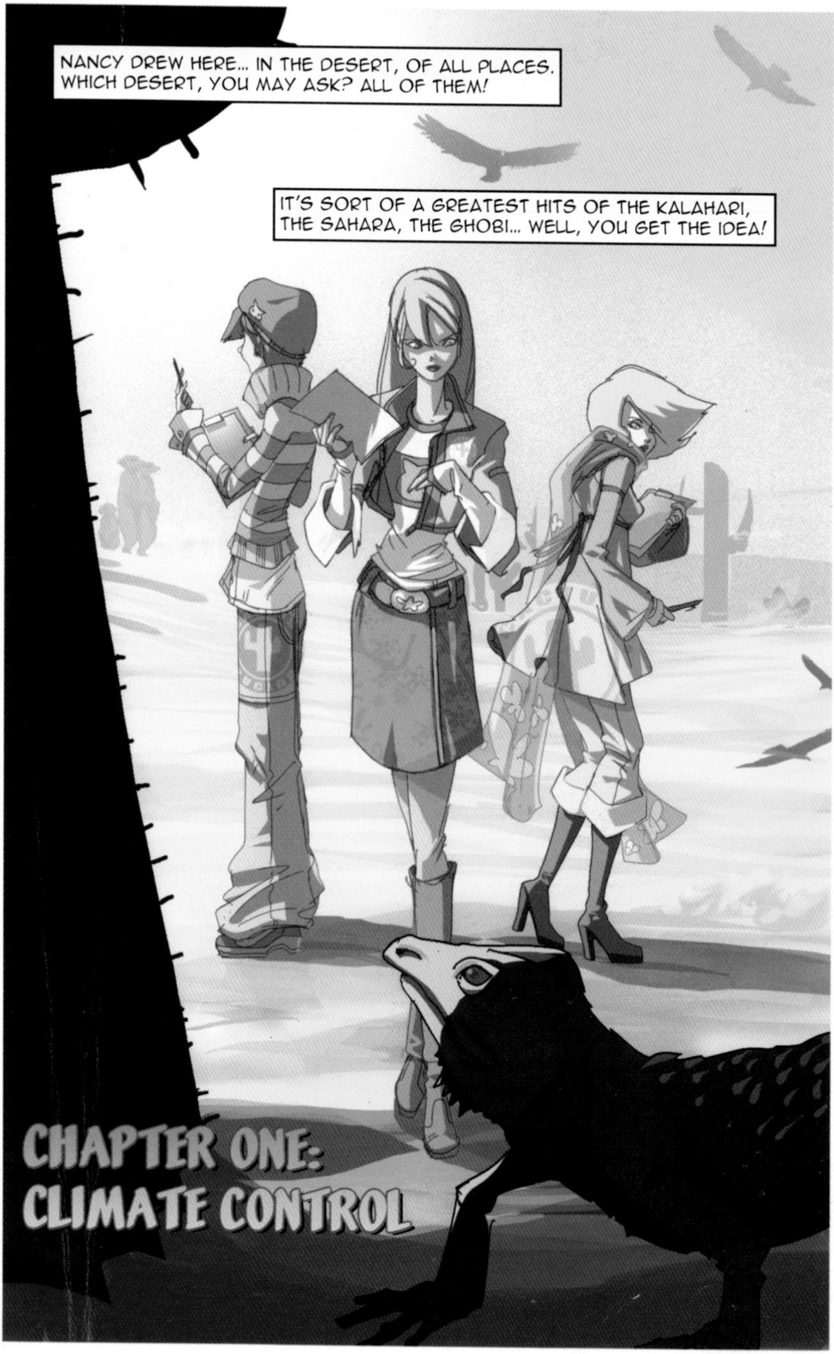
NANCY DREW HERE... IN THE DESERT, OF ALL PLACES. WHICH DESERT, YOU MAY ASK? ALL OF THEM!
IT'S SORT OF A GREATEST HITS OF THE KALAHARI, THE SAHARA, THE GHOBI... WELL, YOU GET THE IDEA!
CHAPTER ONE: CLIMATE CONTROL

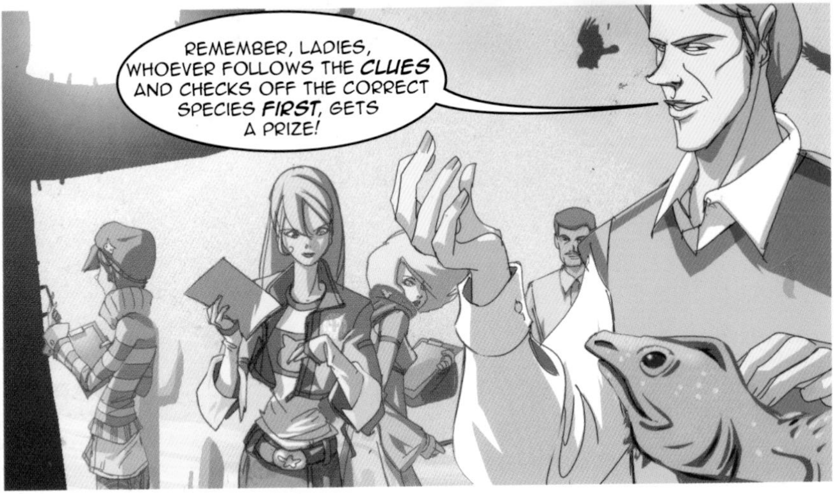
REMEMBER, LADIES, WHOEVER FOLLOWS THE CLUES AND CHECKS OFF THE CORRECT SPECIES FIRST, GETS A PRIZE!

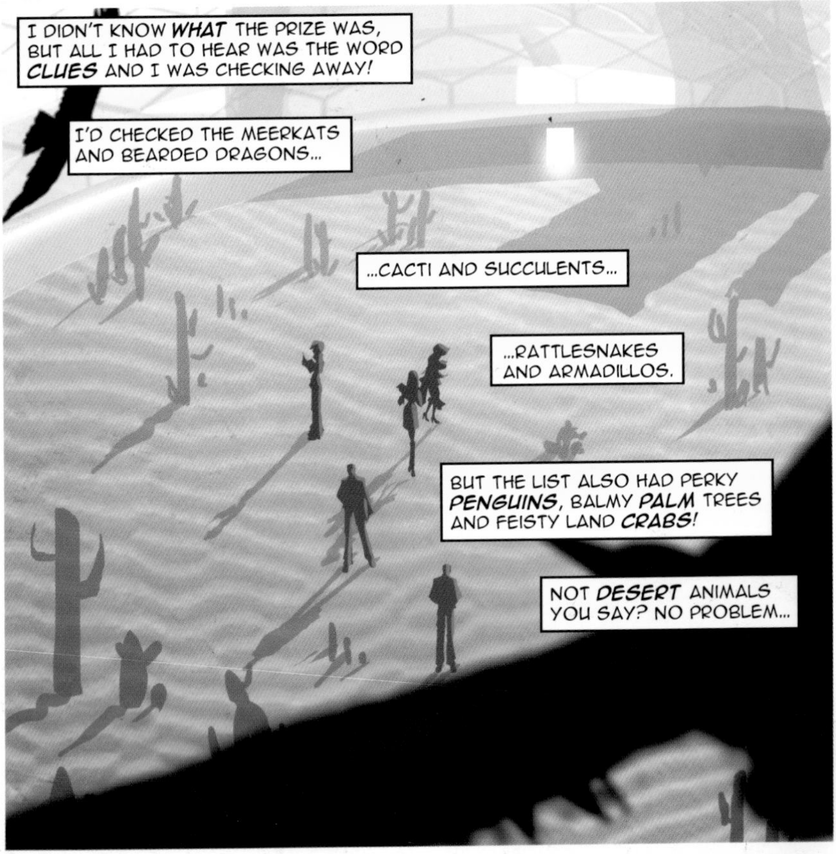
I DIDN'T KNOW WHAT THE PRIZE WAS, BUT ALL I HAD TO HEAR WAS THE WORD CLUES AND I WAS CHECKING AWAY!
I'D CHECKED THE MEERKATS AND BEARDED DRAGONS...
...CACTI AND SUCCULENTS...
...RATTLESNAKES AND ARMADILLOS.
BUT THE LIST ALSO HAD PERKY PENGUINS, BALMY PALM TREES AND FEISTY LAND CRABS!
NOT DESERT ANIMALS YOU SAY? NO PROBLEM...

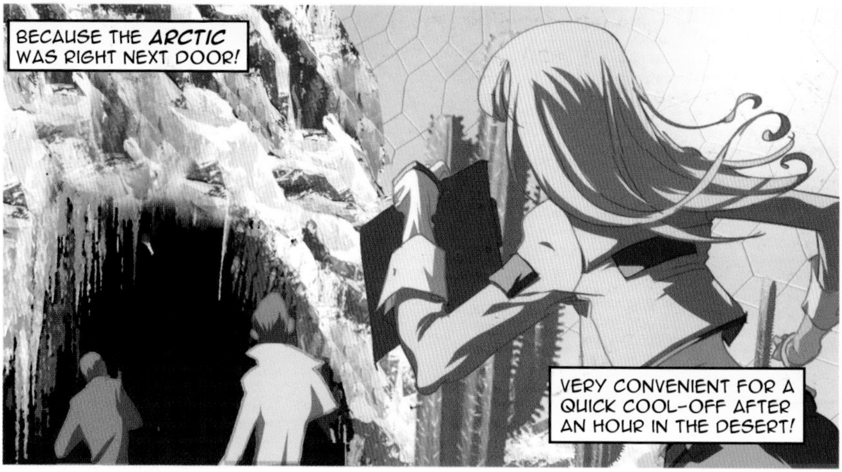
BECAUSE THE ARCTIC WAS RIGHT NEXT DOOR!
VERY CONVENIENT FOR A QUICK COOL-OFF AFTER AN HOUR IN THE DESERT!

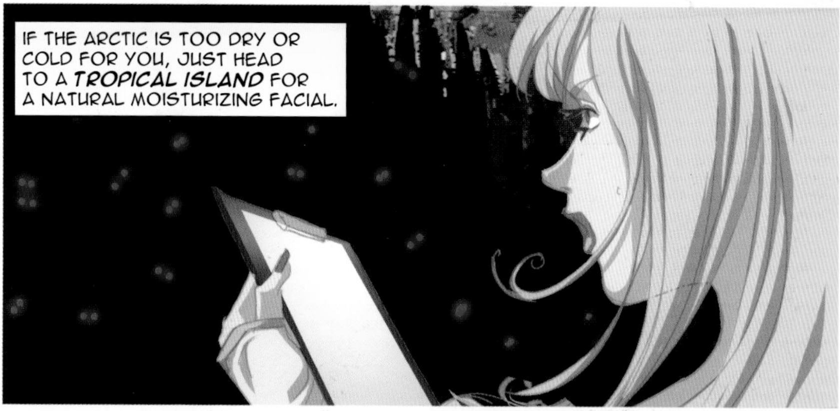
IF THE ARCTIC IS TOO DRY OR COLD FOR YOU, JUST HEAD TO A TROPICAL ISLAND FOR A NATURAL MOISTURIZING FACIAL.

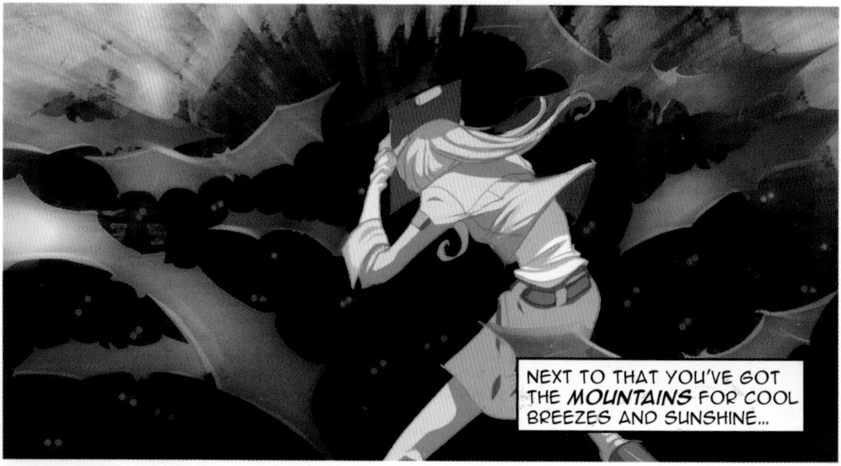
NEXT TO THAT YOU'VE GOT THE MOUNTAINS FOR COOL BREEZES AND SUNSHINE...

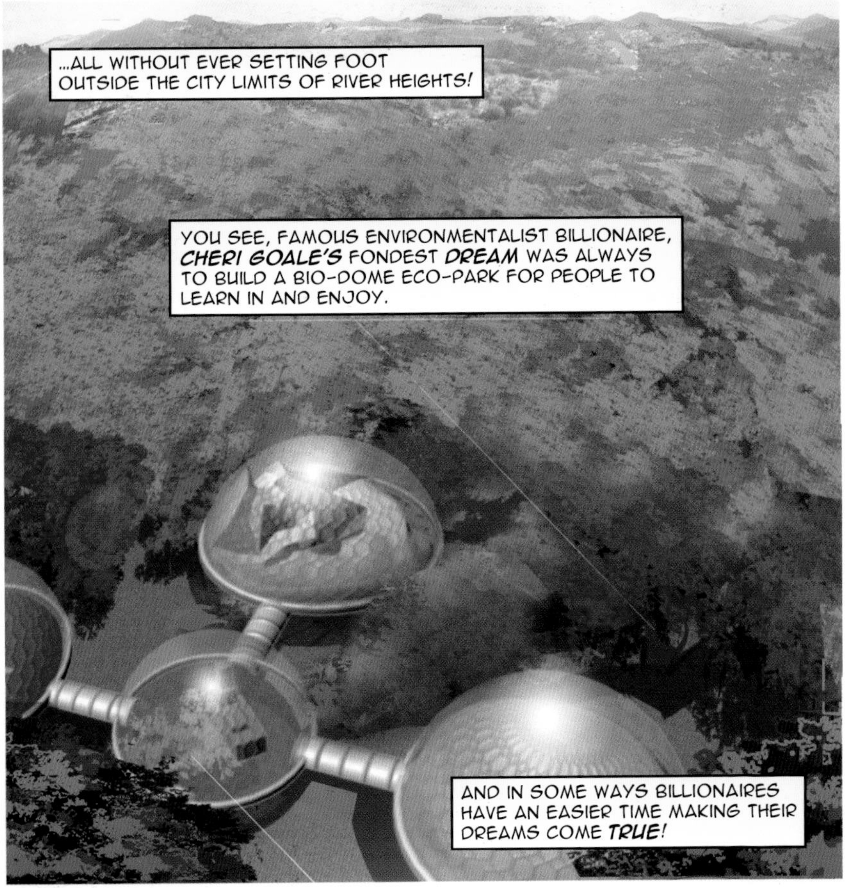
...ALL WITHOUT EVER SETTING FOOT OUTSIDE THE CITY LIMITS OF RIVER HEIGHTS!
YOU SEE, FAMOUS ENVIRONMENTALIST BILLIONAIRE, CHERI GOALE'S FONDEST DREAM WAS ALWAYS TO BUILD A BIO-DOME ECO-PARK FOR PEOPLE TO LEARN IN AND ENJOY.
AND IN SOME WAYS BILLIONAIRES HAVE AN EASIER TIME MAKING THEIR DREAMS COME TRUE!

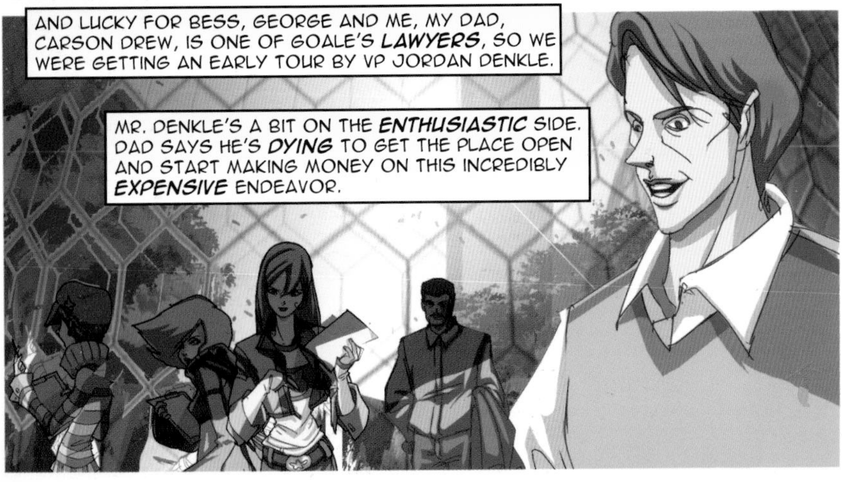
AND LUCKY FOR BESS, GEORGE AND ME, MY DAD, CARSON DREW, IS ONE OF GOALE'S LAWYERS, SO WE WERE GETTING AN EARLY TOUR BY VP JORDAN DENKLE.
MR. DENKLE'S A BIT ON THE ENTHUSIASTIC SIDE. DAD SAYS HE'S DYING TO GET THE PLACE OPEN AND START MAKING MONEY ON THIS INCREDIBLY EXPENSIVE ENDEAVOR.

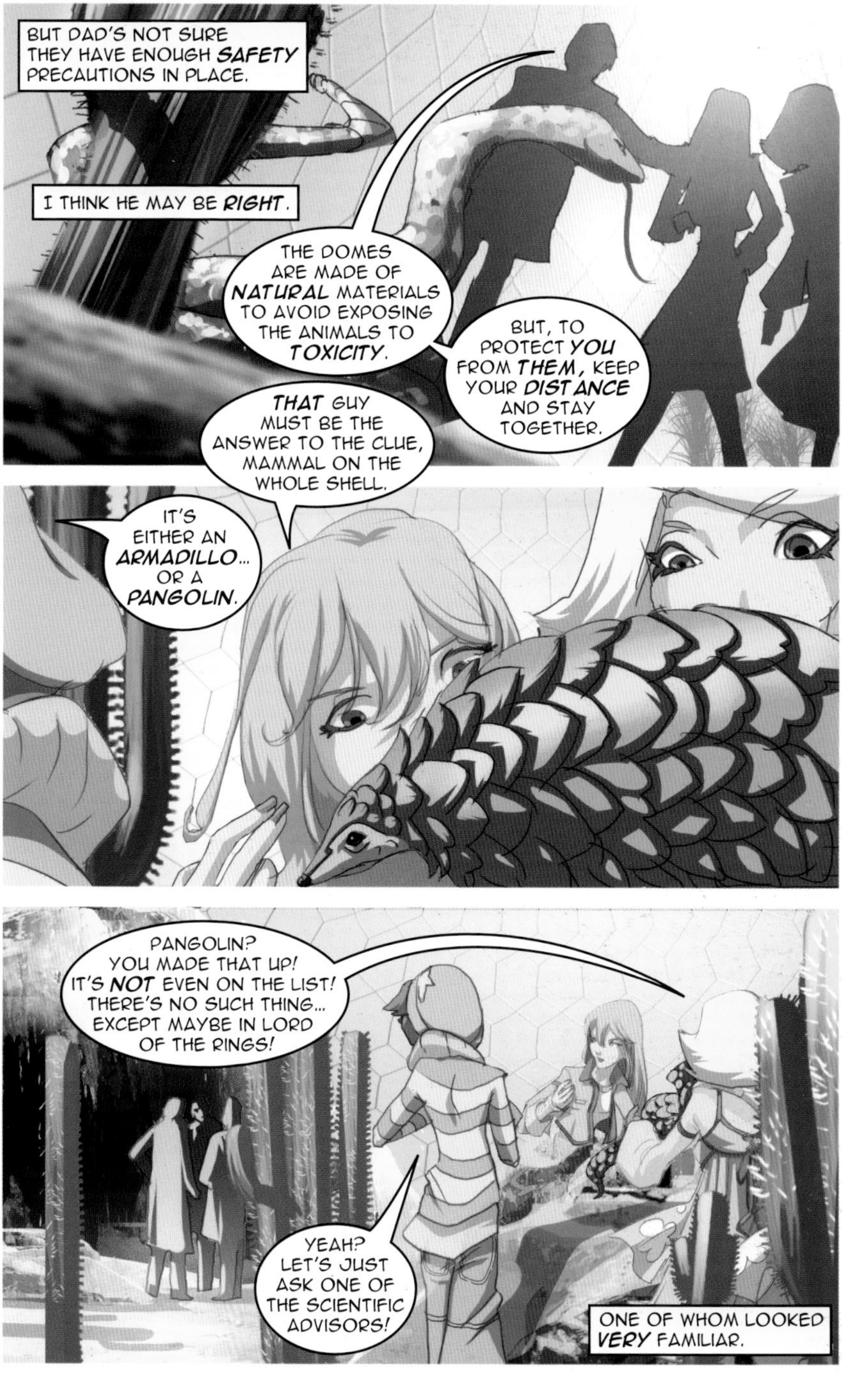
BUT DAD'S NOT SURE THEY HAVE ENOUGH SAFETY PRECAUTIONS IN PLACE.
I THINK HE MAY BE RIGHT.
THE DOMES ARE MADE OF NATURAL MATERIALS TO AVOID EXPOSING THE ANIMALS TO TOXICITY.
BUT, TO PROTECT YOU FROM THEM, KEEP YOUR DISTANCE AND STAY TOGETHER.
THAT GUY MUST BE THE ANSWER TO THE CLUE, MAMMAL ON THE WHOLE SHELL.
IT'S EITHER AN ARMADILLO... OR A PANGOLIN.
PANGOLIN? YOU MADE THAT UP! IT'S NOT EVEN ON THE LIST! THERE'S NO SUCH THING... EXCEPT MAYBE IN LORD OF THE RINGS!
YEAH? LET'S JUST ASK ONE OF THE SCIENTIFIC ADVISORS!
ONE OF WHOM LOOKED VERY FAMILIAR.

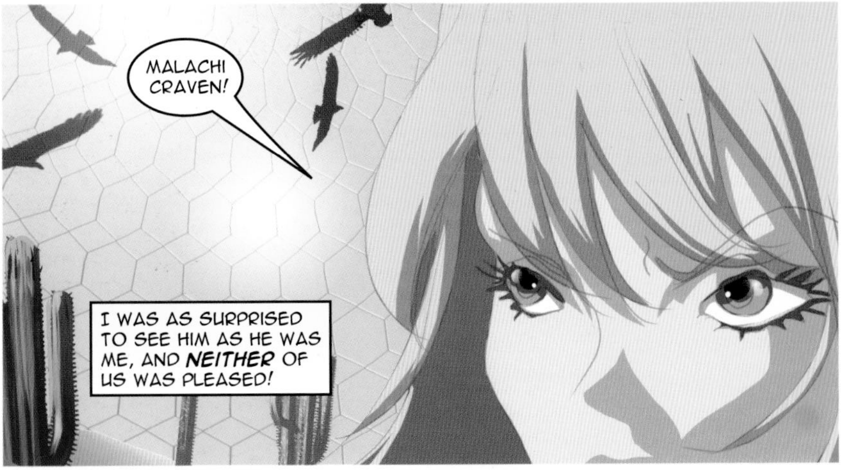
MALACHI CRAVEN!
I WAS AS SURPRISED TO SEE HIM AS HE WAS ME, AND NEITHER OF US WAS PLEASED!

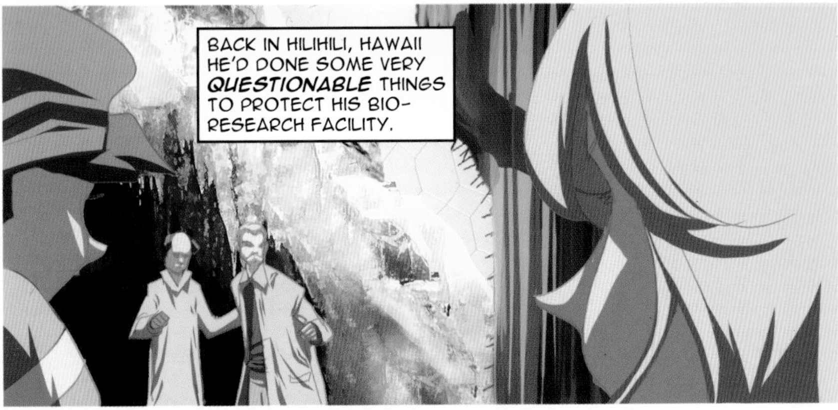
BACK IN HILIHILI, HAWAII HE'D DONE SOME VERY QUESTIONABLE THINGS TO PROTECT HIS BIO-RESEARCH FACILITY.

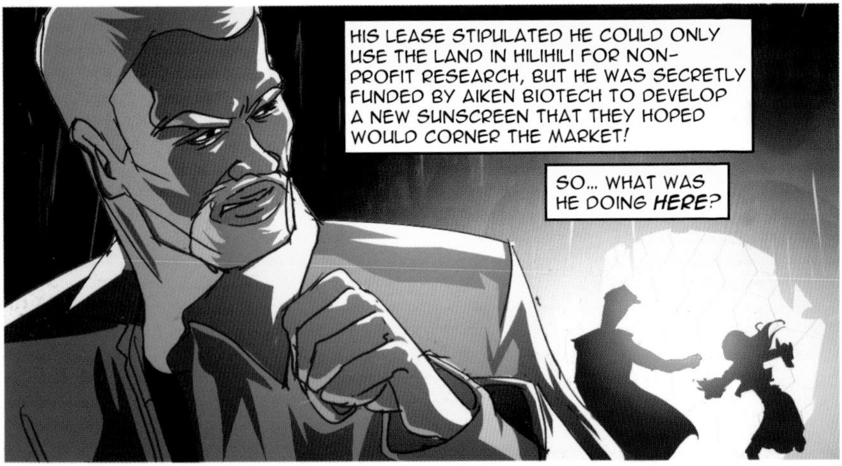
HIS LEASE STIPULATED HE COULD ONLY USE THE LAND IN HILIHILI FOR NON-PROFIT RESEARCH, BUT HE WAS SECRETLY FUNDED BY AIKEN BIOTECH TO DEVELOP A NEW SUNSCREEN THAT THEY HOPED WOULD CORNER THE MARKET!
SO... WHAT WAS HE DOING HERE?

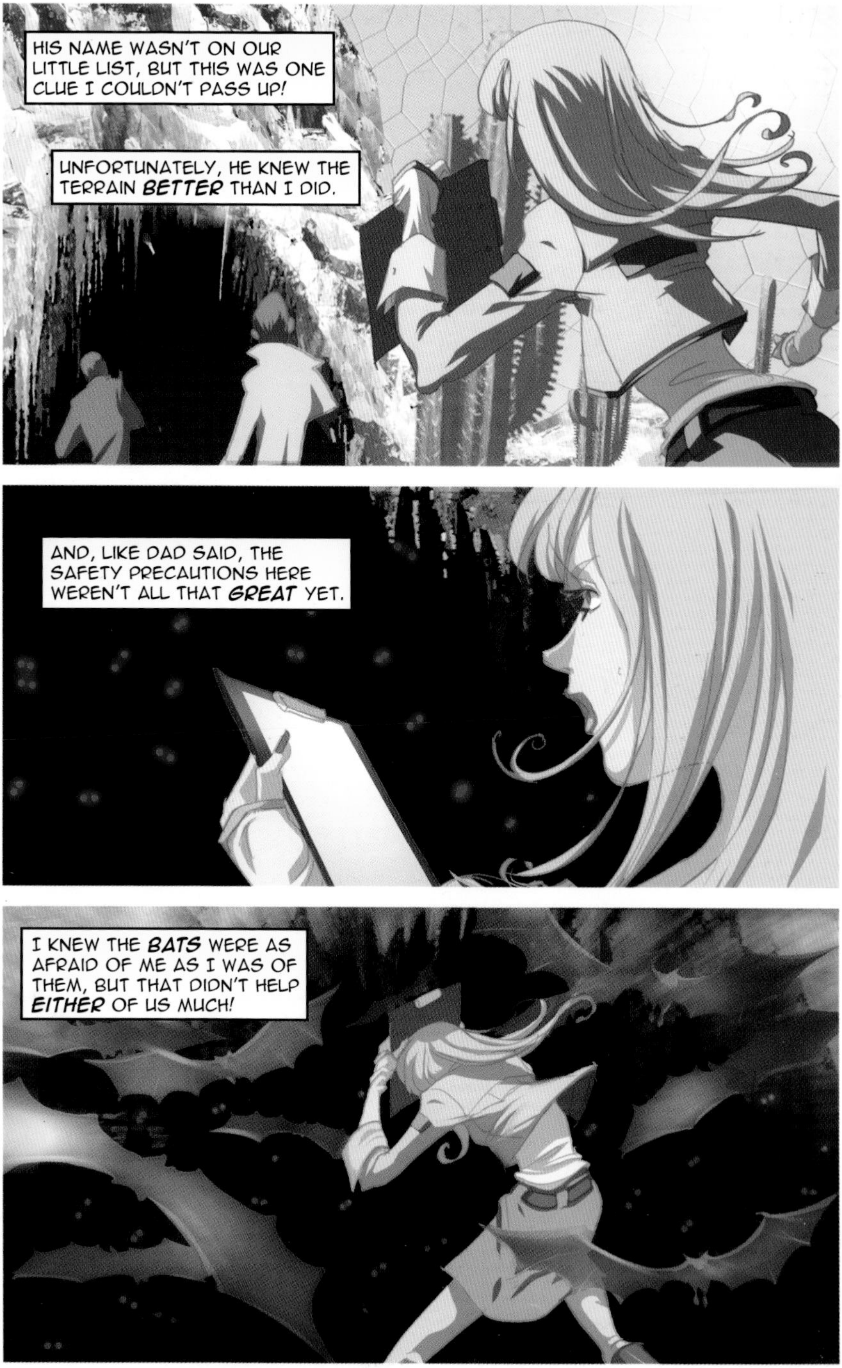
HIS NAME WASN'T ON OUR LITTLE LIST, BUT THIS WAS ONE CLUE I COULDN'T PASS UP!
UNFORTUNATELY, HE KNEW THE TERRAIN BETTER THAN I DID.
AND, LIKE DAD SAID, THE SAFETY PRECAUTIONS HERE WEREN'T ALL THAT GREAT YET.
I KNEW THE BATS WERE AS AFRAID OF ME AS I WAS OF THEM, BUT THAT DIDN'T HELP EITHER OF US MUCH!

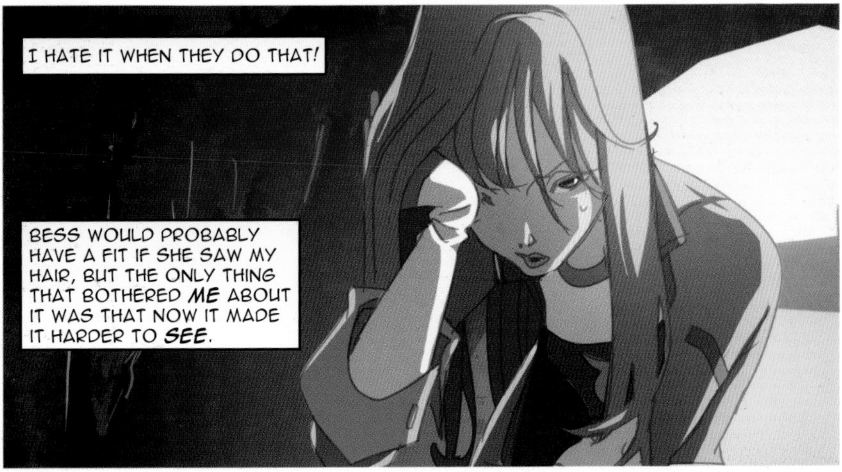
I HATE IT WHEN THEY DO THAT!
BESS WOULD PROBABLY HAVE A FIT IF SHE SAW MY HAIR, BUT THE ONLY THING THAT BOTHERED ME ABOUT IT WAS THAT NOW IT MADE IT HARDER TO SEE.

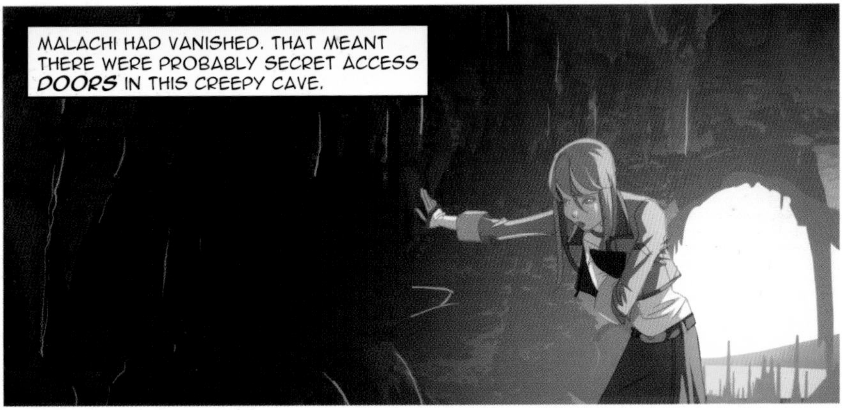
MALACHI HAD VANISHED. THAT MEANT THERE WERE PROBABLY SECRET ACCESS DOORS IN THIS CREEPY CAVE.

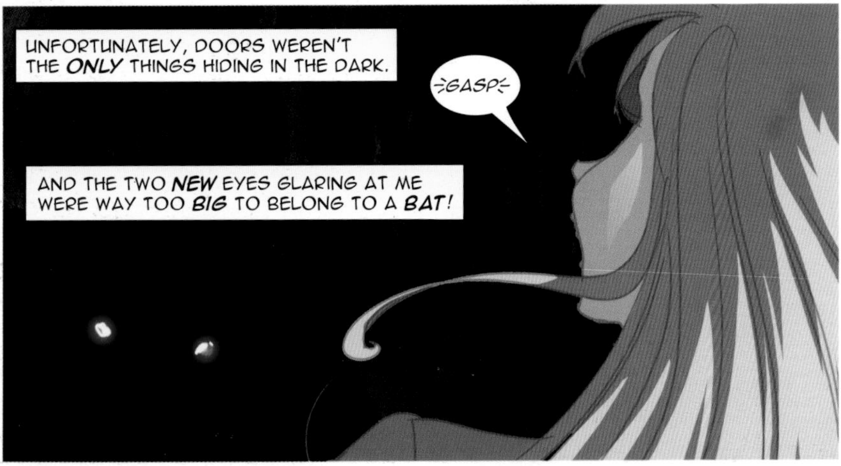
UNFORTUNATELY, DOORS WEREN'T THE ONLY THINGS HIDING IN THE DARK.
GASP
AND THE TWO NEW EYES GLARING AT ME WERE WAY TOO BIG TO BELONG TO A BAT!

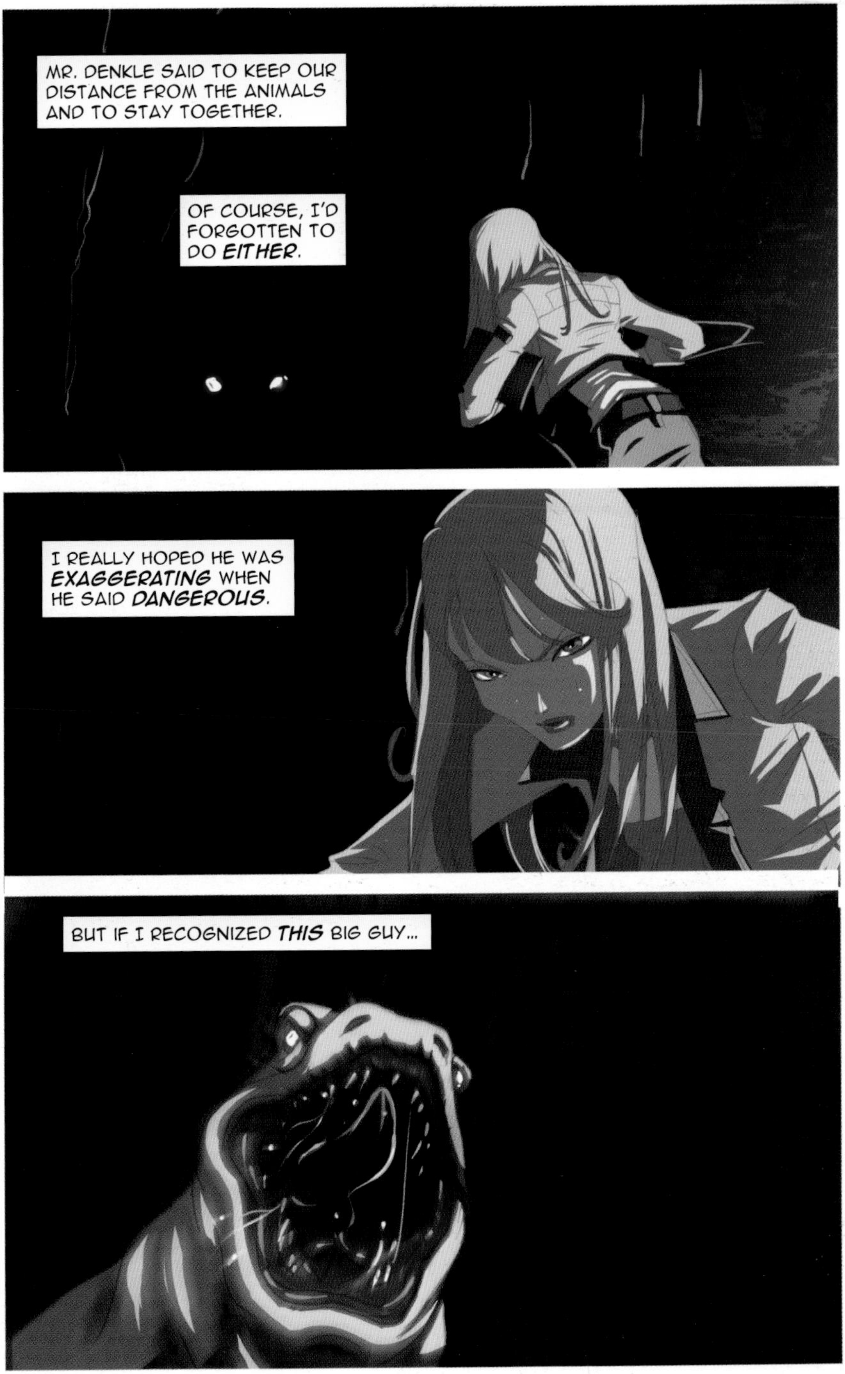
MR. DENKLE SAID TO KEEP OUR DISTANCE FROM THE ANIMALS AND TO STAY TOGETHER.
OF COURSE, I'D FORGOTTEN TO DO *EITHER*.
I REALLY HOPED HE WAS *EXAGGERATING* WHEN HE SAID *DANGEROUS*.
BUT IF I RECOGNIZED *THIS* BIG GUY...

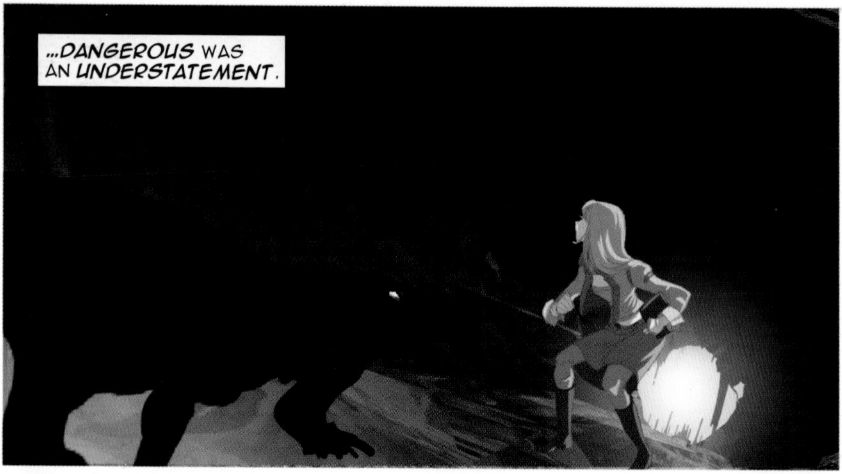
...DANGEROUS WAS AN UNDERSTATEMENT.

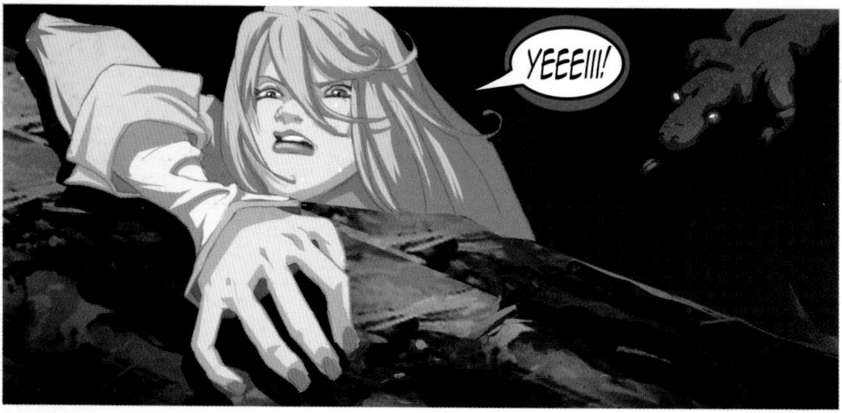
YEEEIII!

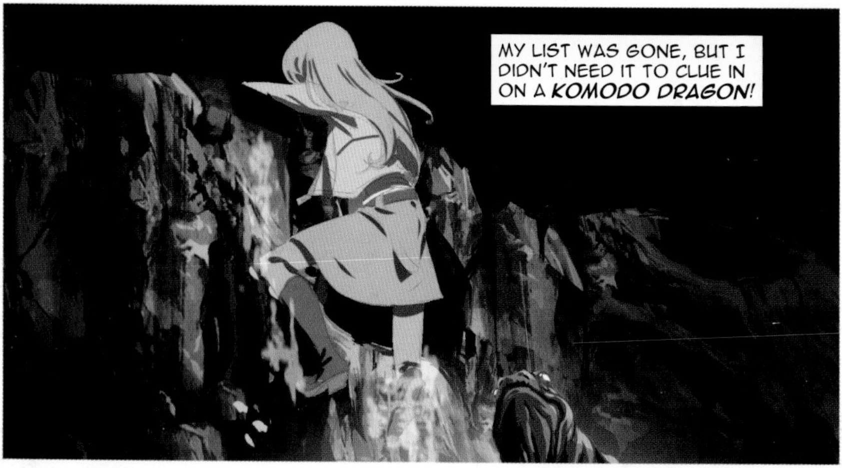
MY LIST WAS GONE, BUT I DIDN'T NEED IT TO CLUE IN ON A KOMODO DRAGON!

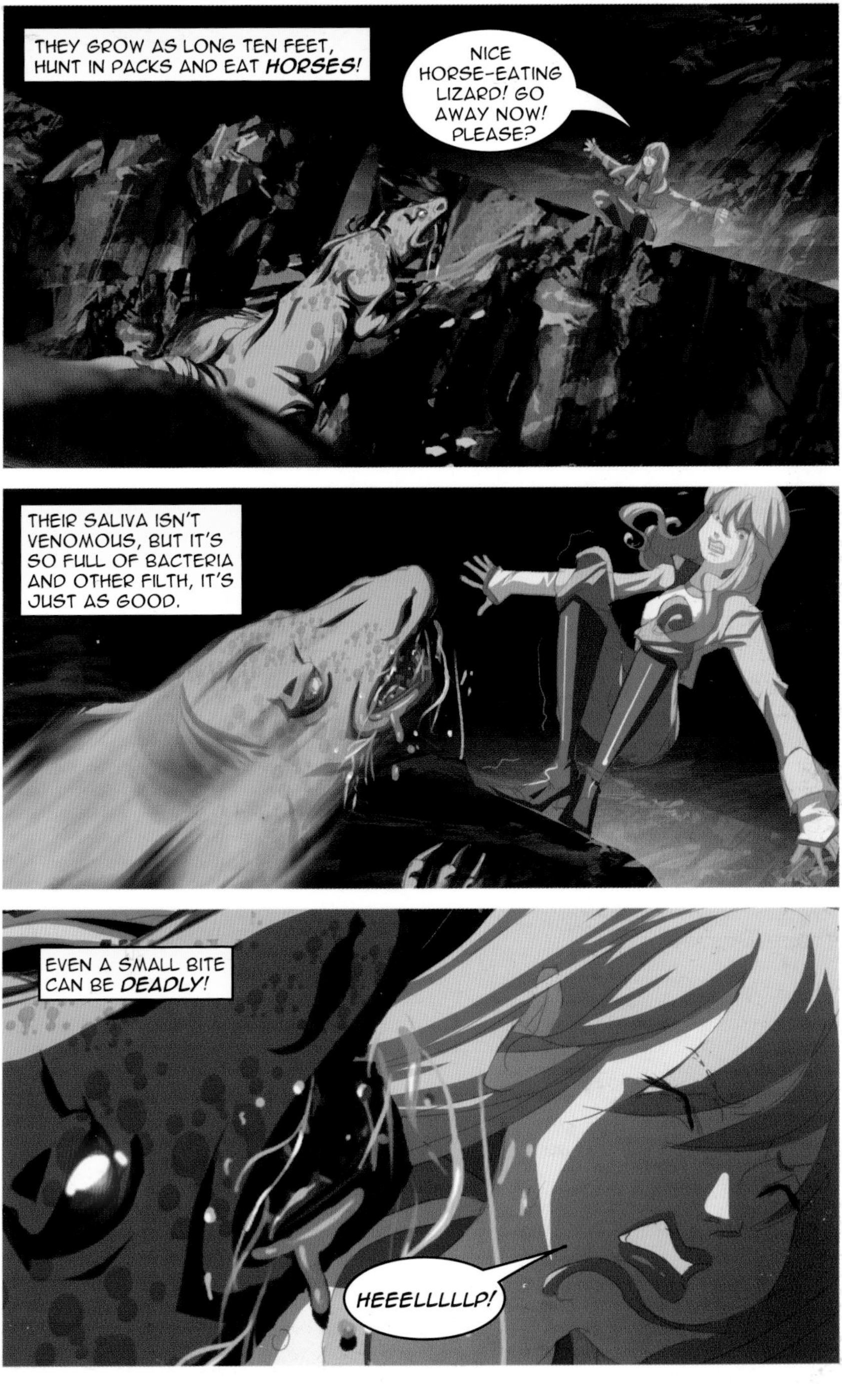
THEY GROW AS LONG TEN FEET, HUNT IN PACKS AND EAT *HORSES*!
NICE HORSE-EATING LIZARD! GO AWAY NOW! PLEASE?
THEIR SALIVA ISN'T VENOMOUS, BUT IT'S SO FULL OF BACTERIA AND OTHER FILTH, IT'S JUST AS GOOD.
EVEN A SMALL BITE CAN BE *DEADLY*!
HEEELLLLLP!

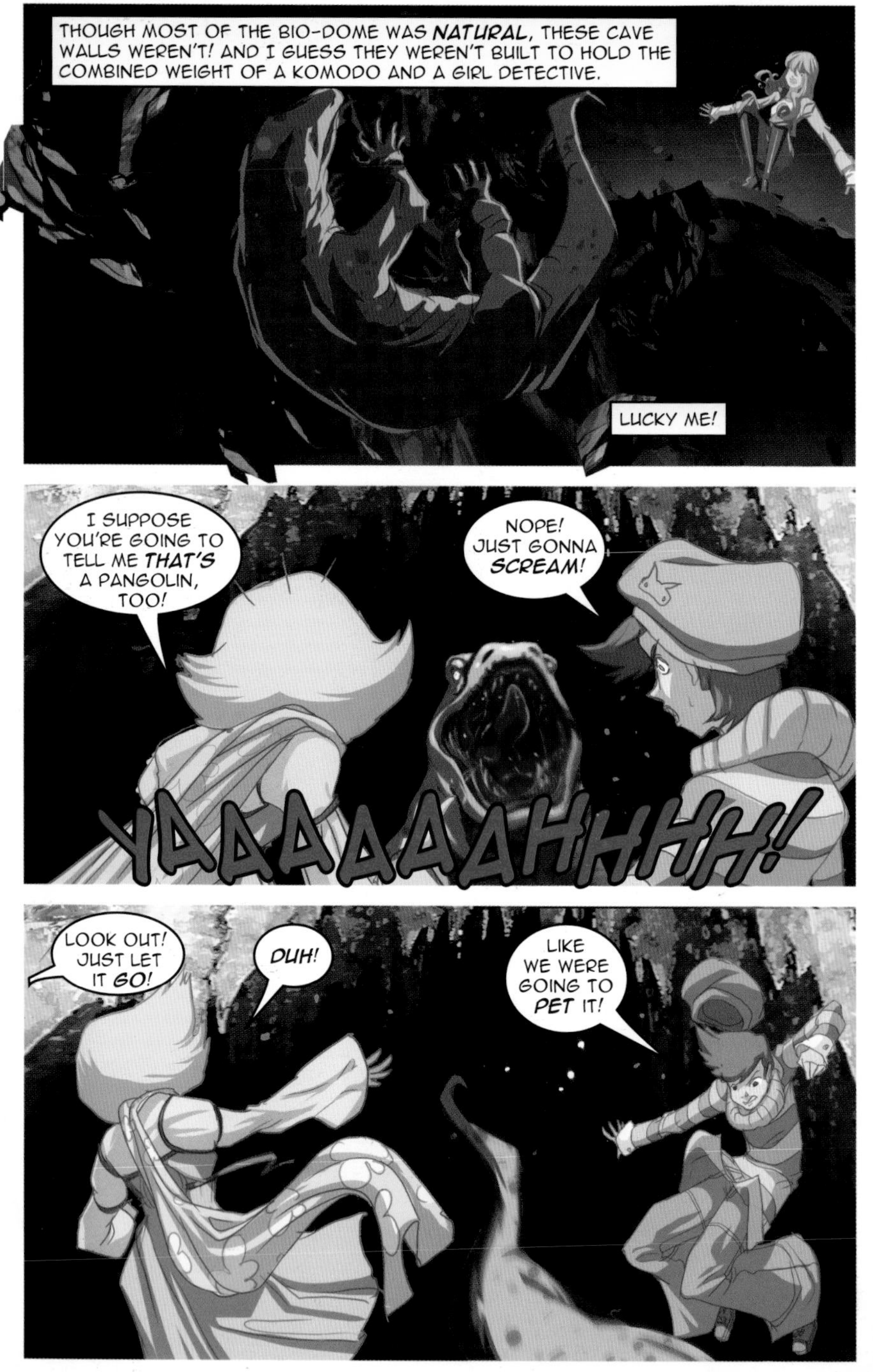
THOUGH MOST OF THE BIO-DOME WAS NATURAL, THESE CAVE WALLS WEREN'T! AND I GUESS THEY WEREN'T BUILT TO HOLD THE COMBINED WEIGHT OF A KOMODO AND A GIRL DETECTIVE.
LUCKY ME!
I SUPPOSE YOU'RE GOING TO TELL ME THAT'S A PANGOLIN, TOO!
NOPE! JUST GONNA SCREAM!
YAAAAAAHHHH!
LOOK OUT! JUST LET IT GO!
DUH!
LIKE WE WERE GOING TO PET IT!

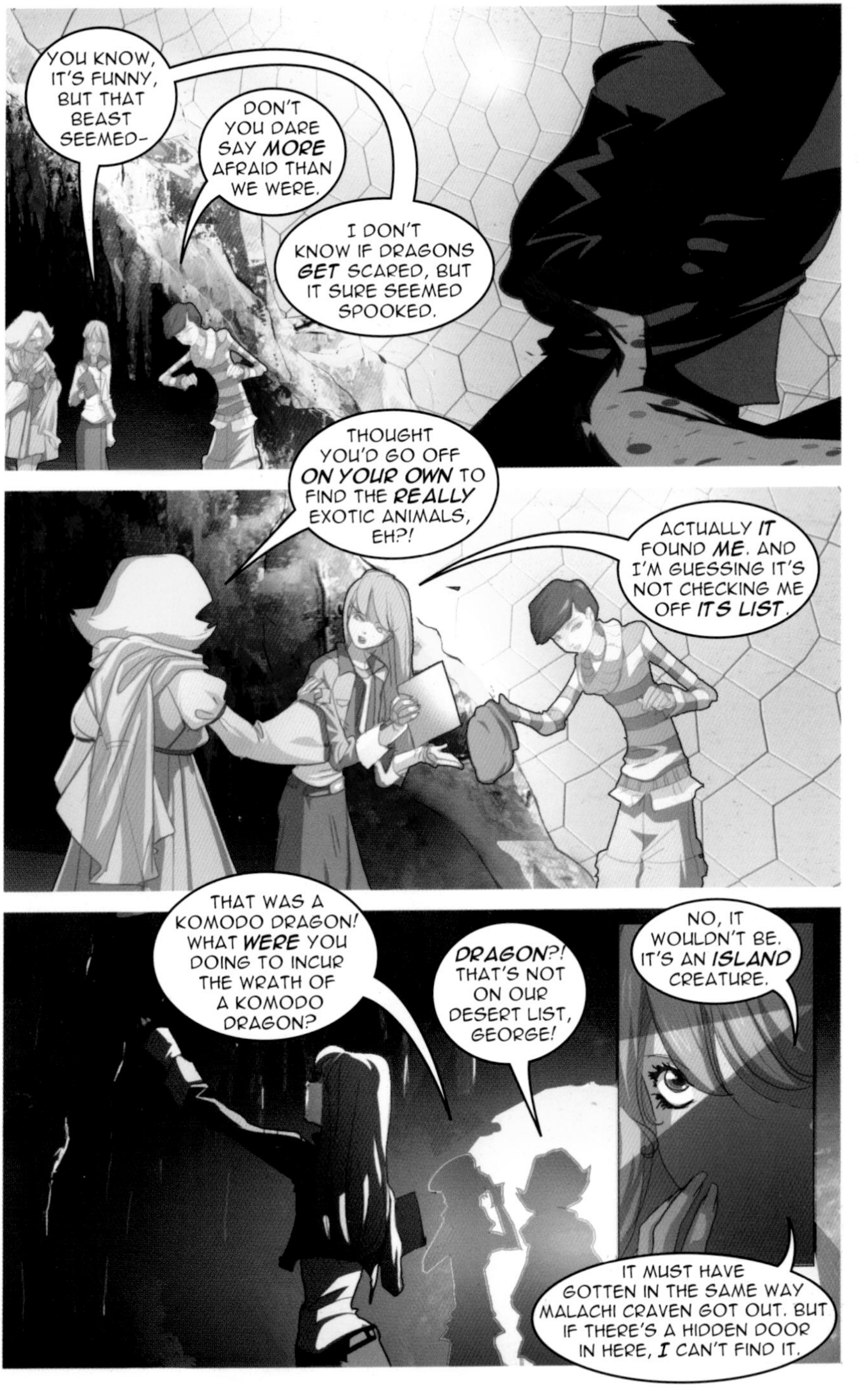
YOU KNOW, IT'S FUNNY, BUT THAT BEAST SEEMED-
DON'T YOU DARE SAY MORE AFRAID THAN WE WERE.
I DON'T KNOW IF DRAGONS GET SCARED, BUT IT SURE SEEMED SPOOKED.
THOUGHT YOU'D GO OFF ON YOUR OWN TO FIND THE REALLY EXOTIC ANIMALS, EH?!
ACTUALLY IT FOUND ME. AND I'M GUESSING IT'S NOT CHECKING ME OFF ITS LIST.
THAT WAS A KOMODO DRAGON! WHAT WERE YOU DOING TO INCUR THE WRATH OF A KOMODO DRAGON?
DRAGON?! THAT'S NOT ON OUR DESERT LIST, GEORGE!
NO, IT WOULDN'T BE. IT'S AN ISLAND CREATURE.
IT MUST HAVE GOTTEN IN THE SAME WAY MALACHI CRAVEN GOT OUT. BUT IF THERE'S A HIDDEN DOOR IN HERE, I CAN'T FIND IT.

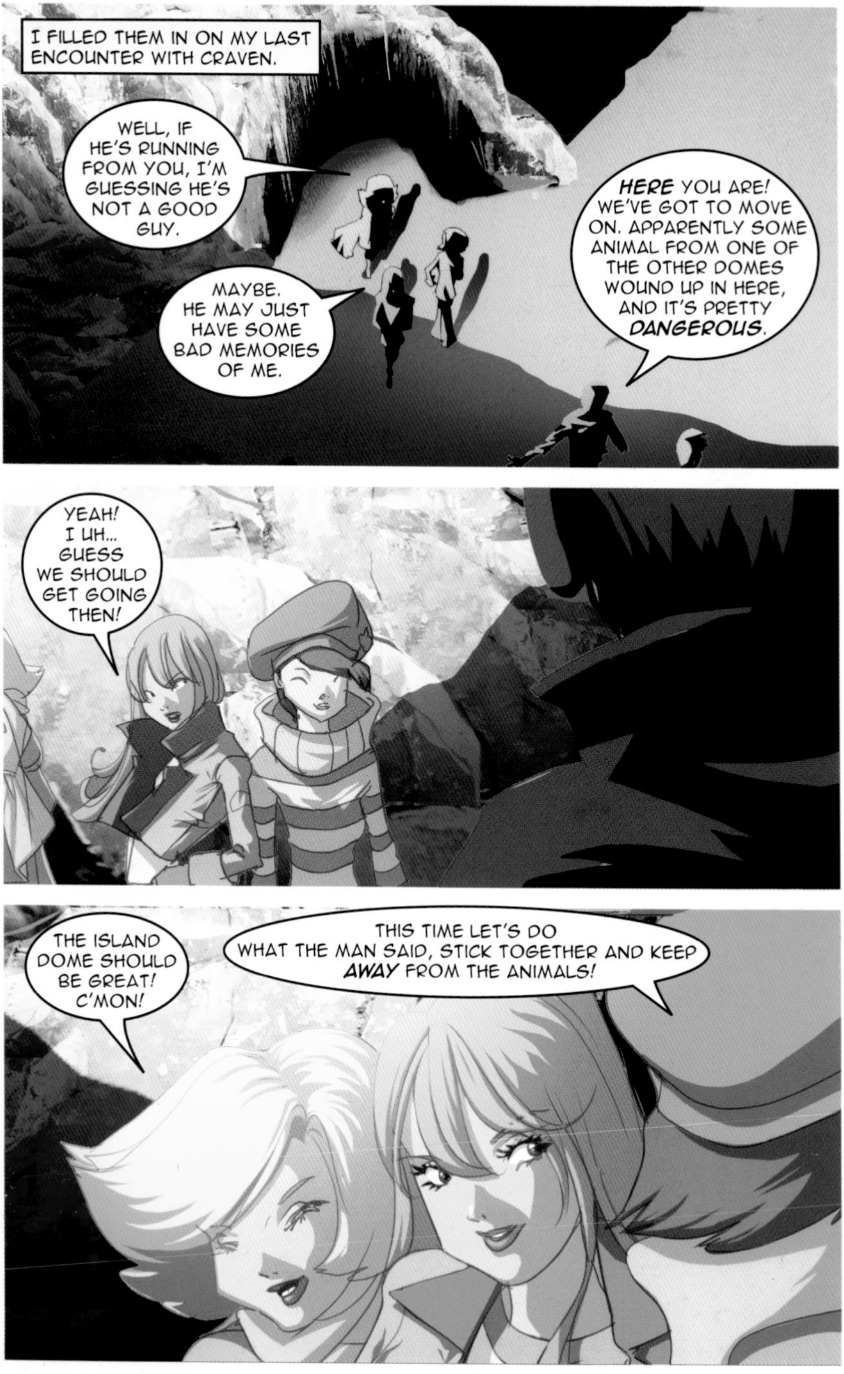
I FILLED THEM IN ON MY LAST ENCOUNTER WITH CRAVEN.
WELL, IF HE'S RUNNING FROM YOU, I'M GUESSING HE'S NOT A GOOD GUY.
MAYBE. HE MAY JUST HAVE SOME BAD MEMORIES OF ME.
HERE YOU ARE! WE'VE GOT TO MOVE ON. APPARENTLY SOME ANIMAL FROM ONE OF THE OTHER DOMES WOUND UP IN HERE, AND IT'S PRETTY DANGEROUS.
YEAH! I UH... GUESS WE SHOULD GET GOING THEN!
THE ISLAND DOME SHOULD BE GREAT! C'MON!
THIS TIME LET'S DO WHAT THE MAN SAID, STICK TOGETHER AND KEEP AWAY FROM THE ANIMALS!

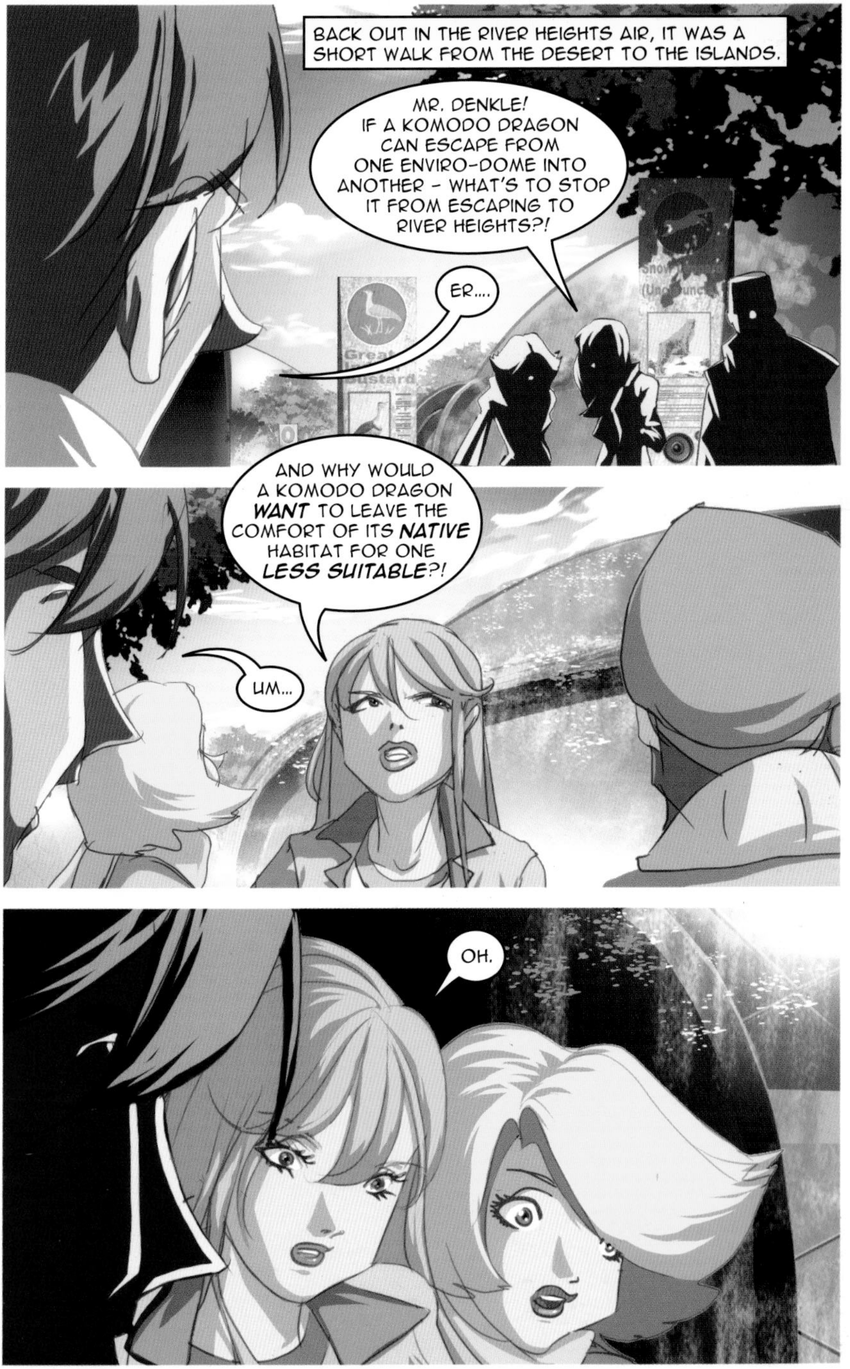
BACK OUT IN THE RIVER HEIGHTS AIR, IT WAS A SHORT WALK FROM THE DESERT TO THE ISLANDS.
MR. DENKLE! IF A KOMODO DRAGON CAN ESCAPE FROM ONE ENVIRO-DOME INTO ANOTHER - WHAT'S TO STOP IT FROM ESCAPING TO RIVER HEIGHTS?!
ER....
AND WHY WOULD A KOMODO DRAGON ***WANT*** TO LEAVE THE COMFORT OF ITS ***NATIVE*** HABITAT FOR ONE ***LESS SUITABLE***?!
UM...
OH.

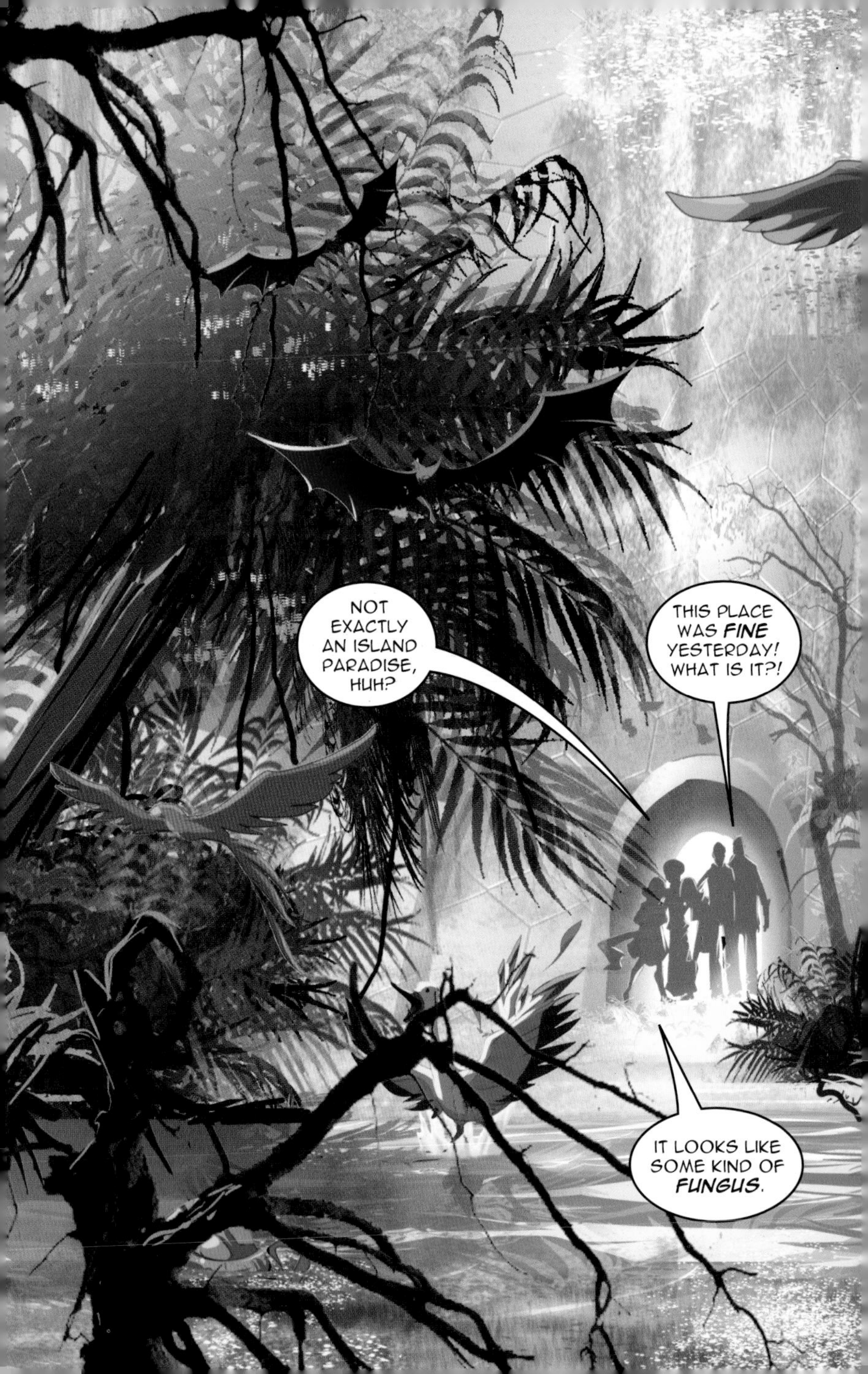
NOT EXACTLY AN ISLAND PARADISE, HUH?
THIS PLACE WAS FINE YESTERDAY! WHAT IS IT?!
IT LOOKS LIKE SOME KIND OF FUNGUS.

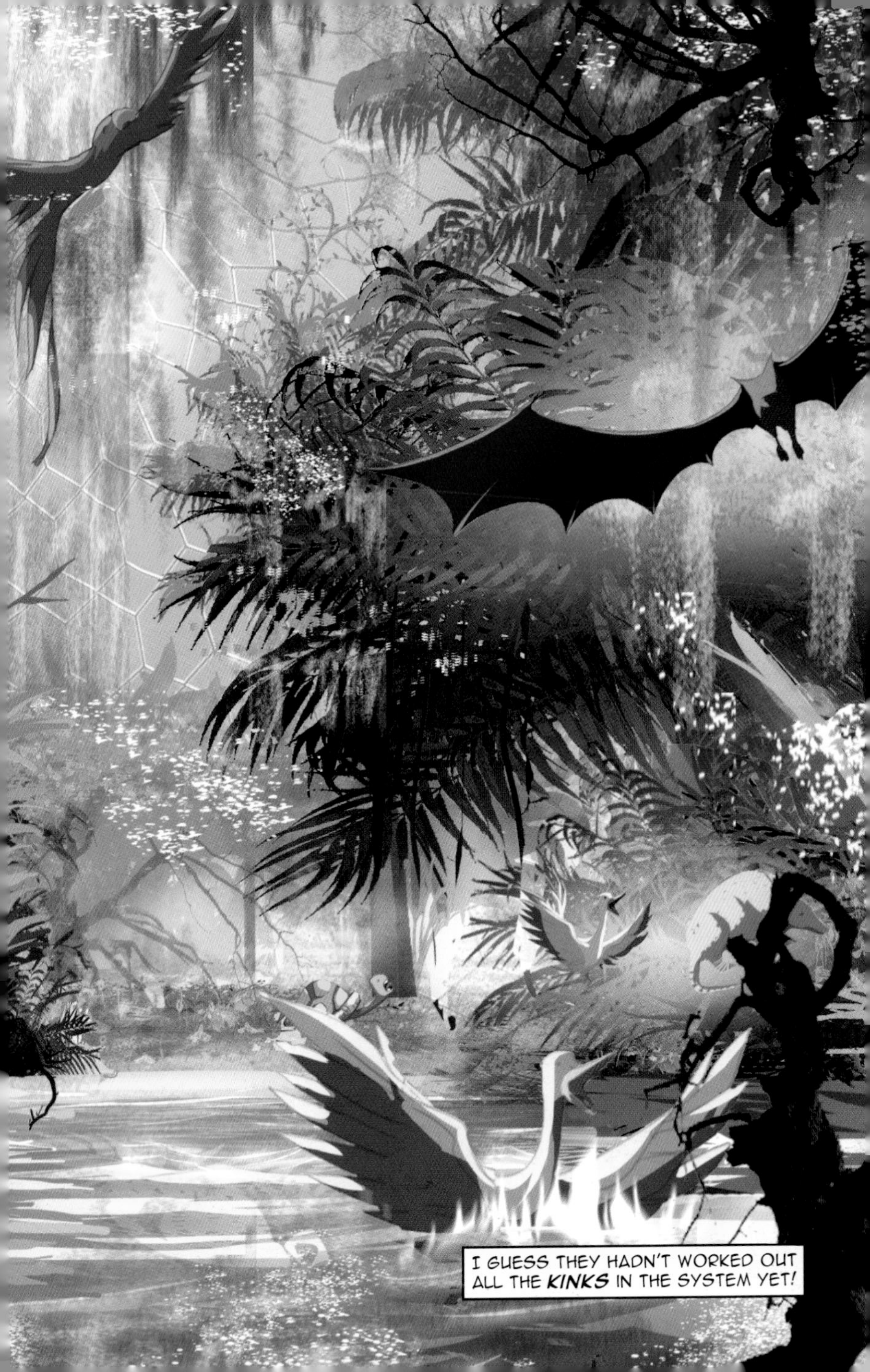
I GUESS THEY HADN'T WORKED OUT ALL THE *KINKS* IN THE SYSTEM YET!

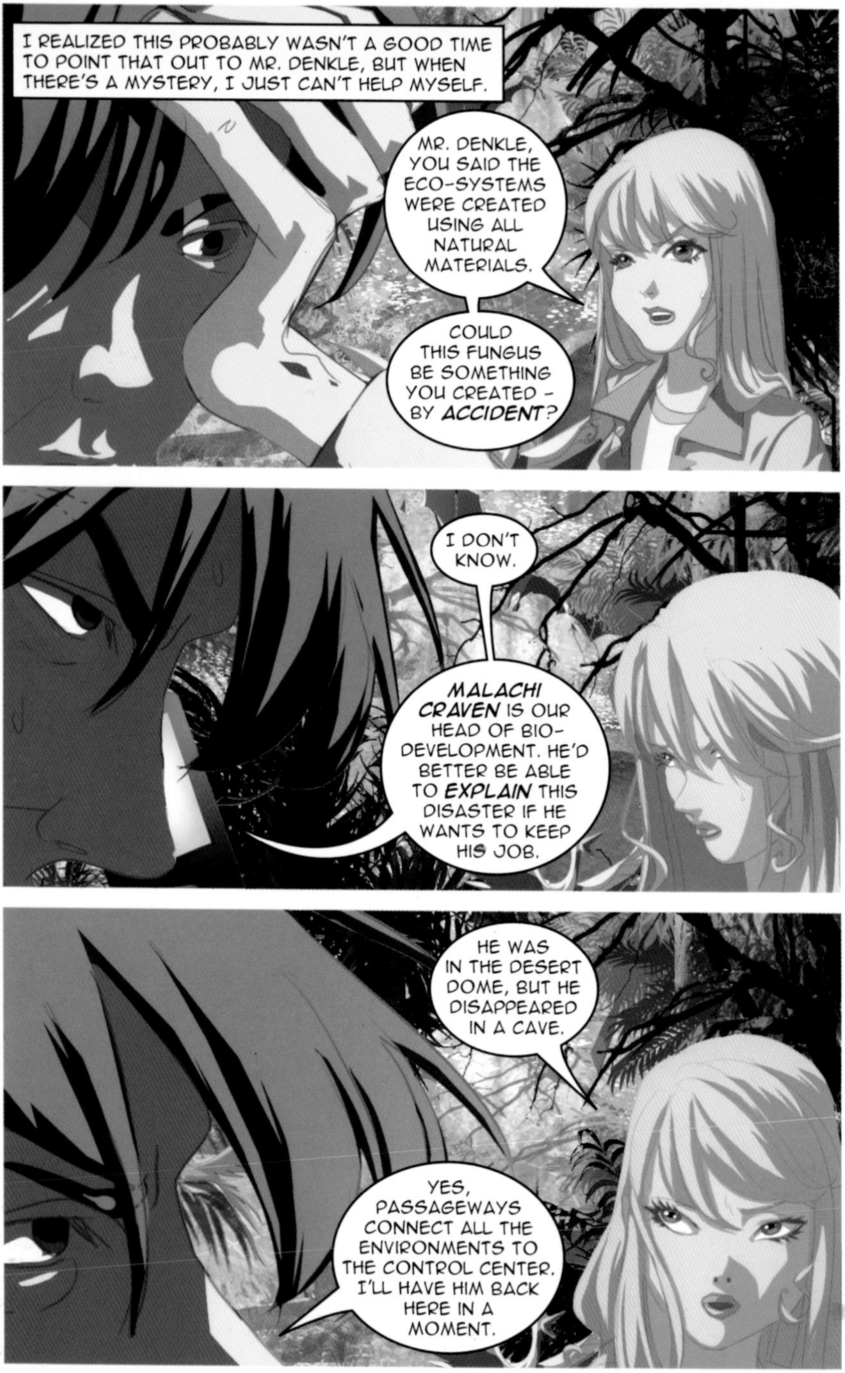
I REALIZED THIS PROBABLY WASN'T A GOOD TIME TO POINT THAT OUT TO MR. DENKLE, BUT WHEN THERE'S A MYSTERY, I JUST CAN'T HELP MYSELF.
MR. DENKLE, YOU SAID THE ECO-SYSTEMS WERE CREATED USING ALL NATURAL MATERIALS.
COULD THIS FUNGUS BE SOMETHING YOU CREATED - BY ACCIDENT?
I DON'T KNOW.
MALACHI CRAVEN IS OUR HEAD OF BIO-DEVELOPMENT. HE'D BETTER BE ABLE TO EXPLAIN THIS DISASTER IF HE WANTS TO KEEP HIS JOB.
HE WAS IN THE DESERT DOME, BUT HE DISAPPEARED IN A CAVE.
YES, PASSAGEWAYS CONNECT ALL THE ENVIRONMENTS TO THE CONTROL CENTER. I'LL HAVE HIM BACK HERE IN A MOMENT.

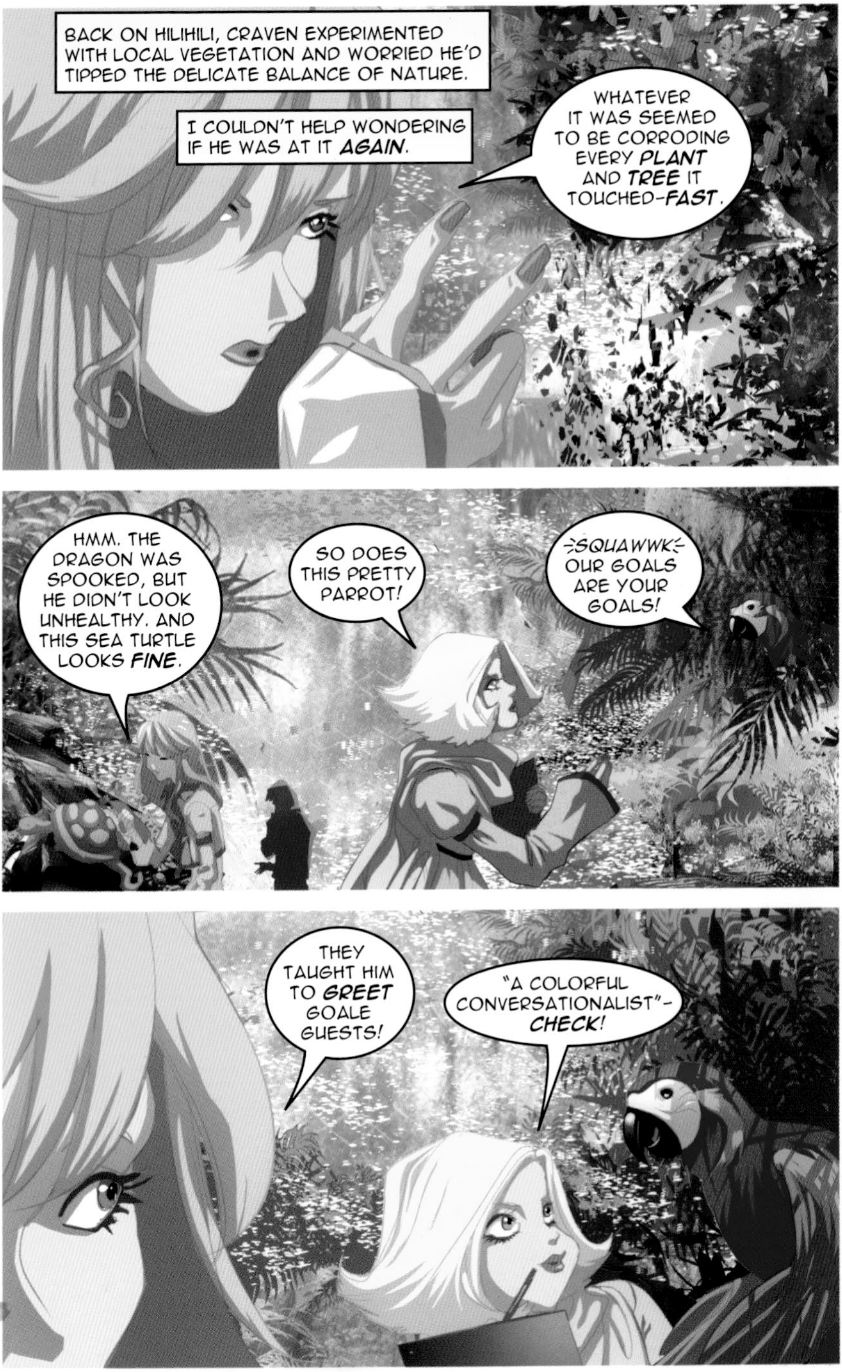
BACK ON HILIHILI, CRAVEN EXPERIMENTED WITH LOCAL VEGETATION AND WORRIED HE'D TIPPED THE DELICATE BALANCE OF NATURE.
I COULDN'T HELP WONDERING IF HE WAS AT IT ***AGAIN***.
WHATEVER IT WAS SEEMED TO BE CORRODING EVERY ***PLANT*** AND ***TREE*** IT TOUCHED-***FAST***.
HMM. THE DRAGON WAS SPOOKED, BUT HE DIDN'T LOOK UNHEALTHY. AND THIS SEA TURTLE LOOKS ***FINE***.
SO DOES THIS PRETTY PARROT!
SQUAWWK OUR GOALS ARE YOUR GOALS!
THEY TAUGHT HIM TO ***GREET*** GOALE GUESTS!
"A COLORFUL CONVERSATIONALIST"-***CHECK***!

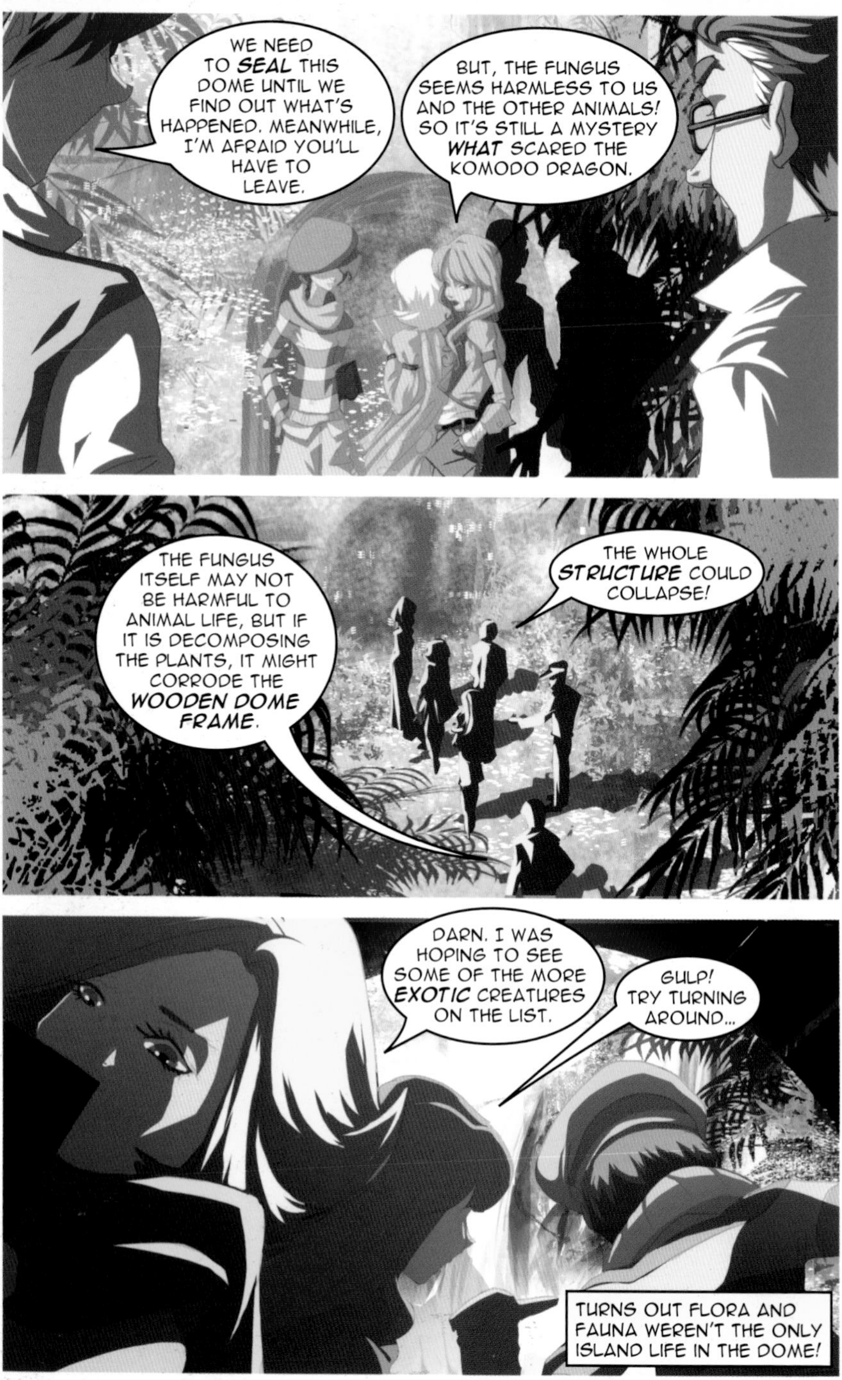
WE NEED TO SEAL THIS DOME UNTIL WE FIND OUT WHAT'S HAPPENED. MEANWHILE, I'M AFRAID YOU'LL HAVE TO LEAVE.
BUT, THE FUNGUS SEEMS HARMLESS TO US AND THE OTHER ANIMALS! SO IT'S STILL A MYSTERY WHAT SCARED THE KOMODO DRAGON.
THE FUNGUS ITSELF MAY NOT BE HARMFUL TO ANIMAL LIFE, BUT IF IT IS DECOMPOSING THE PLANTS, IT MIGHT CORRODE THE WOODEN DOME FRAME.
THE WHOLE STRUCTURE COULD COLLAPSE!
DARN. I WAS HOPING TO SEE SOME OF THE MORE EXOTIC CREATURES ON THE LIST.
GULP! TRY TURNING AROUND...
TURNS OUT FLORA AND FAUNA WEREN'T THE ONLY ISLAND LIFE IN THE DOME!

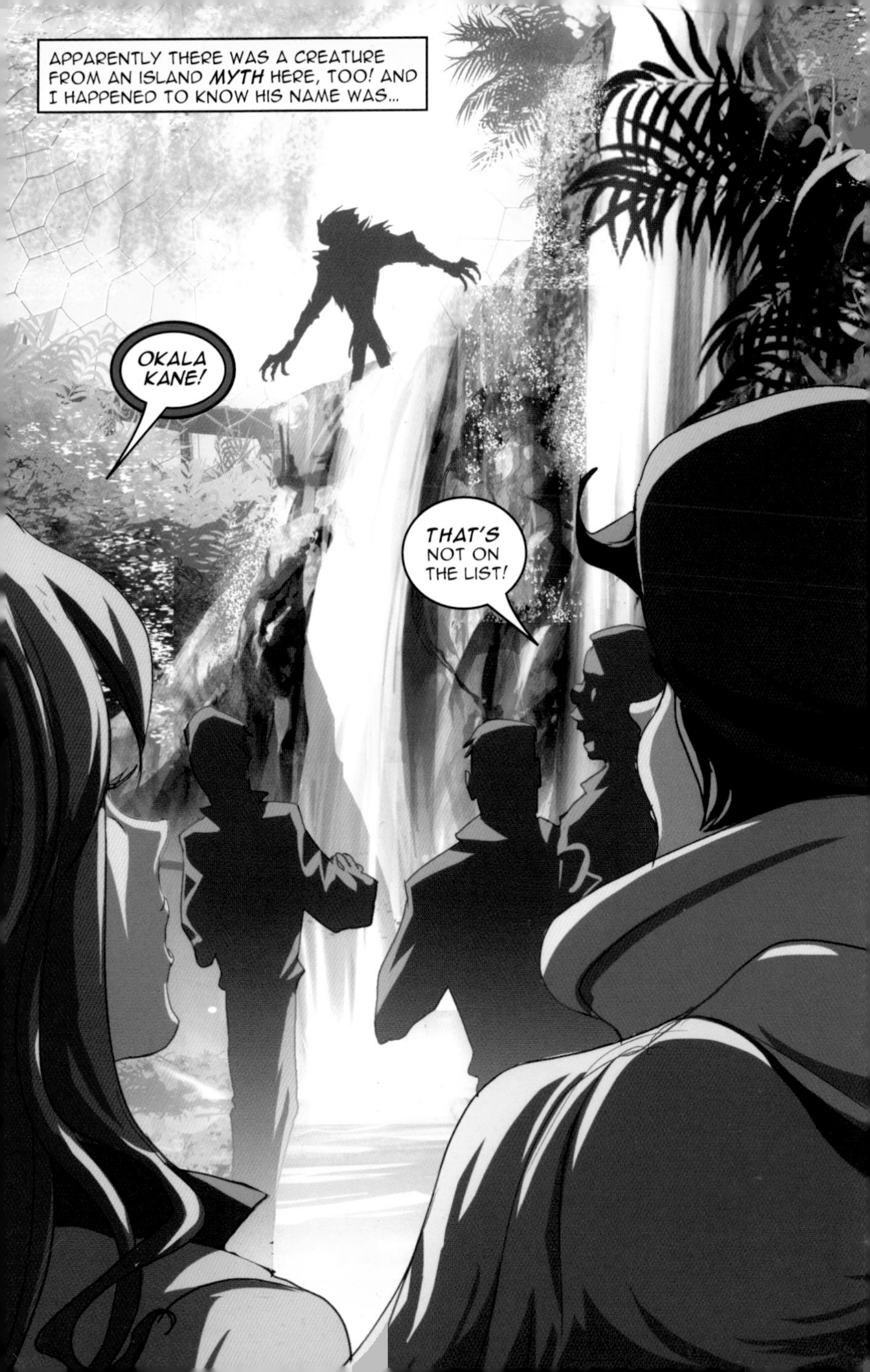
APPARENTLY THERE WAS A CREATURE FROM AN ISLAND *MYTH* HERE, TOO! AND I HAPPENED TO KNOW HIS NAME WAS...
OKALA KANE!
THAT'S NOT ON THE LIST!

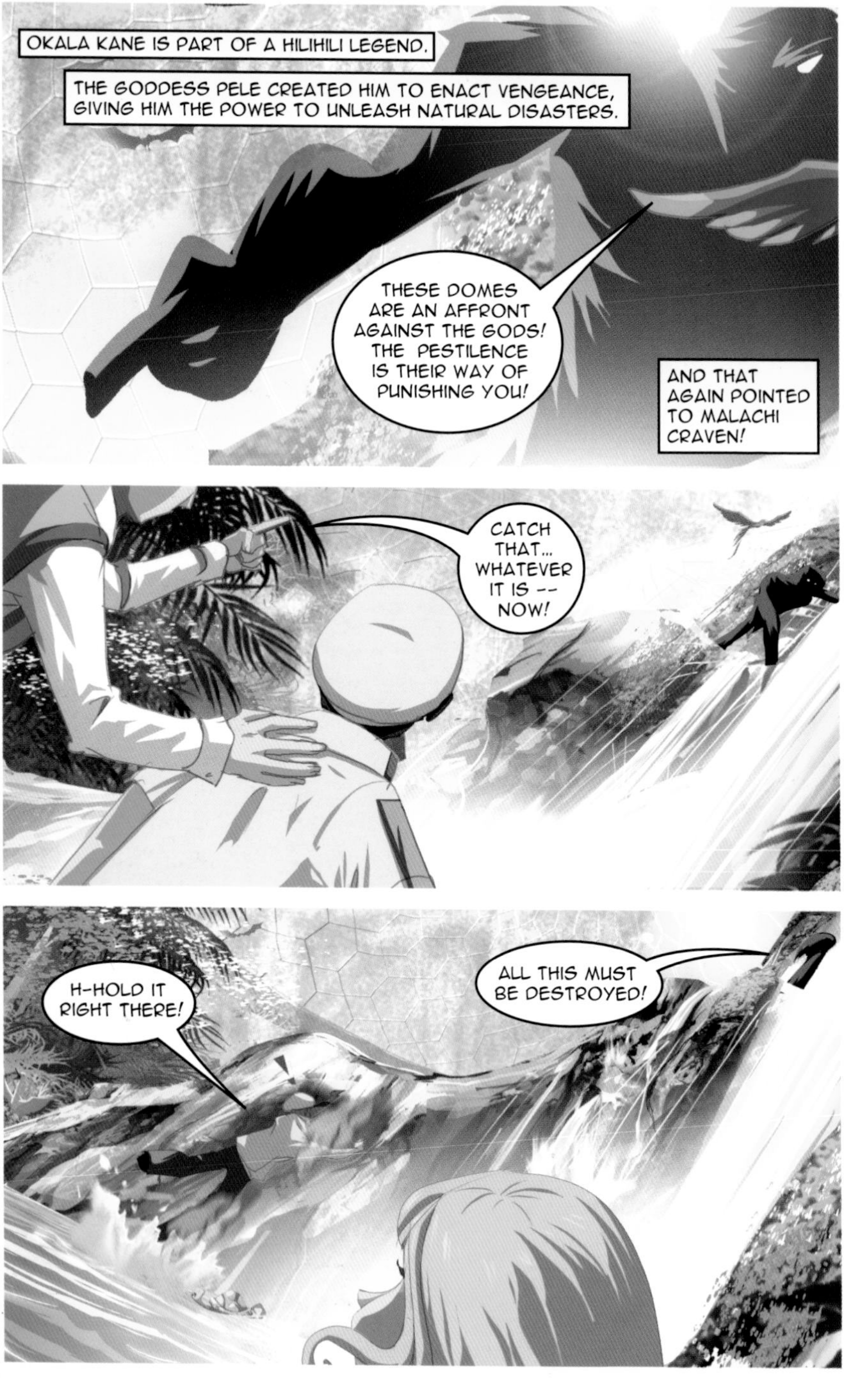
OKALA KANE IS PART OF A HILIHILI LEGEND.
THE GODDESS PELE CREATED HIM TO ENACT VENGEANCE, GIVING HIM THE POWER TO UNLEASH NATURAL DISASTERS.
THESE DOMES ARE AN AFFRONT AGAINST THE GODS! THE PESTILENCE IS THEIR WAY OF PUNISHING YOU!
AND THAT AGAIN POINTED TO MALACHI CRAVEN!
CATCH THAT... WHATEVER IT IS -- NOW!
H-HOLD IT RIGHT THERE!
ALL THIS MUST BE DESTROYED!

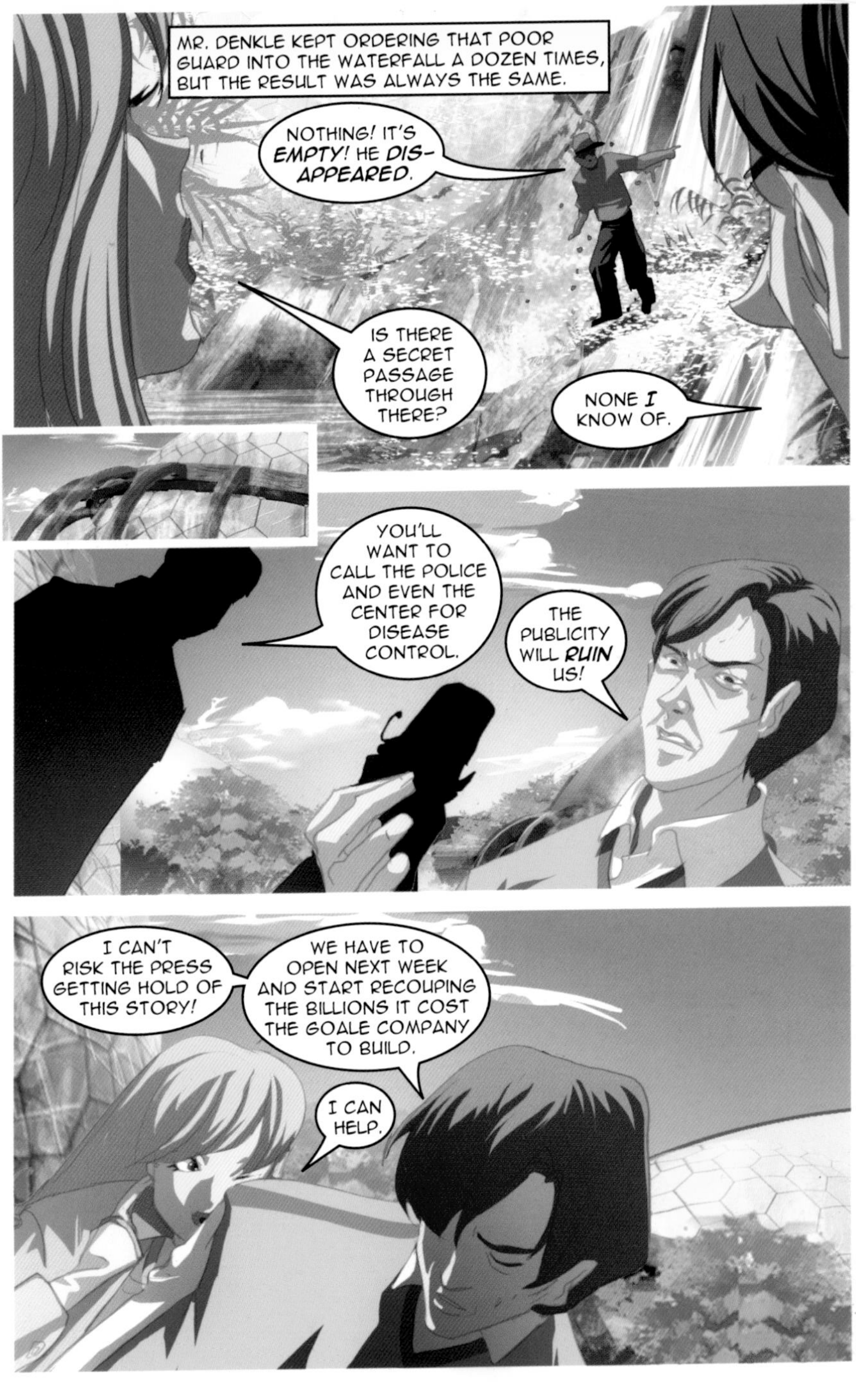
MR. DENKLE KEPT ORDERING THAT POOR GUARD INTO THE WATERFALL A DOZEN TIMES, BUT THE RESULT WAS ALWAYS THE SAME.
NOTHING! IT'S EMPTY! HE DIS-APPEARED.
IS THERE A SECRET PASSAGE THROUGH THERE?
NONE I KNOW OF.
YOU'LL WANT TO CALL THE POLICE AND EVEN THE CENTER FOR DISEASE CONTROL.
THE PUBLICITY WILL RUIN US!
I CAN'T RISK THE PRESS GETTING HOLD OF THIS STORY!
WE HAVE TO OPEN NEXT WEEK AND START RECOUPING THE BILLIONS IT COST THE GOALE COMPANY TO BUILD.
I CAN HELP.

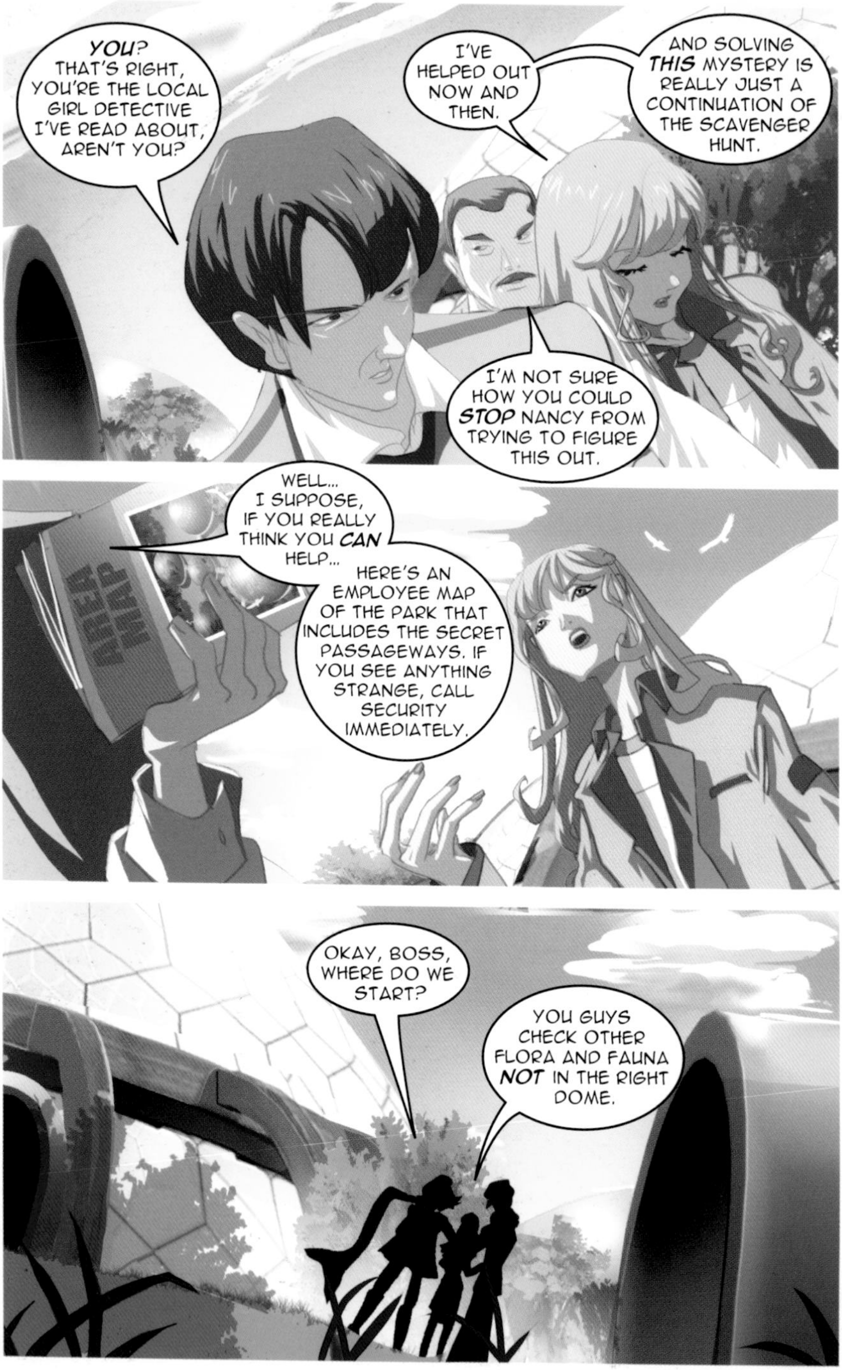
YOU? THAT'S RIGHT, YOU'RE THE LOCAL GIRL DETECTIVE I'VE READ ABOUT, AREN'T YOU?
I'VE HELPED OUT NOW AND THEN.
AND SOLVING THIS MYSTERY IS REALLY JUST A CONTINUATION OF THE SCAVENGER HUNT.
I'M NOT SURE HOW YOU COULD STOP NANCY FROM TRYING TO FIGURE THIS OUT.
AREA MAP
WELL... I SUPPOSE, IF YOU REALLY THINK YOU CAN HELP...
HERE'S AN EMPLOYEE MAP OF THE PARK THAT INCLUDES THE SECRET PASSAGEWAYS. IF YOU SEE ANYTHING STRANGE, CALL SECURITY IMMEDIATELY.
OKAY, BOSS, WHERE DO WE START?
YOU GUYS CHECK OTHER FLORA AND FAUNA NOT IN THE RIGHT DOME.

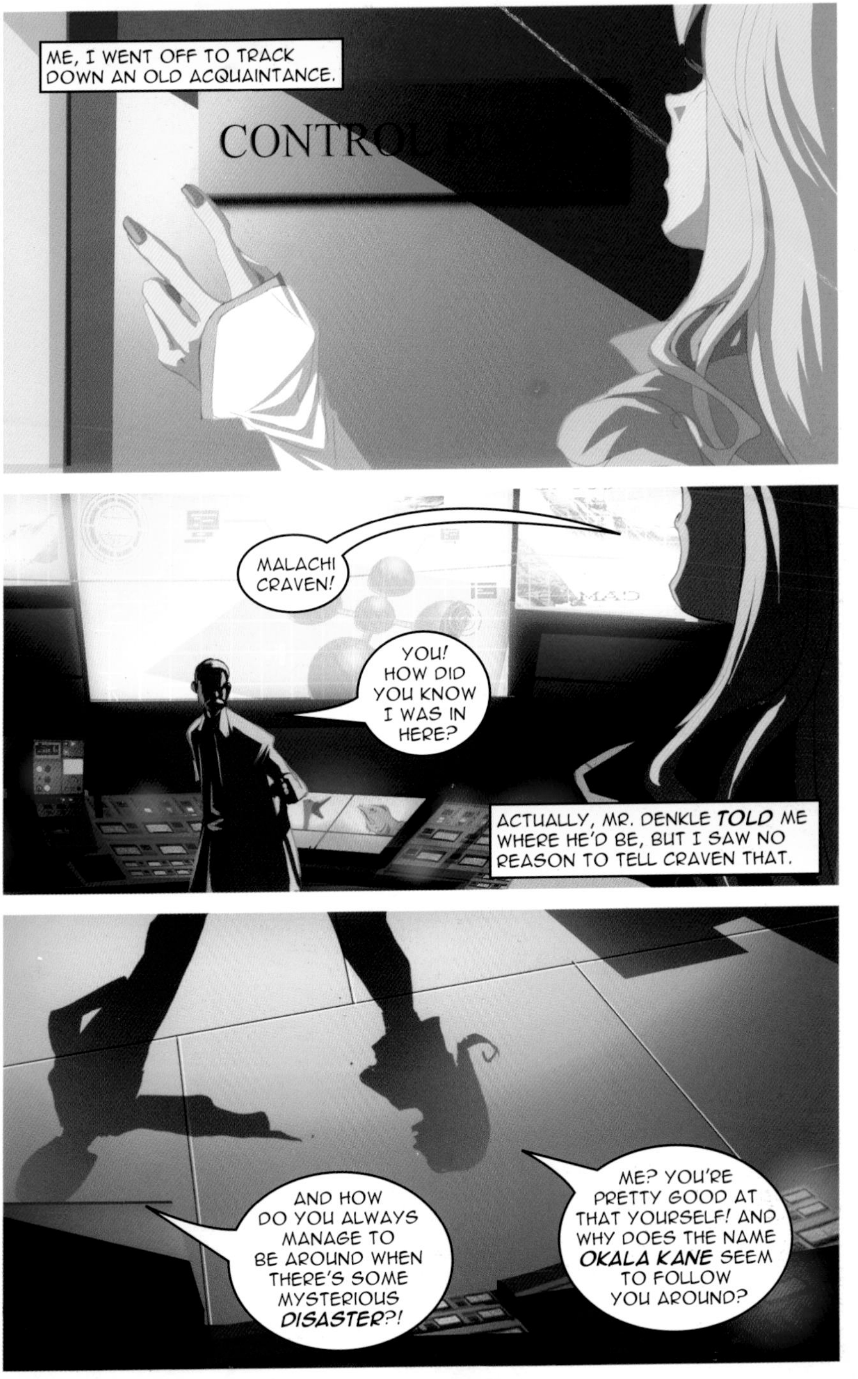
ME, I WENT OFF TO TRACK DOWN AN OLD ACQUAINTANCE.
MALACHI CRAVEN!
YOU! HOW DID YOU KNOW I WAS IN HERE?
ACTUALLY, MR. DENKLE **TOLD** ME WHERE HE'D BE, BUT I SAW NO REASON TO TELL CRAVEN THAT.
AND HOW DO YOU ALWAYS MANAGE TO BE AROUND WHEN THERE'S SOME MYSTERIOUS ***DISASTER***?!
ME? YOU'RE PRETTY GOOD AT THAT YOURSELF! AND WHY DOES THE NAME ***OKALA KANE*** SEEM TO FOLLOW YOU AROUND?

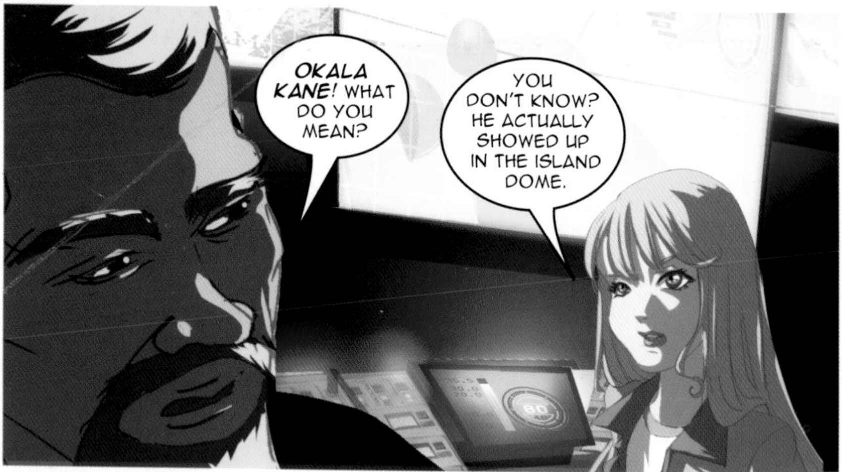
OKALA KANE! WHAT DO YOU MEAN?
YOU DON'T KNOW? HE ACTUALLY SHOWED UP IN THE ISLAND DOME.

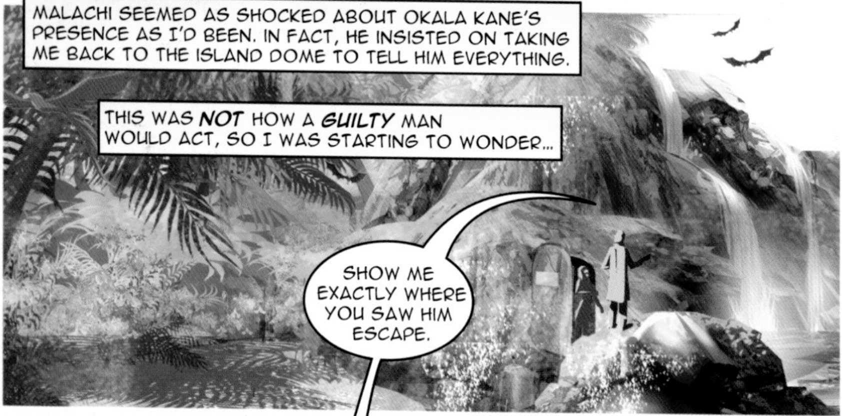
MALACHI SEEMED AS SHOCKED ABOUT OKALA KANE'S PRESENCE AS I'D BEEN. IN FACT, HE INSISTED ON TAKING ME BACK TO THE ISLAND DOME TO TELL HIM EVERYTHING.
THIS WAS NOT HOW A GUILTY MAN WOULD ACT, SO I WAS STARTING TO WONDER...
SHOW ME EXACTLY WHERE YOU SAW HIM ESCAPE.

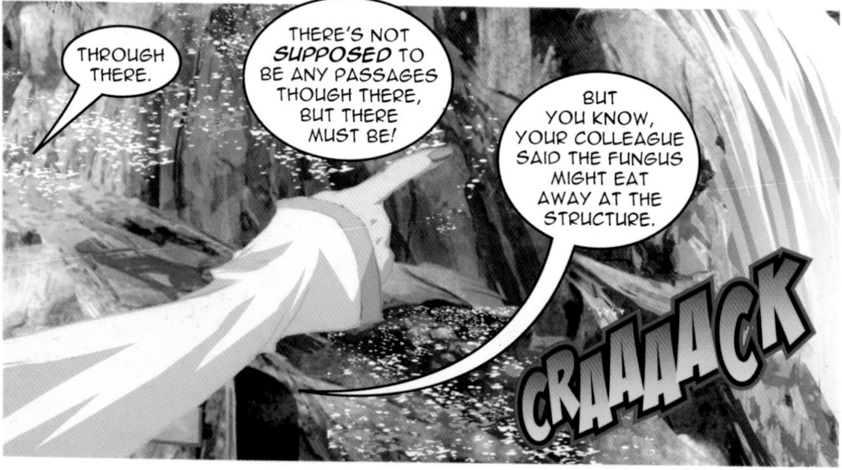
THROUGH THERE.
THERE'S NOT SUPPOSED TO BE ANY PASSAGES THOUGH THERE, BUT THERE MUST BE!
BUT YOU KNOW, YOUR COLLEAGUE SAID THE FUNGUS MIGHT EAT AWAY AT THE STRUCTURE.
CRAAAACK

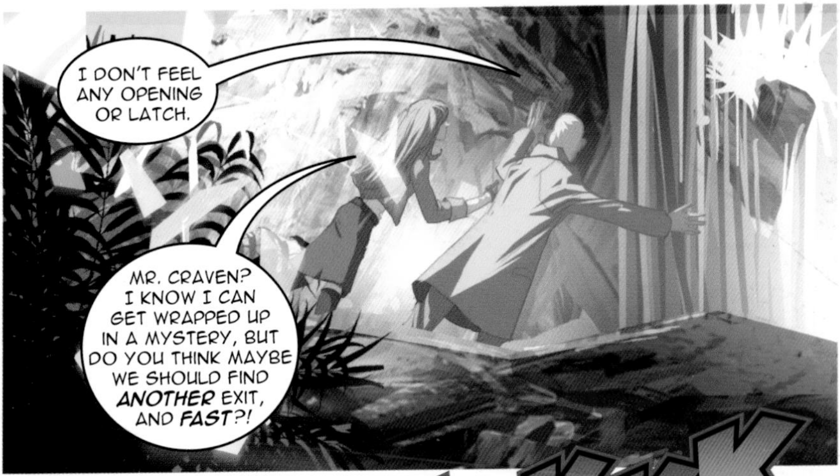
I DON'T FEEL ANY OPENING OR LATCH.
MR. CRAVEN? I KNOW I CAN GET WRAPPED UP IN A MYSTERY, BUT DO YOU THINK MAYBE WE SHOULD FIND *ANOTHER* EXIT, AND *FAST*?!

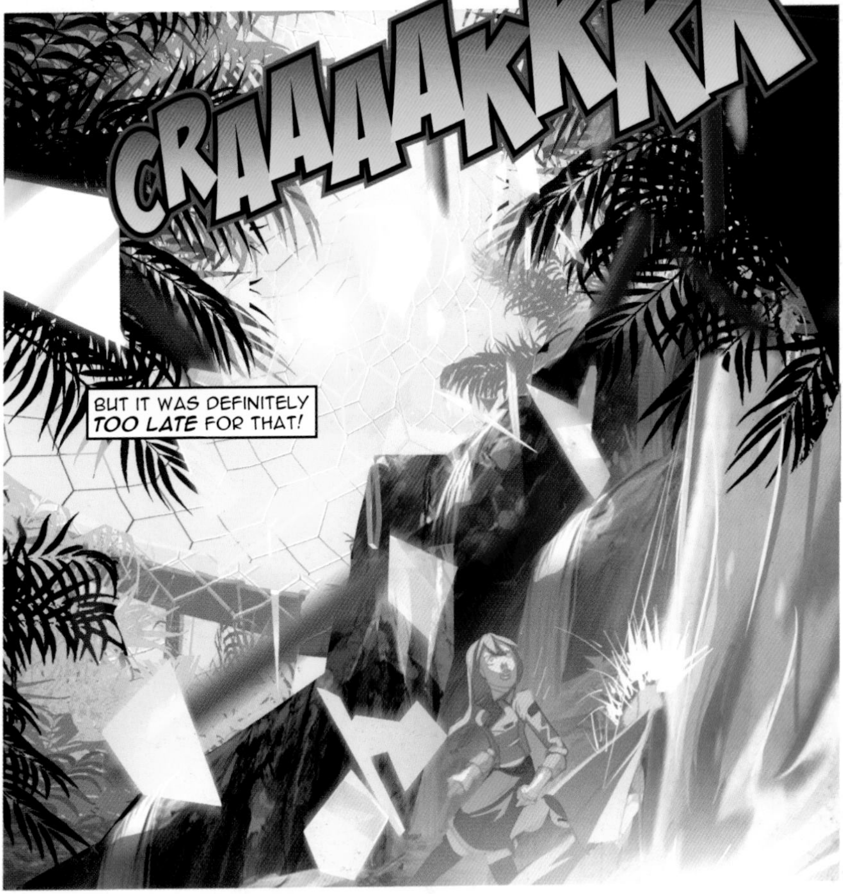
CRAAAAKKKK
BUT IT WAS DEFINITELY *TOO LATE* FOR THAT!

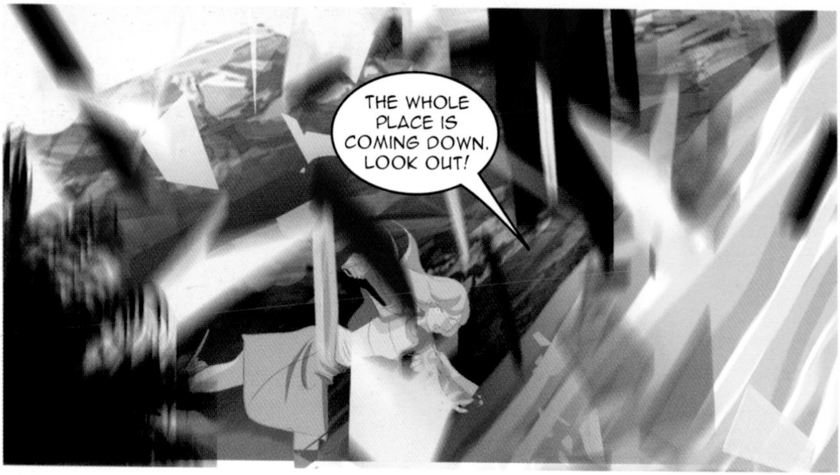
THE WHOLE PLACE IS COMING DOWN. LOOK OUT!

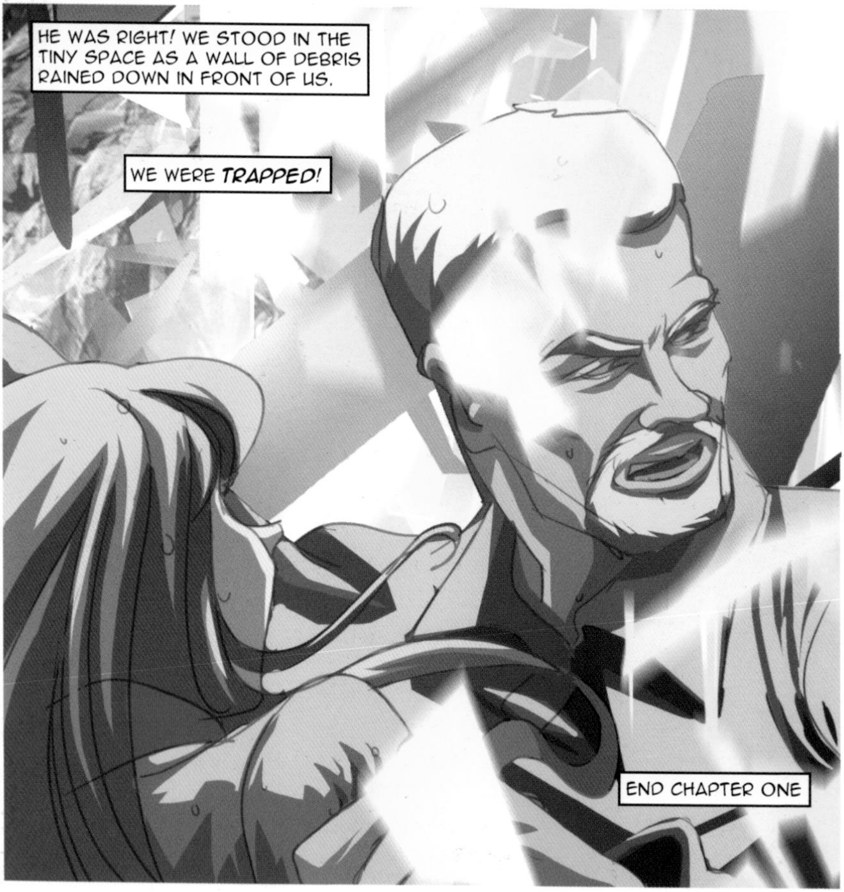
HE WAS RIGHT! WE STOOD IN THE TINY SPACE AS A WALL OF DEBRIS RAINED DOWN IN FRONT OF US.
WE WERE TRAPPED!
END CHAPTER ONE

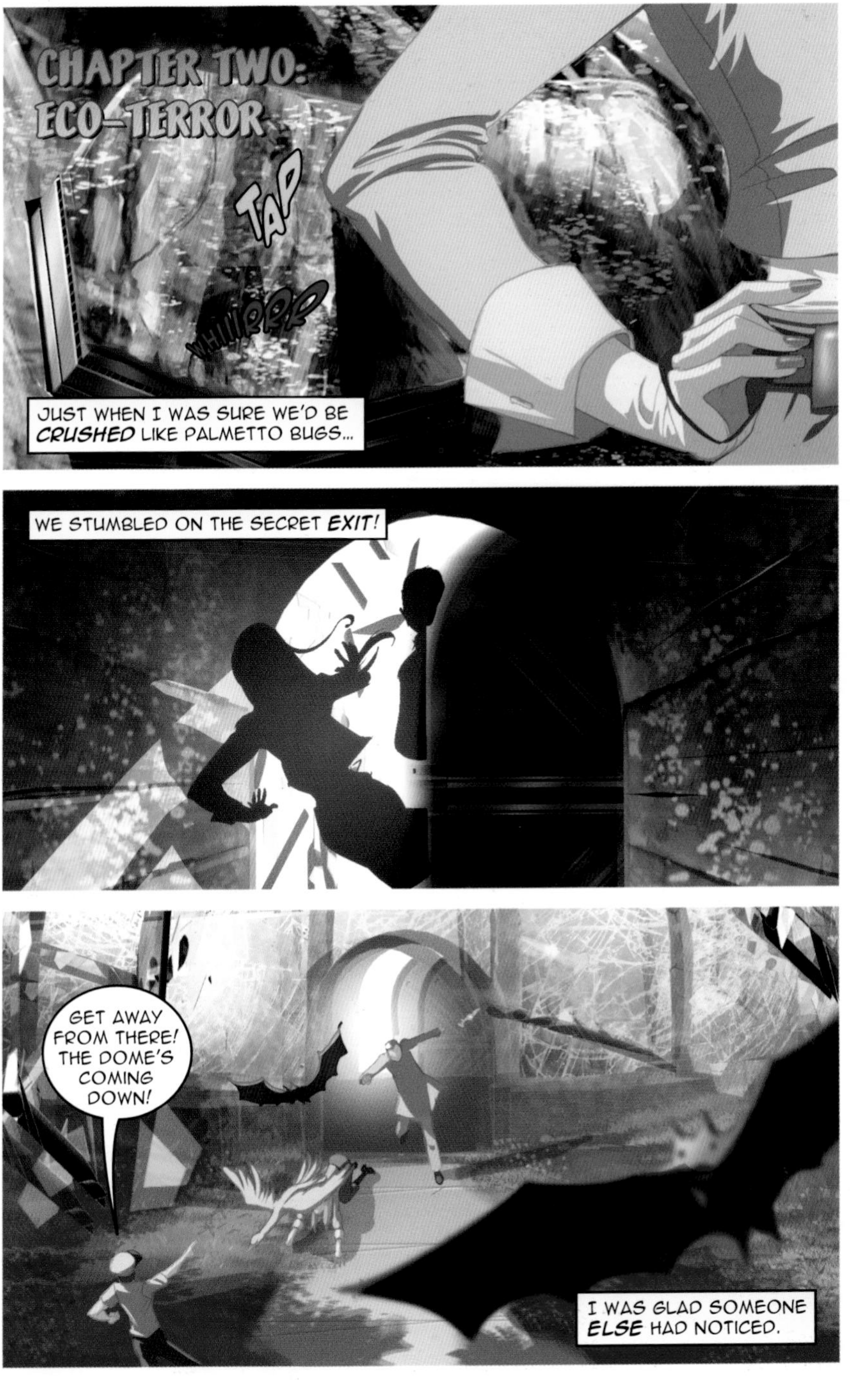
CHAPTER TWO: ECO-TERROR
TAP
WHIIIRRR
JUST WHEN I WAS SURE WE'D BE CRUSHED LIKE PALMETTO BUGS...
WE STUMBLED ON THE SECRET EXIT!
GET AWAY FROM THERE! THE DOME'S COMING DOWN!
I WAS GLAD SOMEONE ELSE HAD NOTICED.

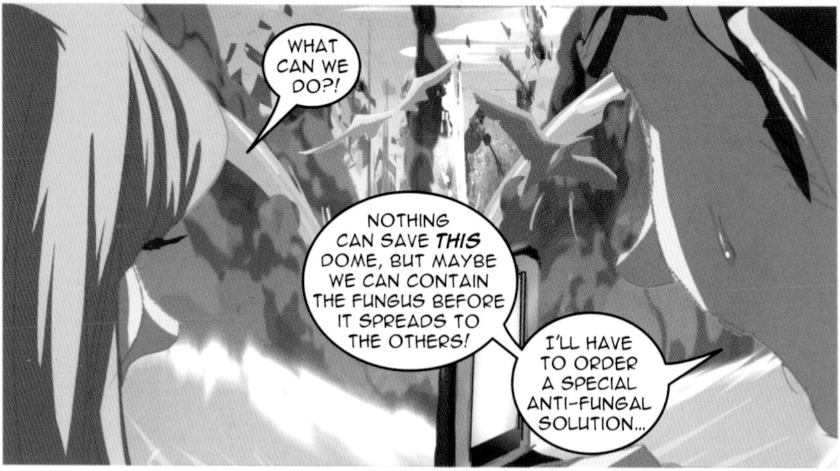
WHAT CAN WE DO?!
NOTHING CAN SAVE **THIS** DOME, BUT MAYBE WE CAN CONTAIN THE FUNGUS BEFORE IT SPREADS TO THE OTHERS!
I'LL HAVE TO ORDER A SPECIAL ANTI-FUNGAL SOLUTION...

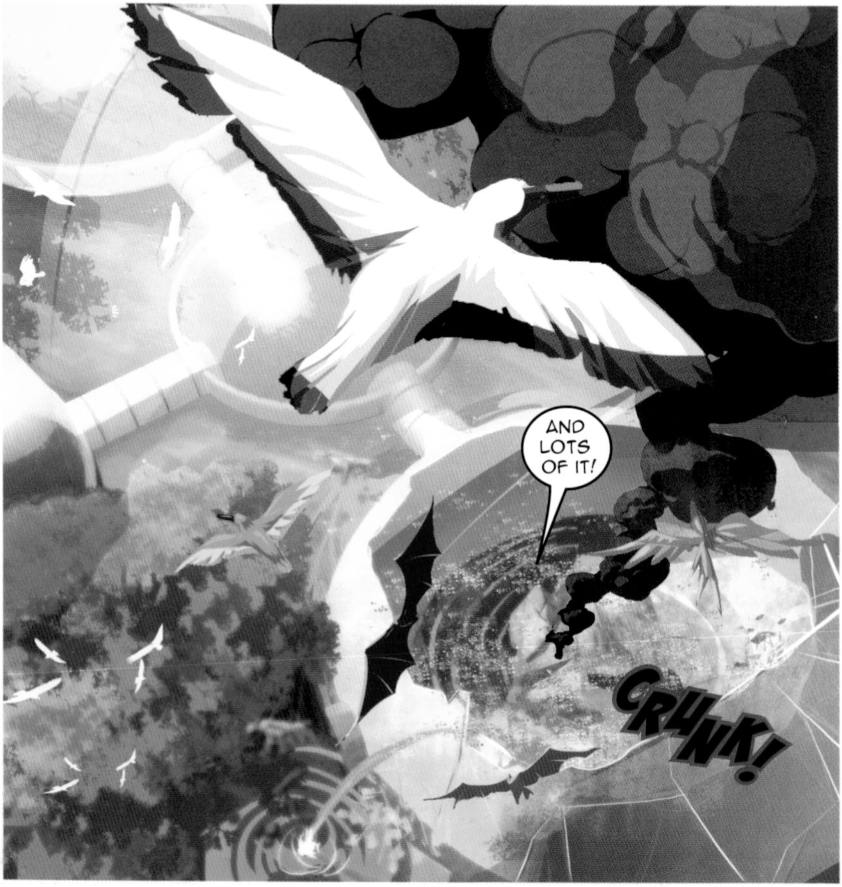
AND LOTS OF IT!
CRUNK!

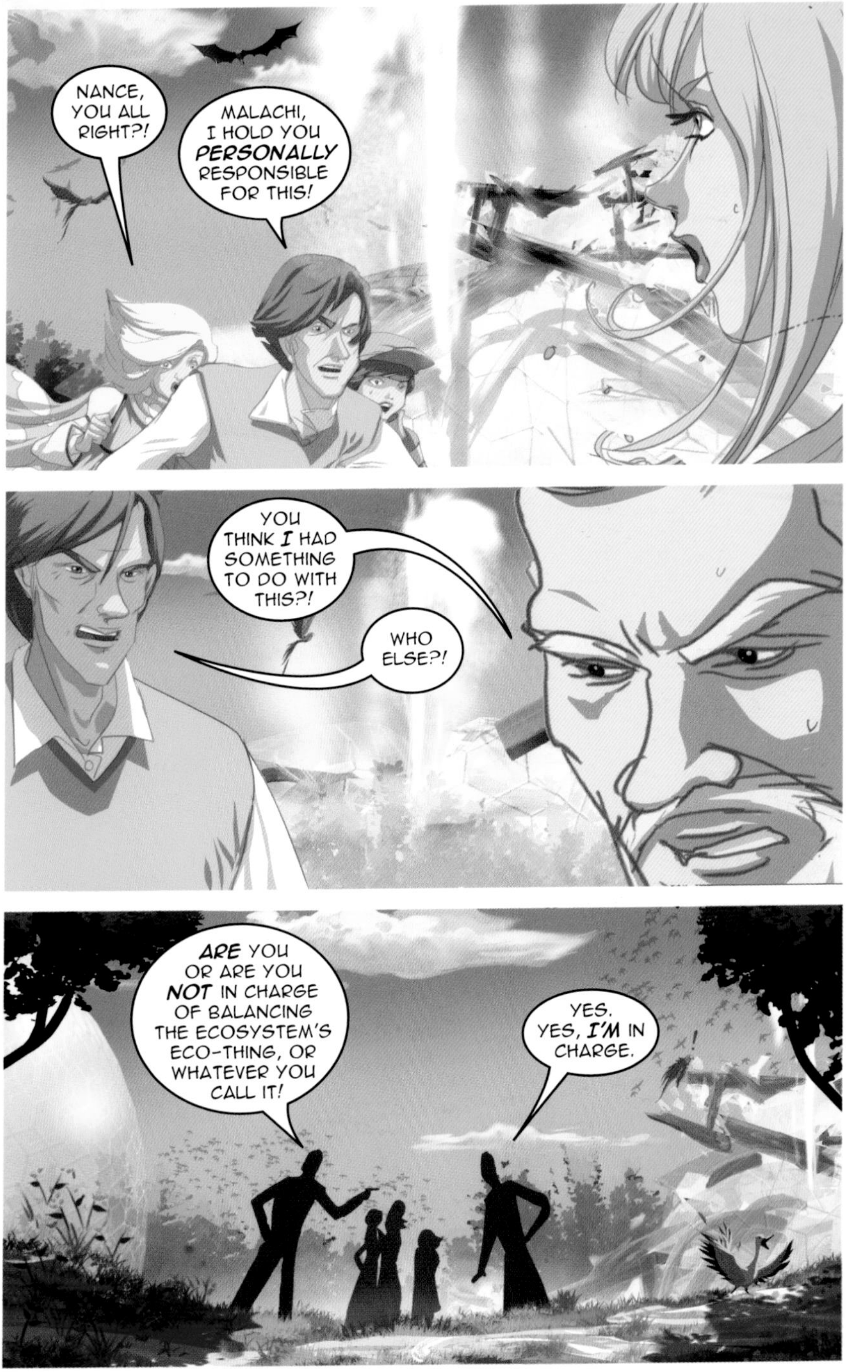
NANCE, YOU ALL RIGHT?!
MALACHI, I HOLD YOU *PERSONALLY* RESPONSIBLE FOR THIS!
YOU THINK *I* HAD SOMETHING TO DO WITH THIS?!
WHO ELSE?!
ARE YOU OR ARE YOU *NOT* IN CHARGE OF BALANCING THE ECOSYSTEM'S ECO-THING, OR WHATEVER YOU CALL IT!
YES. YES, *I'M* IN CHARGE.

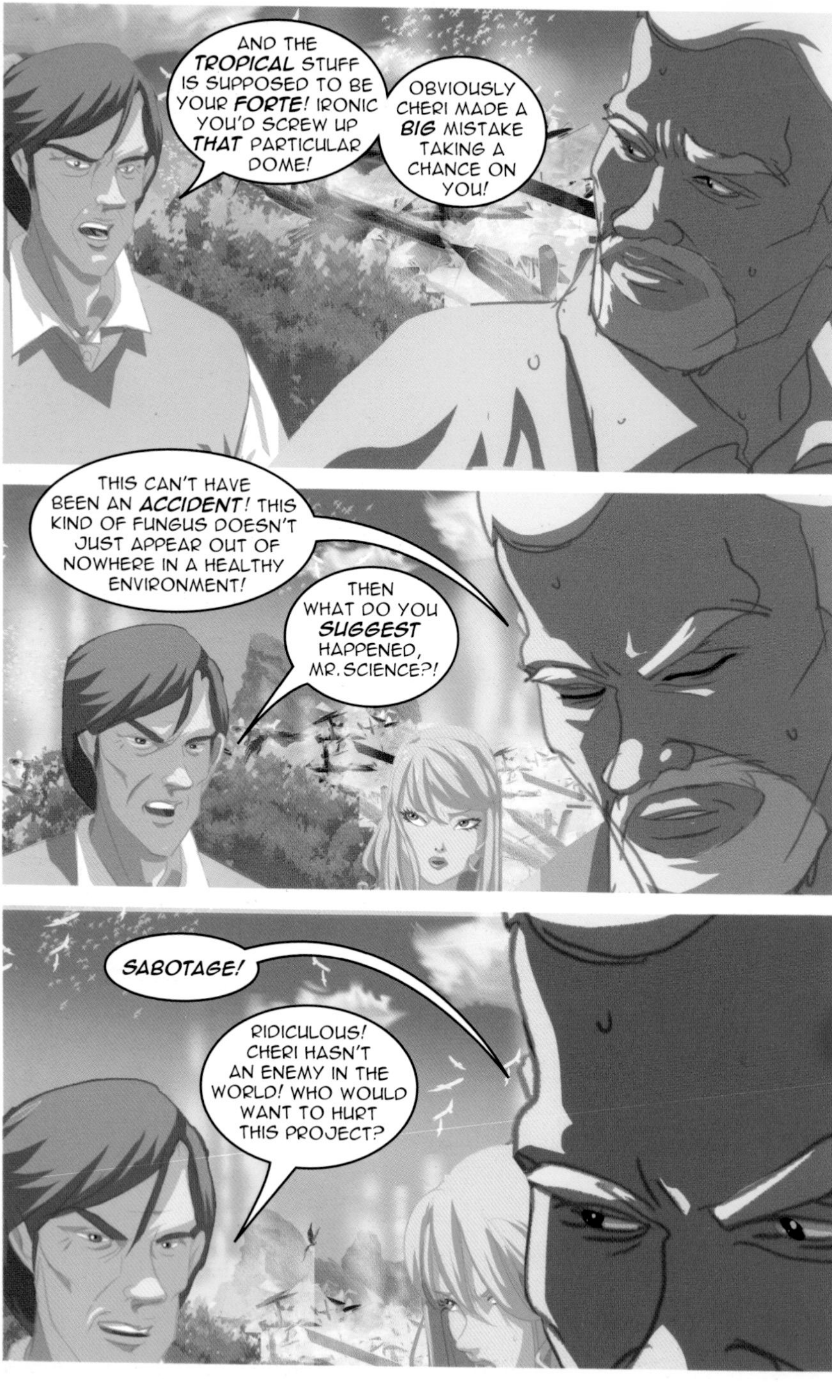
AND THE TROPICAL STUFF IS SUPPOSED TO BE YOUR FORTE! IRONIC YOU'D SCREW UP THAT PARTICULAR DOME!
OBVIOUSLY CHERI MADE A BIG MISTAKE TAKING A CHANCE ON YOU!
THIS CAN'T HAVE BEEN AN ACCIDENT! THIS KIND OF FUNGUS DOESN'T JUST APPEAR OUT OF NOWHERE IN A HEALTHY ENVIRONMENT!
THEN WHAT DO YOU SUGGEST HAPPENED, MR. SCIENCE?!
SABOTAGE!
RIDICULOUS! CHERI HASN'T AN ENEMY IN THE WORLD! WHO WOULD WANT TO HURT THIS PROJECT?

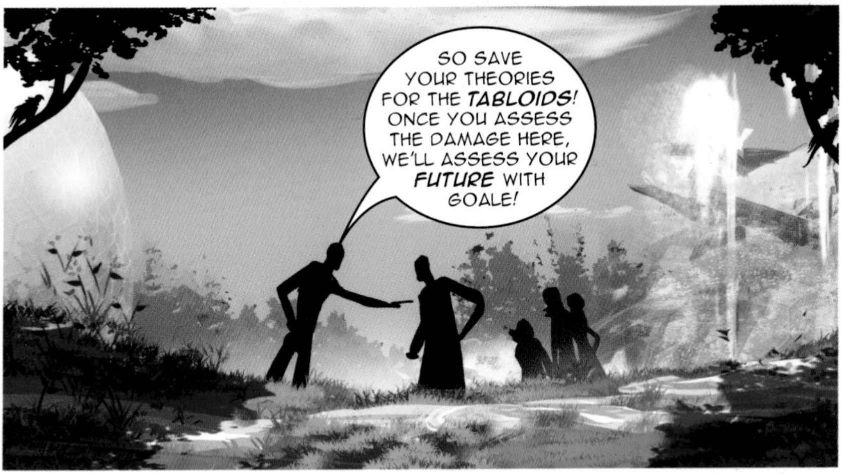
SO SAVE YOUR THEORIES FOR THE TABLOIDS! ONCE YOU ASSESS THE DAMAGE HERE, WE'LL ASSESS YOUR FUTURE WITH GOALE!

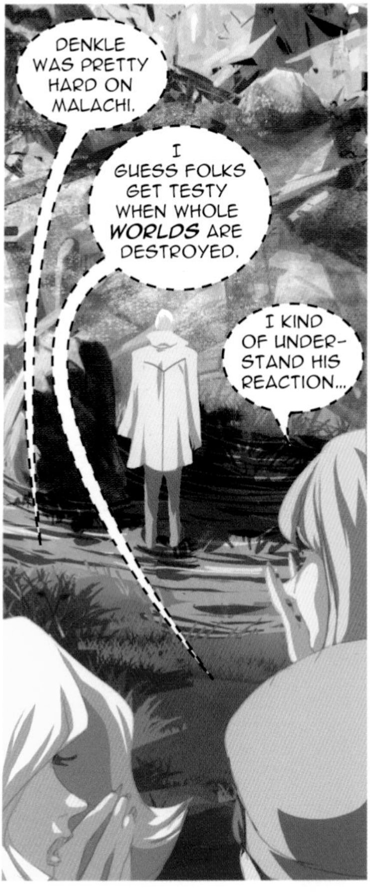
DENKLE WAS PRETTY HARD ON MALACHI.
I GUESS FOLKS GET TESTY WHEN WHOLE WORLDS ARE DESTROYED.
I KIND OF UNDER-STAND HIS REACTION...

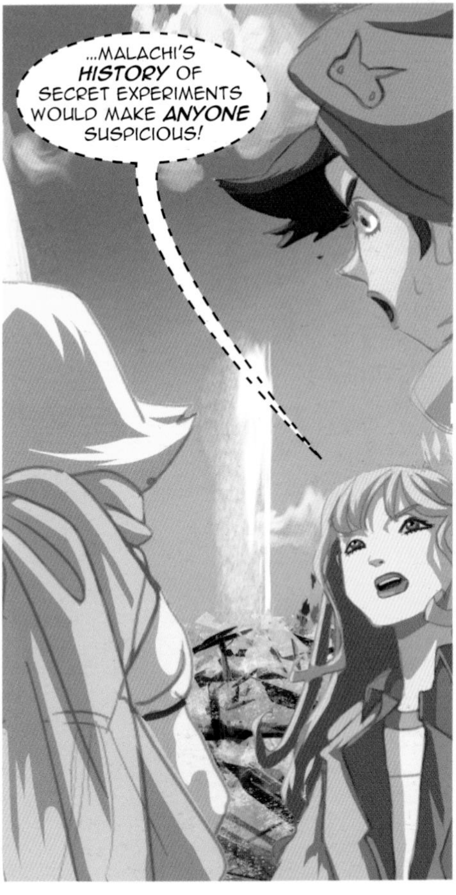
...MALACHI'S HISTORY OF SECRET EXPERIMENTS WOULD MAKE ANYONE SUSPICIOUS!

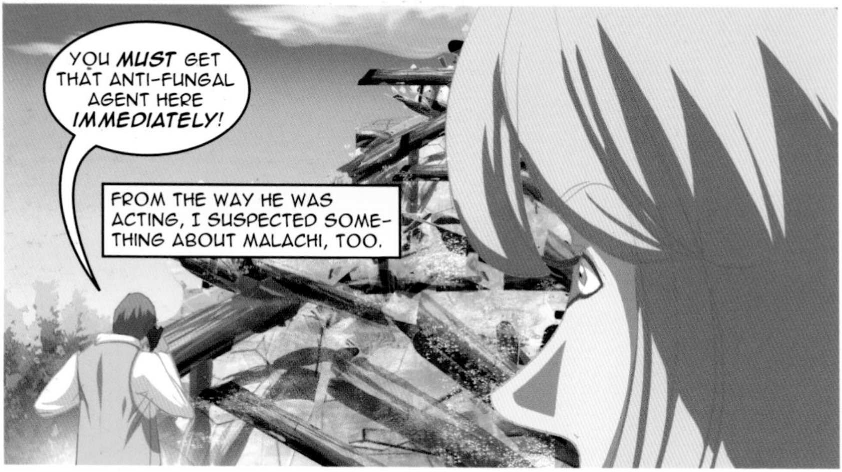
YOU MUST GET THAT ANTI-FUNGAL AGENT HERE IMMEDIATELY!
FROM THE WAY HE WAS ACTING, I SUSPECTED SOMETHING ABOUT MALACHI, TOO.

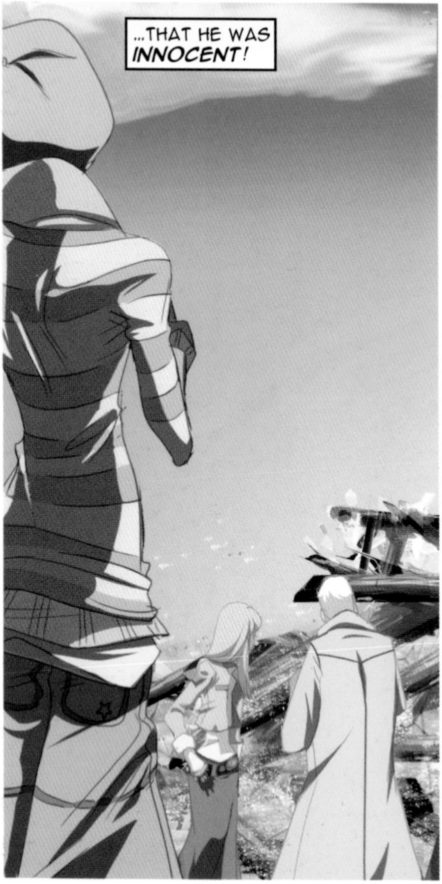
...THAT HE WAS INNOCENT!

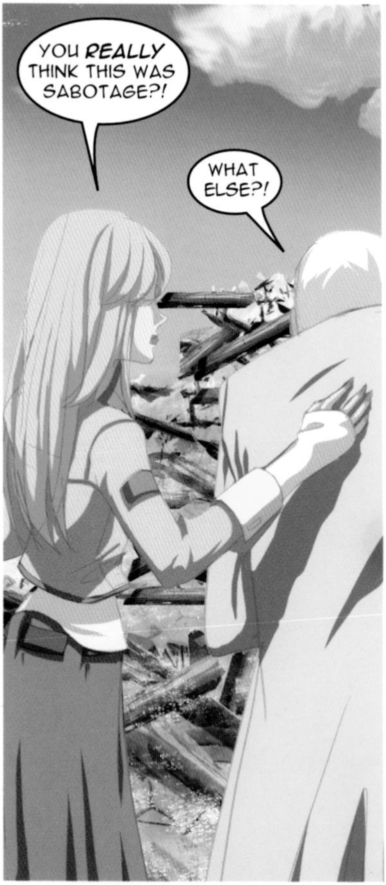
YOU REALLY THINK THIS WAS SABOTAGE?!
WHAT ELSE?!

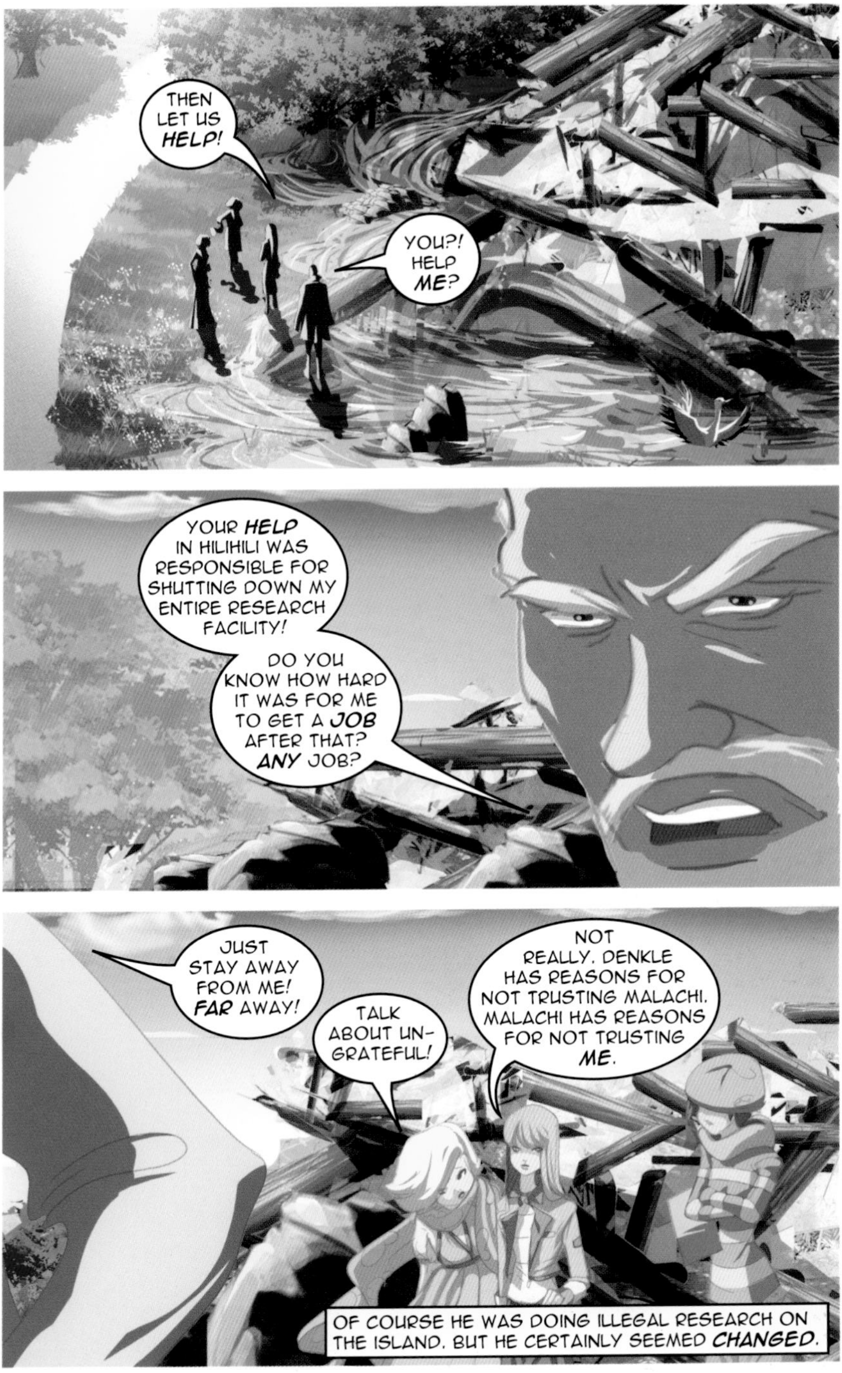
THEN LET US HELP!
YOU?! HELP ME?
YOUR HELP IN HILIHILI WAS RESPONSIBLE FOR SHUTTING DOWN MY ENTIRE RESEARCH FACILITY!
DO YOU KNOW HOW HARD IT WAS FOR ME TO GET A JOB AFTER THAT? ANY JOB?
JUST STAY AWAY FROM ME! FAR AWAY!
TALK ABOUT UN-GRATEFUL!
NOT REALLY. DENKLE HAS REASONS FOR NOT TRUSTING MALACHI. MALACHI HAS REASONS FOR NOT TRUSTING ME.
OF COURSE HE WAS DOING ILLEGAL RESEARCH ON THE ISLAND. BUT HE CERTAINLY SEEMED CHANGED.

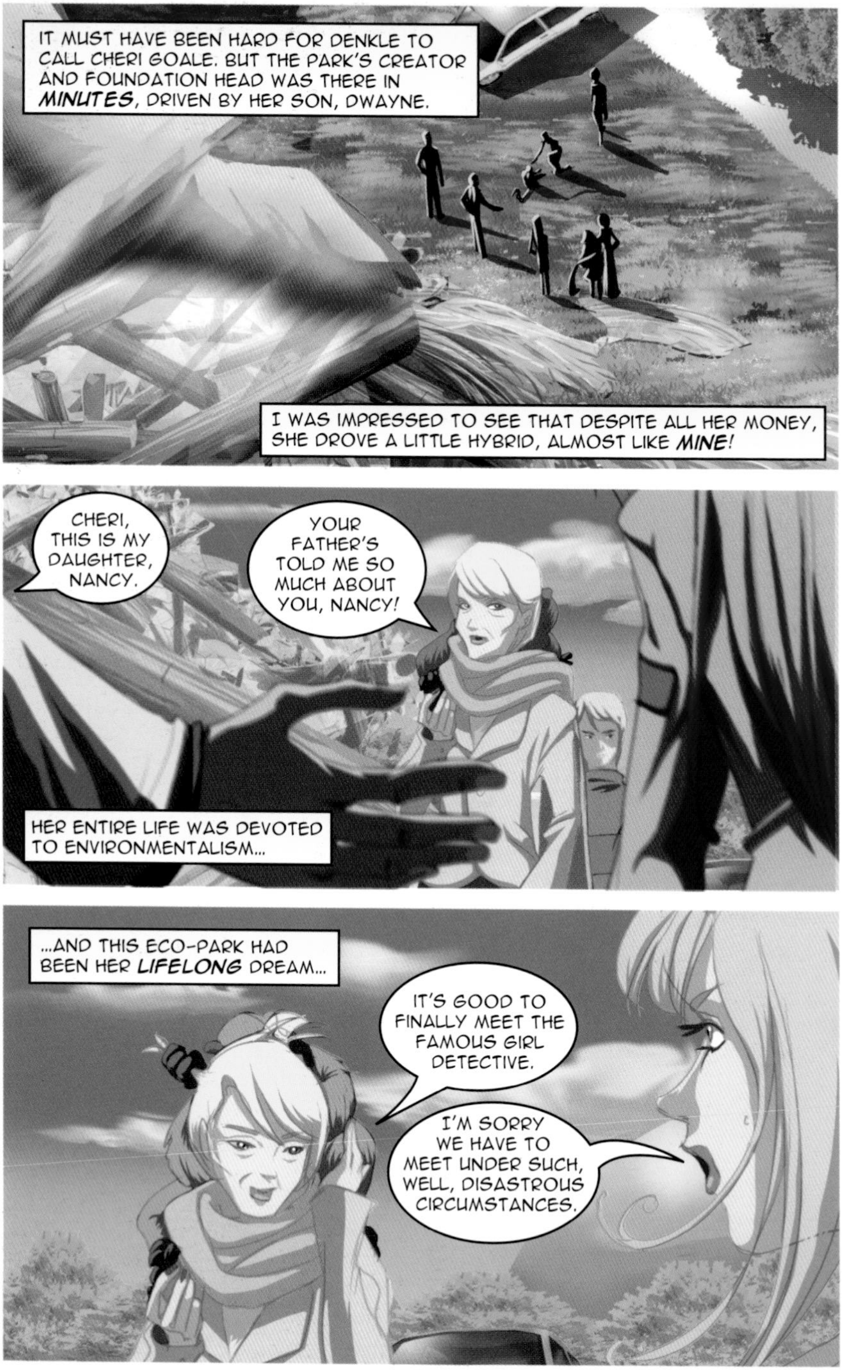
IT MUST HAVE BEEN HARD FOR DENKLE TO CALL CHERI GOALE. BUT THE PARK'S CREATOR AND FOUNDATION HEAD WAS THERE IN MINUTES, DRIVEN BY HER SON, DWAYNE.
I WAS IMPRESSED TO SEE THAT DESPITE ALL HER MONEY, SHE DROVE A LITTLE HYBRID, ALMOST LIKE MINE!
CHERI, THIS IS MY DAUGHTER, NANCY.
YOUR FATHER'S TOLD ME SO MUCH ABOUT YOU, NANCY!
HER ENTIRE LIFE WAS DEVOTED TO ENVIRONMENTALISM...
...AND THIS ECO-PARK HAD BEEN HER LIFELONG DREAM...
IT'S GOOD TO FINALLY MEET THE FAMOUS GIRL DETECTIVE.
I'M SORRY WE HAVE TO MEET UNDER SUCH, WELL, DISASTROUS CIRCUMSTANCES.

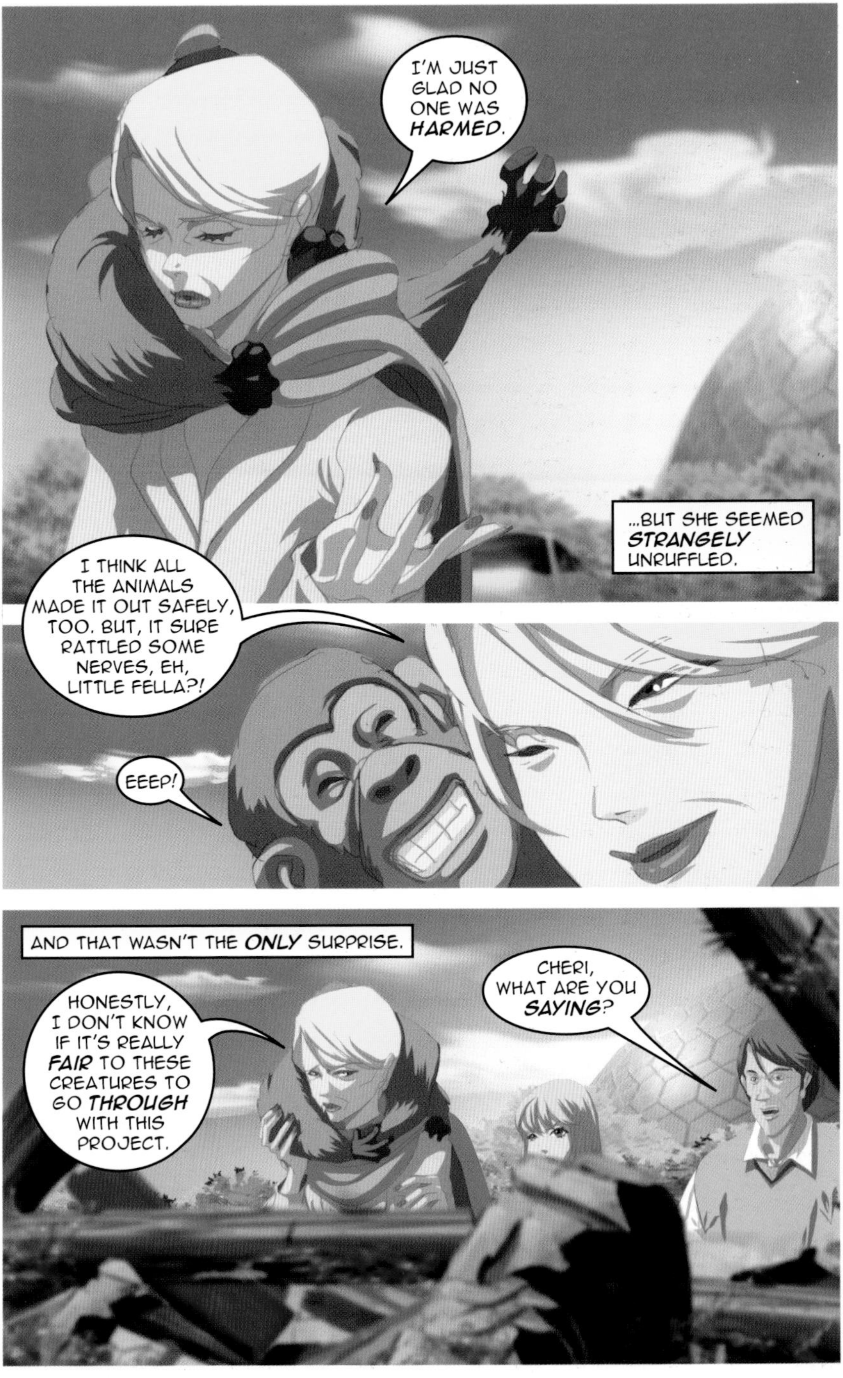
I'M JUST GLAD NO ONE WAS HARMED.
...BUT SHE SEEMED STRANGELY UNRUFFLED.
I THINK ALL THE ANIMALS MADE IT OUT SAFELY, TOO. BUT, IT SURE RATTLED SOME NERVES, EH, LITTLE FELLA?!
EEEP!
AND THAT WASN'T THE ONLY SURPRISE.
HONESTLY, I DON'T KNOW IF IT'S REALLY FAIR TO THESE CREATURES TO GO THROUGH WITH THIS PROJECT.
CHERI, WHAT ARE YOU SAYING?

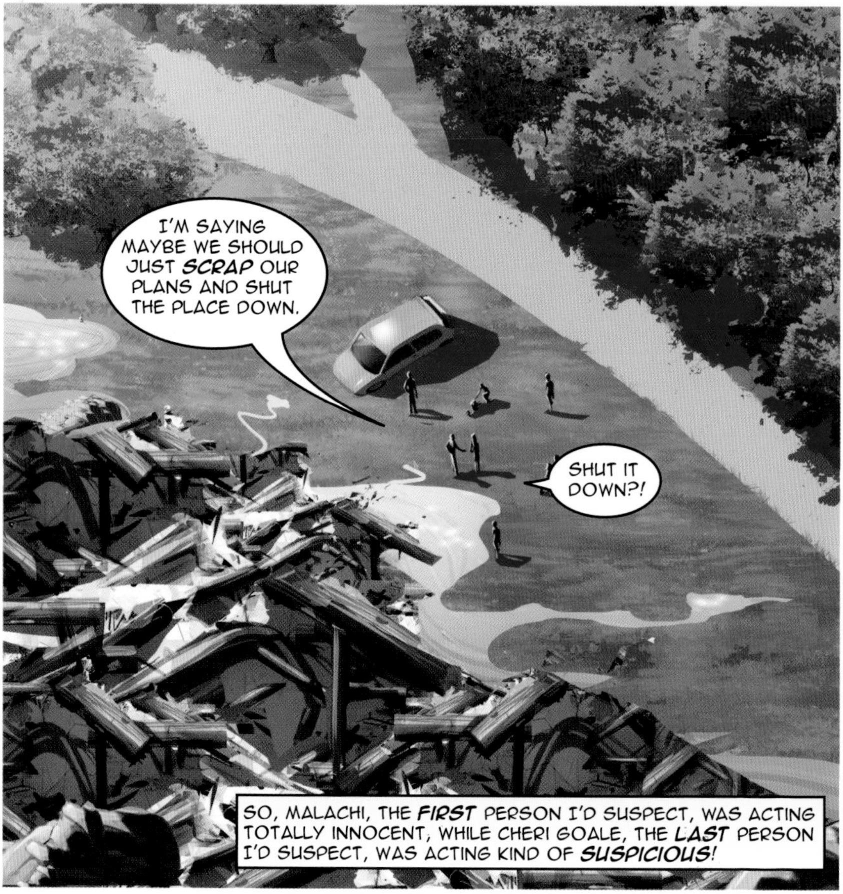
I'M SAYING MAYBE WE SHOULD JUST SCRAP OUR PLANS AND SHUT THE PLACE DOWN.
SHUT IT DOWN?!
SO, MALACHI, THE FIRST PERSON I'D SUSPECT, WAS ACTING TOTALLY INNOCENT, WHILE CHERI GOALE, THE LAST PERSON I'D SUSPECT, WAS ACTING KIND OF SUSPICIOUS!

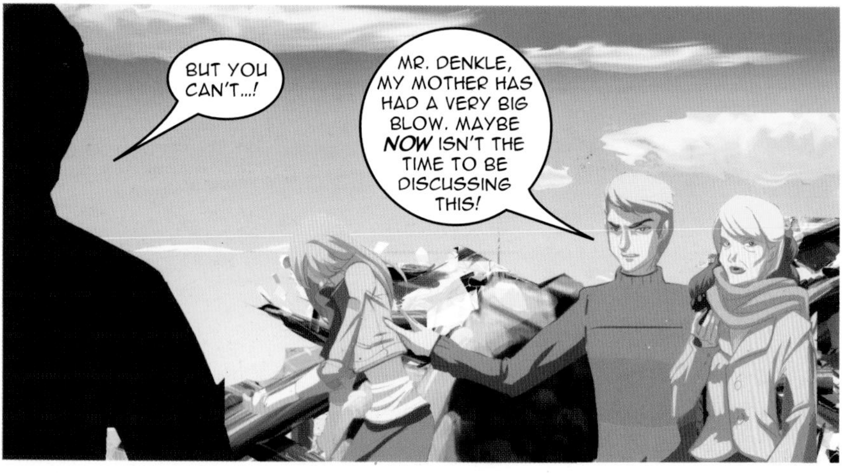
BUT YOU CAN'T...!
MR. DENKLE, MY MOTHER HAS HAD A VERY BIG BLOW. MAYBE NOW ISN'T THE TIME TO BE DISCUSSING THIS!

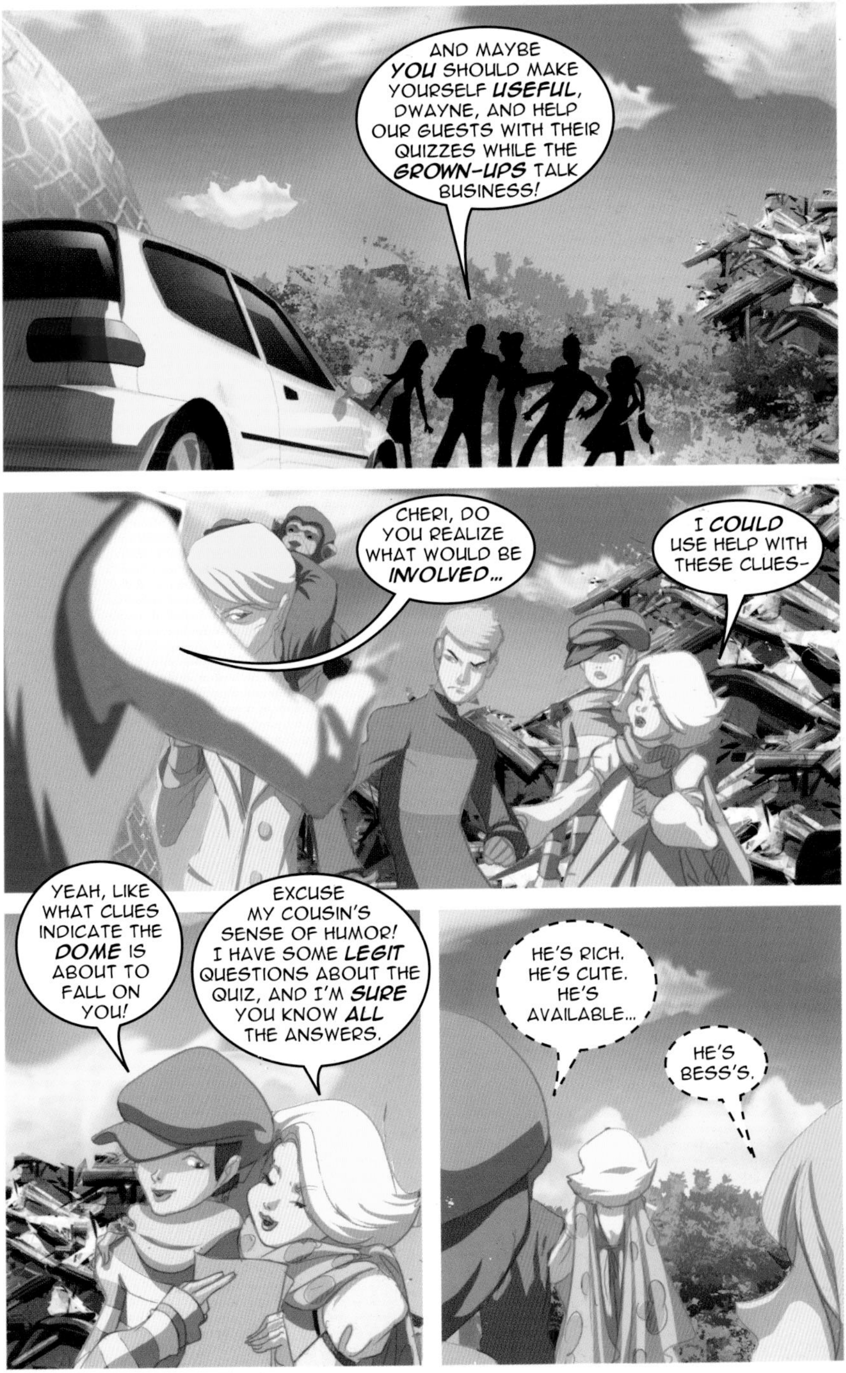
AND MAYBE YOU SHOULD MAKE YOURSELF USEFUL, DWAYNE, AND HELP OUR GUESTS WITH THEIR QUIZZES WHILE THE GROWN-UPS TALK BUSINESS!
CHERI, DO YOU REALIZE WHAT WOULD BE INVOLVED...
I COULD USE HELP WITH THESE CLUES-
YEAH, LIKE WHAT CLUES INDICATE THE DOME IS ABOUT TO FALL ON YOU!
EXCUSE MY COUSIN'S SENSE OF HUMOR! I HAVE SOME LEGIT QUESTIONS ABOUT THE QUIZ, AND I'M SURE YOU KNOW ALL THE ANSWERS.
HE'S RICH. HE'S CUTE. HE'S AVAILABLE...
HE'S BESS'S.

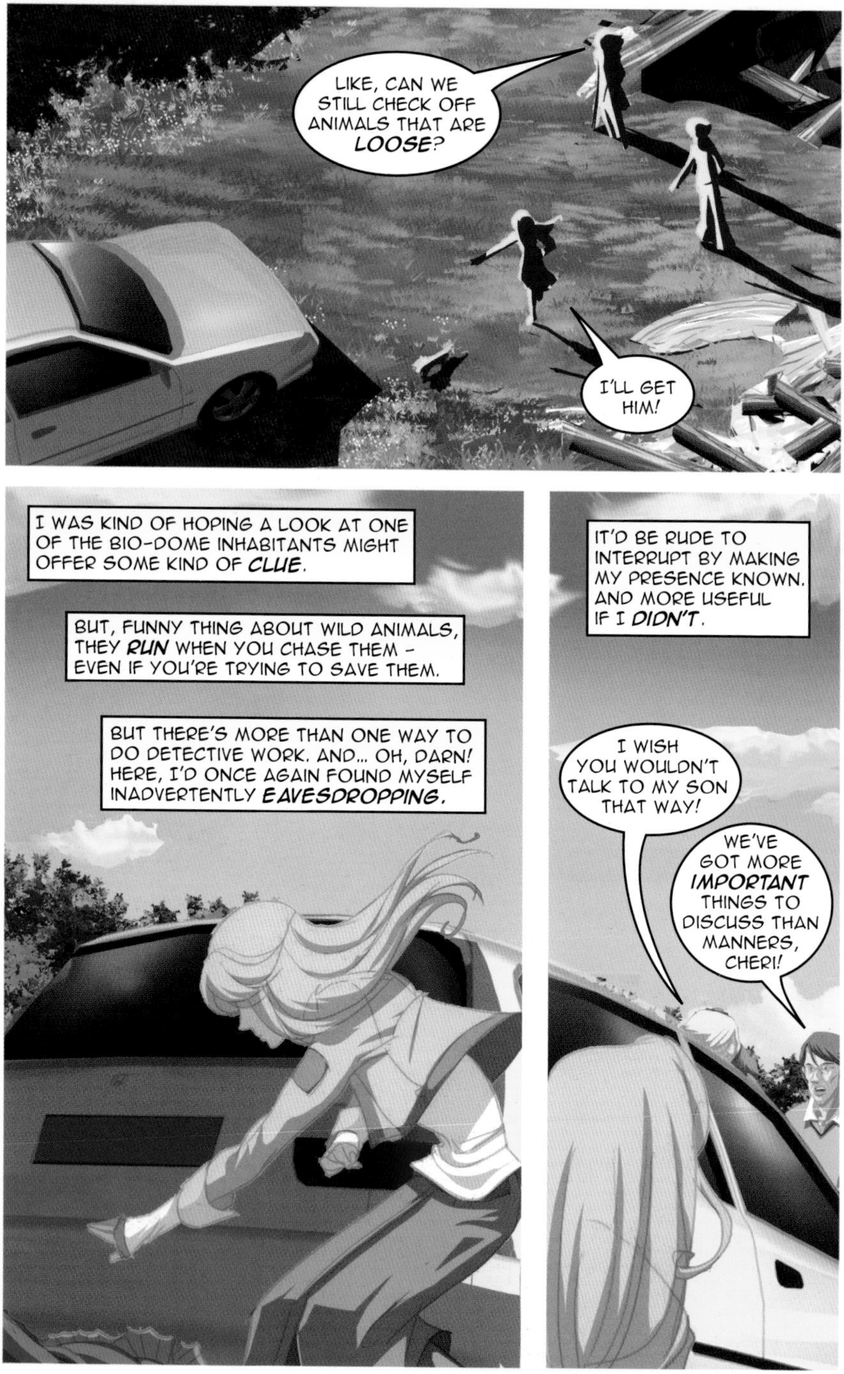
LIKE, CAN WE STILL CHECK OFF ANIMALS THAT ARE LOOSE?
I'LL GET HIM!
I WAS KIND OF HOPING A LOOK AT ONE OF THE BIO-DOME INHABITANTS MIGHT OFFER SOME KIND OF CLUE.
BUT, FUNNY THING ABOUT WILD ANIMALS, THEY RUN WHEN YOU CHASE THEM - EVEN IF YOU'RE TRYING TO SAVE THEM.
BUT THERE'S MORE THAN ONE WAY TO DO DETECTIVE WORK. AND... OH, DARN! HERE, I'D ONCE AGAIN FOUND MYSELF INADVERTENTLY EAVESDROPPING.
IT'D BE RUDE TO INTERRUPT BY MAKING MY PRESENCE KNOWN. AND MORE USEFUL IF I DIDN'T.
I WISH YOU WOULDN'T TALK TO MY SON THAT WAY!
WE'VE GOT MORE IMPORTANT THINGS TO DISCUSS THAN MANNERS, CHERI!

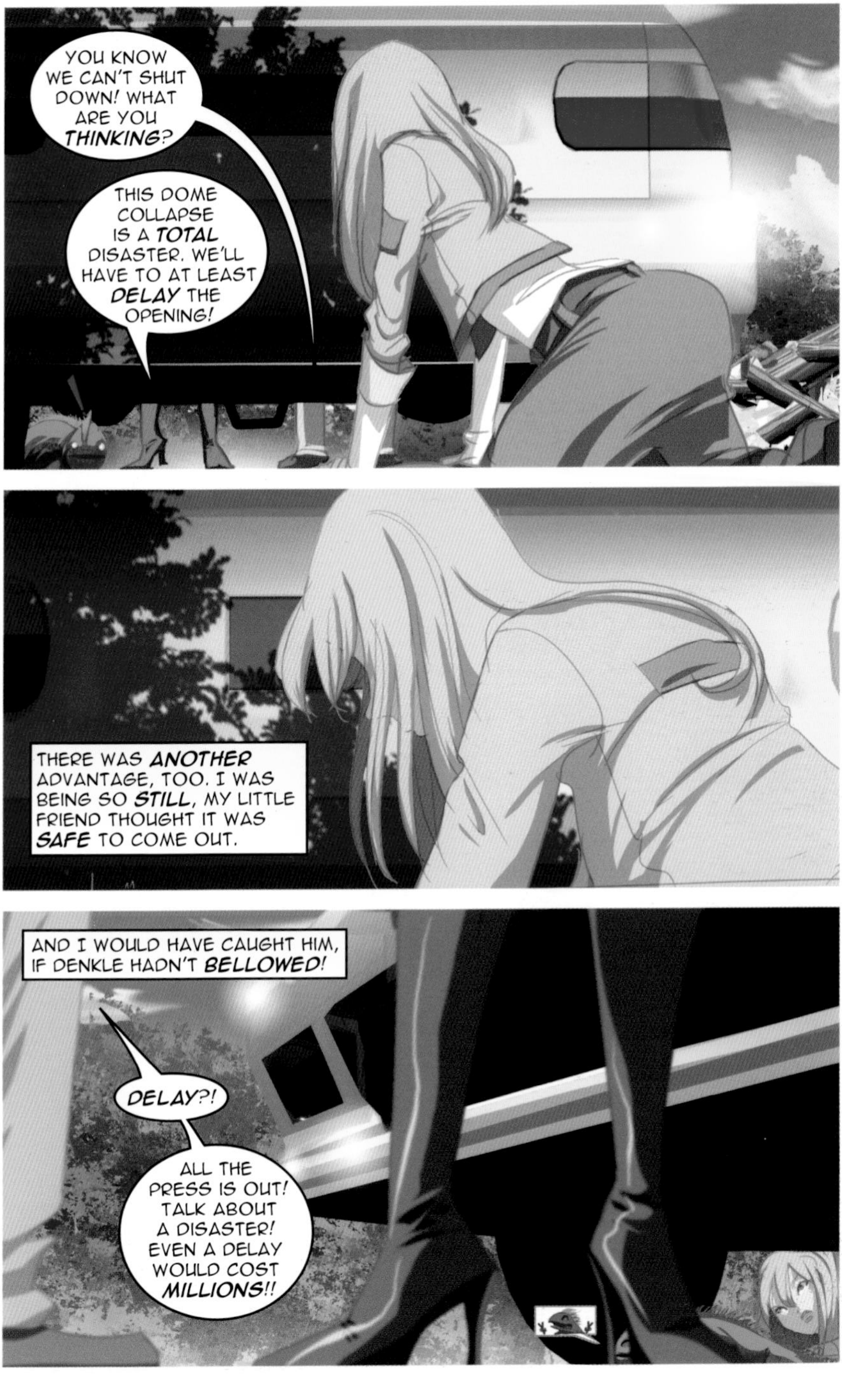
YOU KNOW WE CAN'T SHUT DOWN! WHAT ARE YOU THINKING?
THIS DOME COLLAPSE IS A TOTAL DISASTER. WE'LL HAVE TO AT LEAST DELAY THE OPENING!
THERE WAS ANOTHER ADVANTAGE, TOO. I WAS BEING SO STILL, MY LITTLE FRIEND THOUGHT IT WAS SAFE TO COME OUT.
AND I WOULD HAVE CAUGHT HIM, IF DENKLE HADN'T BELLOWED!
DELAY?!
ALL THE PRESS IS OUT! TALK ABOUT A DISASTER! EVEN A DELAY WOULD COST MILLIONS!!

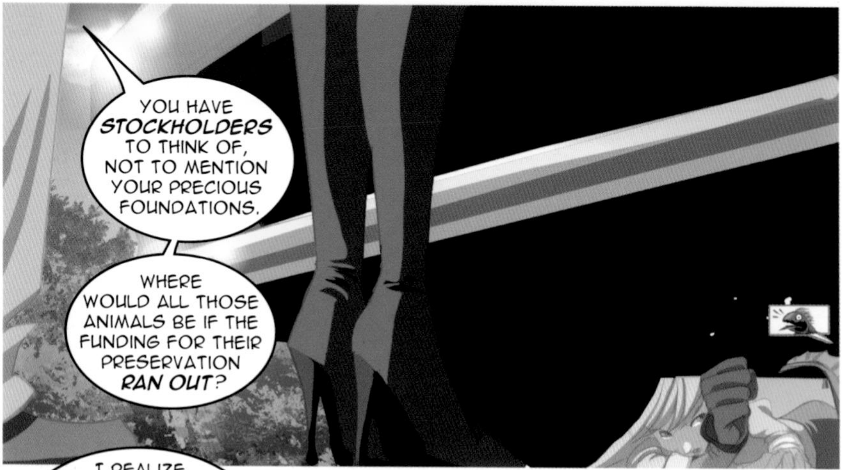
YOU HAVE STOCKHOLDERS TO THINK OF, NOT TO MENTION YOUR PRECIOUS FOUNDATIONS.
WHERE WOULD ALL THOSE ANIMALS BE IF THE FUNDING FOR THEIR PRESERVATION RAN OUT?

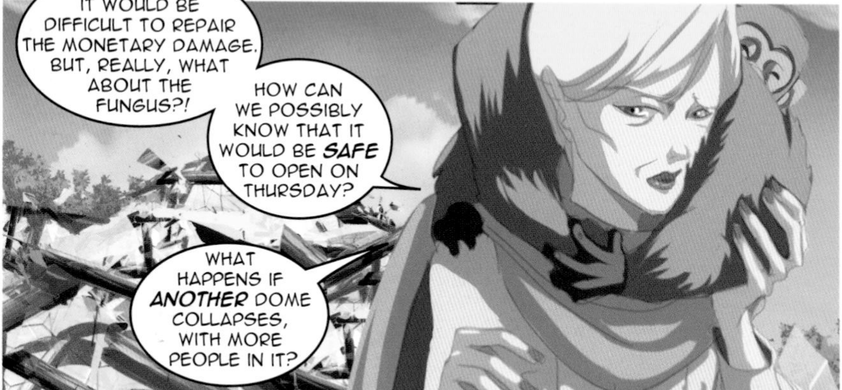
I REALIZE IT WOULD BE DIFFICULT TO REPAIR THE MONETARY DAMAGE. BUT, REALLY, WHAT ABOUT THE FUNGUS?!
HOW CAN WE POSSIBLY KNOW THAT IT WOULD BE SAFE TO OPEN ON THURSDAY?
WHAT HAPPENS IF ANOTHER DOME COLLAPSES, WITH MORE PEOPLE IN IT?

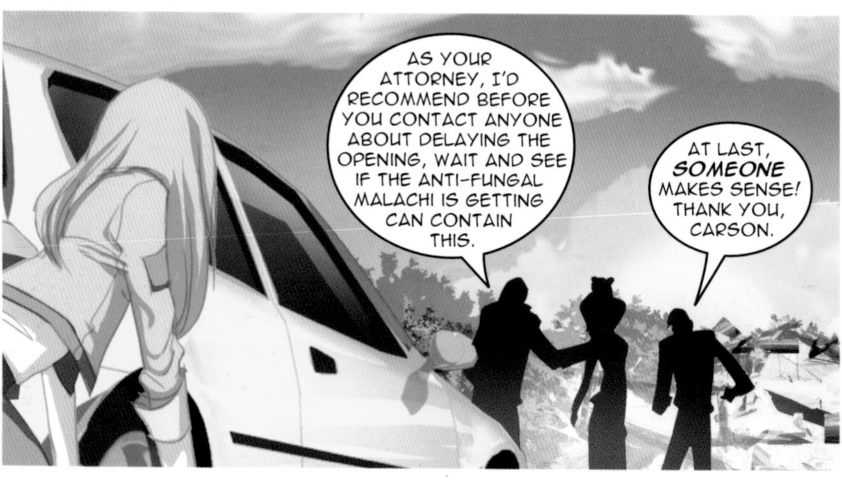
AS YOUR ATTORNEY, I'D RECOMMEND BEFORE YOU CONTACT ANYONE ABOUT DELAYING THE OPENING, WAIT AND SEE IF THE ANTI-FUNGAL MALACHI IS GETTING CAN CONTAIN THIS.
AT LAST, SOMEONE MAKES SENSE! THANK YOU, CARSON.

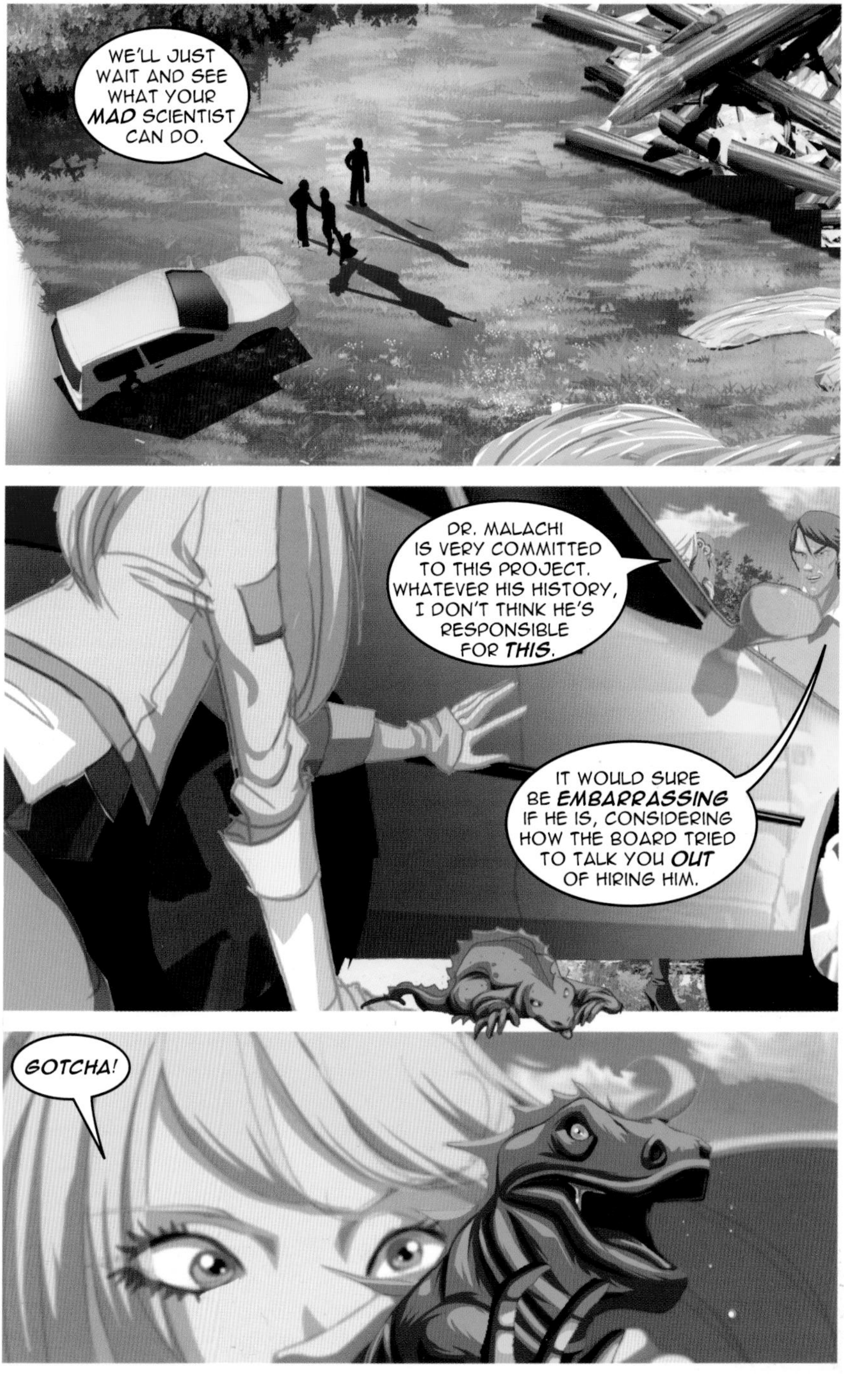
WE'LL JUST WAIT AND SEE WHAT YOUR *MAD* SCIENTIST CAN DO.
DR. MALACHI IS VERY COMMITTED TO THIS PROJECT. WHATEVER HIS HISTORY, I DON'T THINK HE'S RESPONSIBLE FOR *THIS*.
IT WOULD SURE BE *EMBARRASSING* IF HE IS, CONSIDERING HOW THE BOARD TRIED TO TALK YOU *OUT* OF HIRING HIM.
GOTCHA!

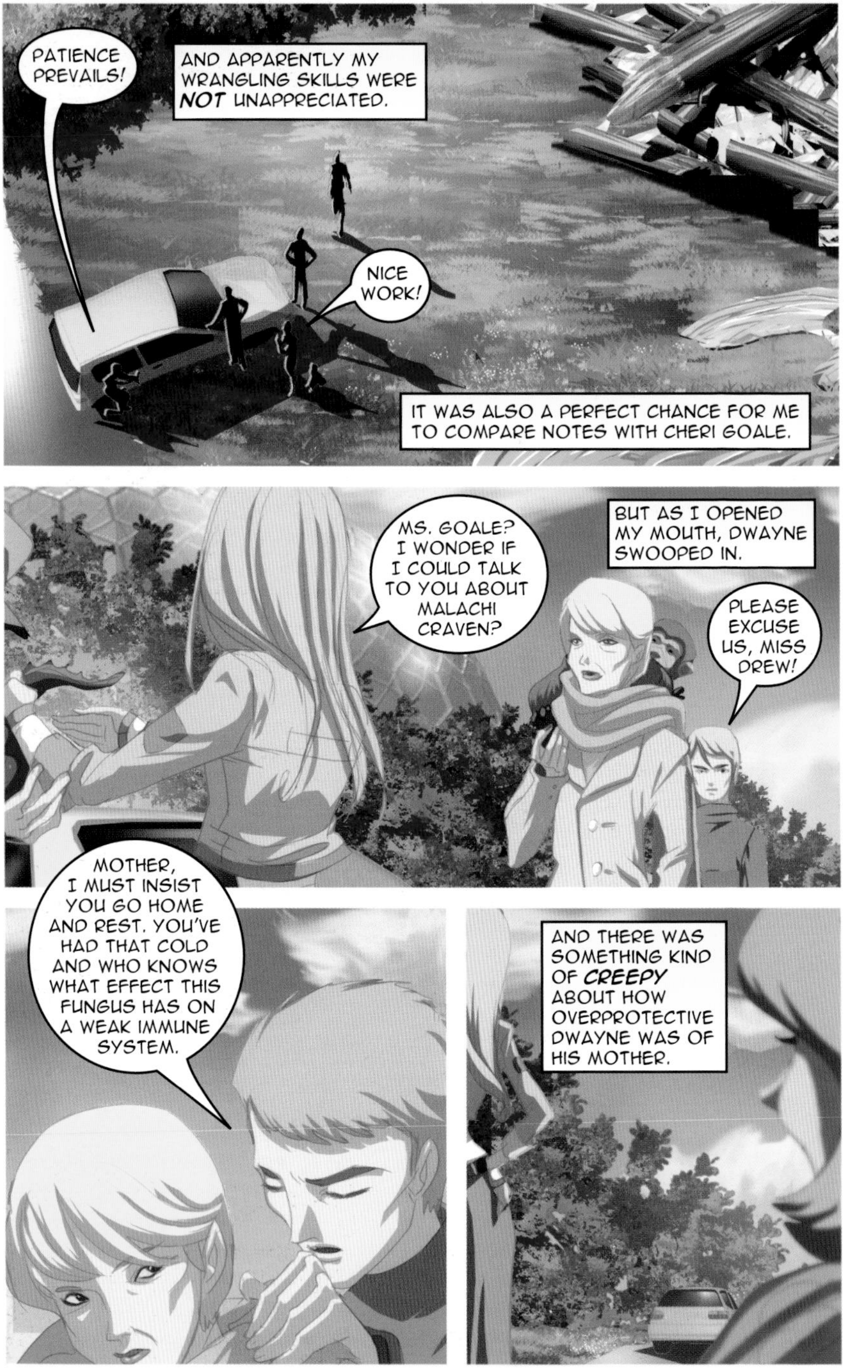
PATIENCE PREVAILS!
AND APPARENTLY MY WRANGLING SKILLS WERE NOT UNAPPRECIATED.
NICE WORK!
IT WAS ALSO A PERFECT CHANCE FOR ME TO COMPARE NOTES WITH CHERI GOALE.
MS. GOALE? I WONDER IF I COULD TALK TO YOU ABOUT MALACHI CRAVEN?
BUT AS I OPENED MY MOUTH, DWAYNE SWOOPED IN.
PLEASE EXCUSE US, MISS DREW!
MOTHER, I MUST INSIST YOU GO HOME AND REST. YOU'VE HAD THAT COLD AND WHO KNOWS WHAT EFFECT THIS FUNGUS HAS ON A WEAK IMMUNE SYSTEM.
AND THERE WAS SOMETHING KIND OF CREEPY ABOUT HOW OVERPROTECTIVE DWAYNE WAS OF HIS MOTHER.

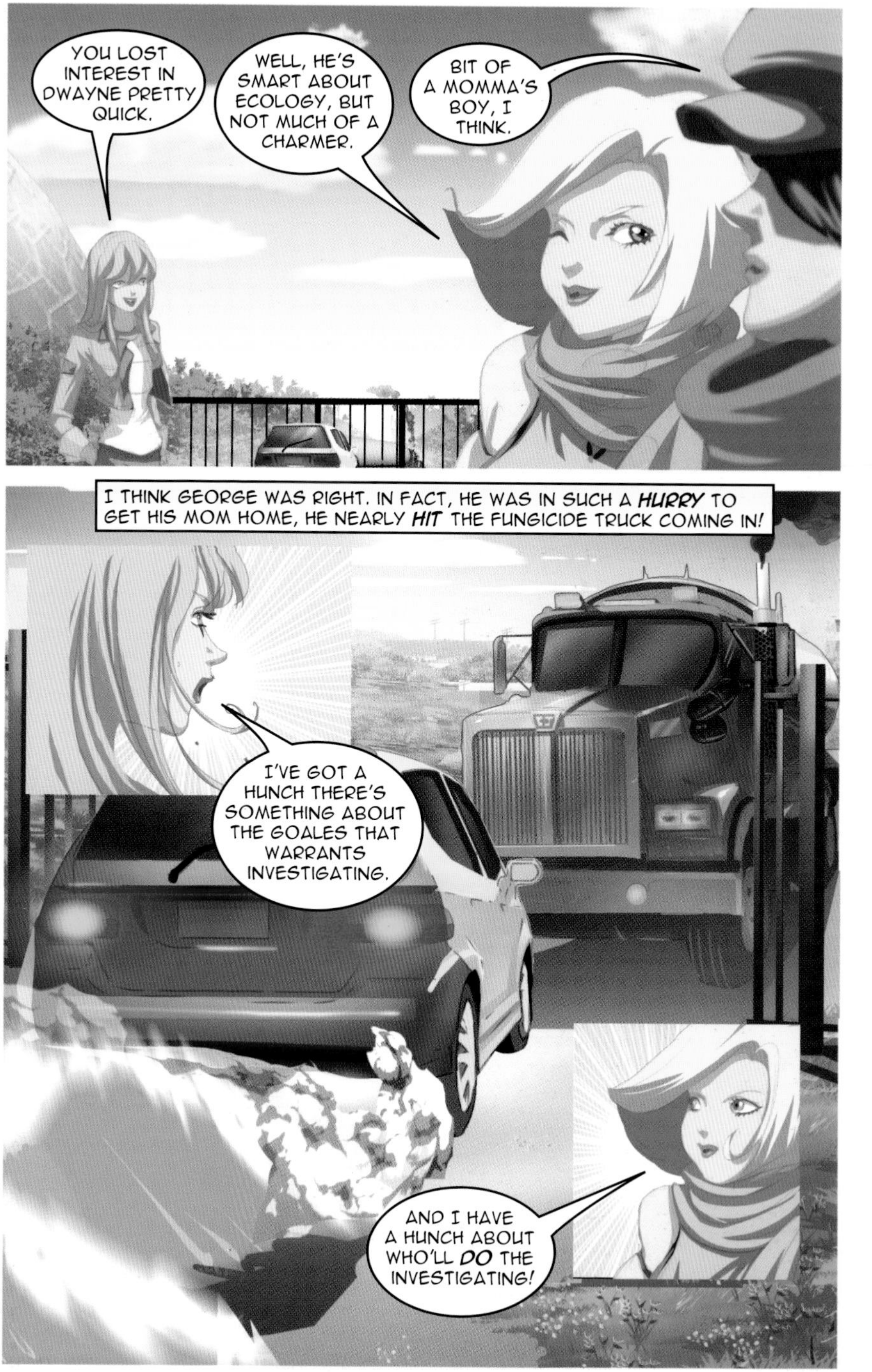
YOU LOST INTEREST IN DWAYNE PRETTY QUICK.
WELL, HE'S SMART ABOUT ECOLOGY, BUT NOT MUCH OF A CHARMER.
BIT OF A MOMMA'S BOY, I THINK.
I THINK GEORGE WAS RIGHT. IN FACT, HE WAS IN SUCH A HURRY TO GET HIS MOM HOME, HE NEARLY HIT THE FUNGICIDE TRUCK COMING IN!
I'VE GOT A HUNCH THERE'S SOMETHING ABOUT THE GOALES THAT WARRANTS INVESTIGATING.
AND I HAVE A HUNCH ABOUT WHO'LL DO THE INVESTIGATING!

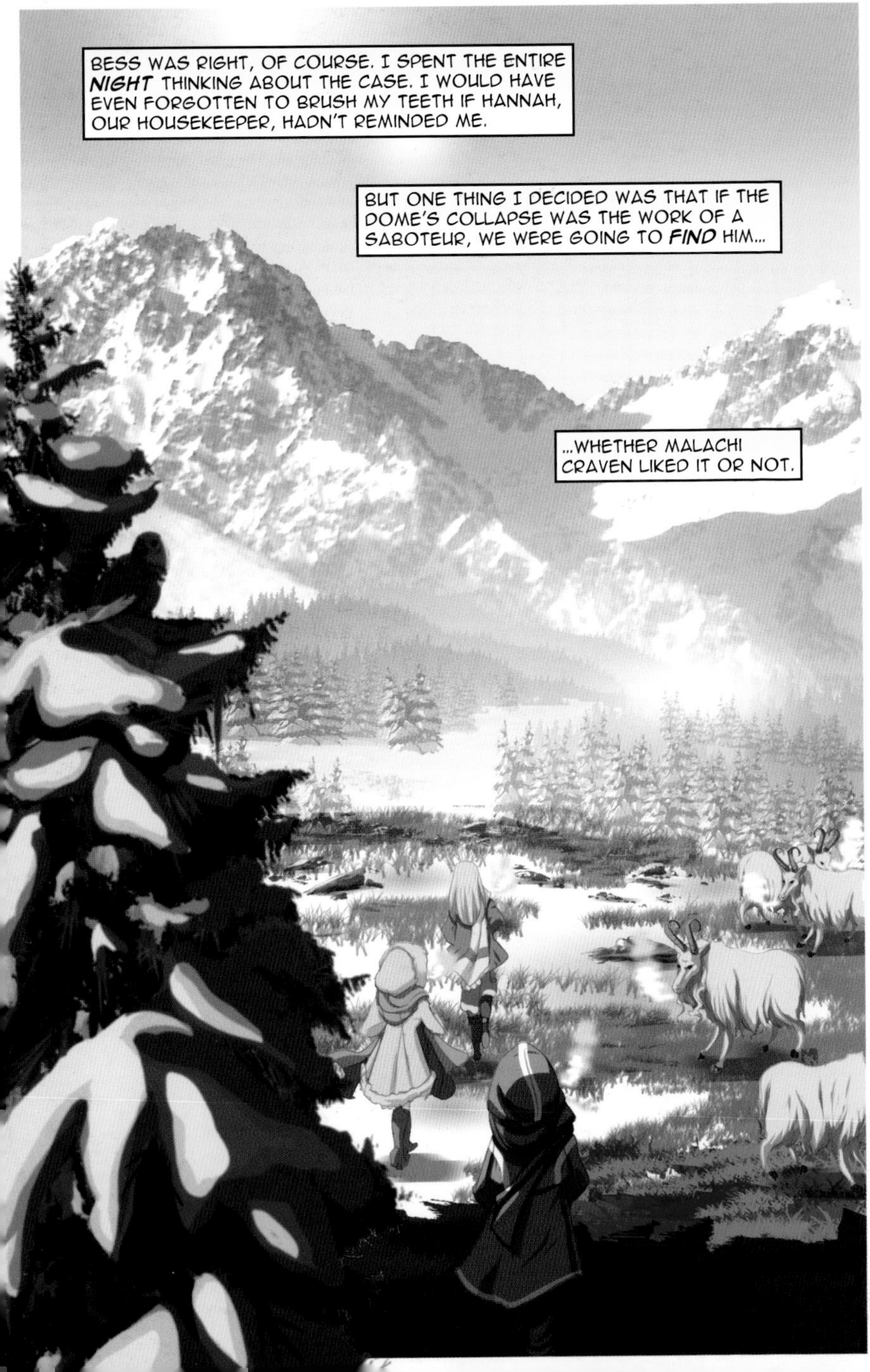
BESS WAS RIGHT, OF COURSE. I SPENT THE ENTIRE NIGHT THINKING ABOUT THE CASE. I WOULD HAVE EVEN FORGOTTEN TO BRUSH MY TEETH IF HANNAH, OUR HOUSEKEEPER, HADN'T REMINDED ME.
BUT ONE THING I DECIDED WAS THAT IF THE DOME'S COLLAPSE WAS THE WORK OF A SABOTEUR, WE WERE GOING TO FIND HIM...
...WHETHER MALACHI CRAVEN LIKED IT OR NOT.

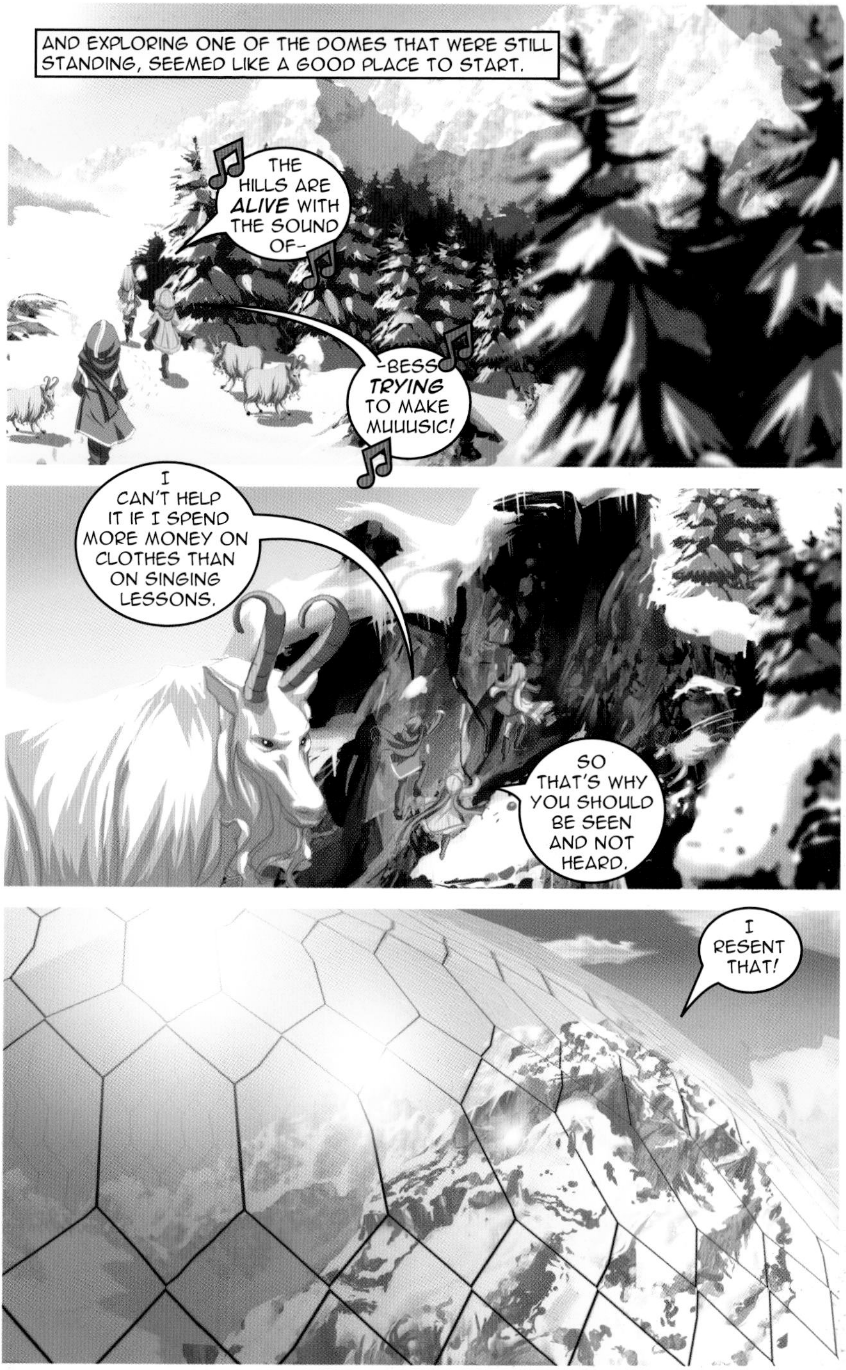
AND EXPLORING ONE OF THE DOMES THAT WERE STILL STANDING, SEEMED LIKE A GOOD PLACE TO START.
THE HILLS ARE ALIVE WITH THE SOUND OF-
-BESS TRYING TO MAKE MUUUSIC!
I CAN'T HELP IT IF I SPEND MORE MONEY ON CLOTHES THAN ON SINGING LESSONS.
SO THAT'S WHY YOU SHOULD BE SEEN AND NOT HEARD.
I RESENT THAT!

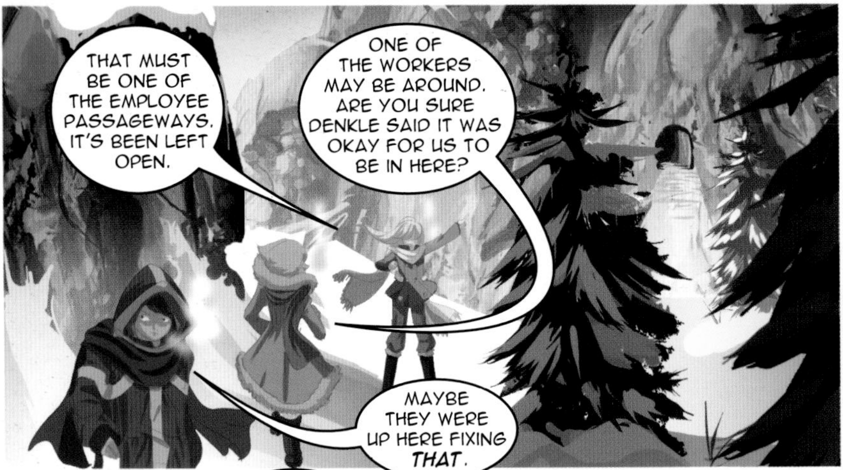
THAT MUST BE ONE OF THE EMPLOYEE PASSAGEWAYS. IT'S BEEN LEFT OPEN.
ONE OF THE WORKERS MAY BE AROUND. ARE YOU SURE DENKLE SAID IT WAS OKAY FOR US TO BE IN HERE?
MAYBE THEY WERE UP HERE FIXING *THAT*.

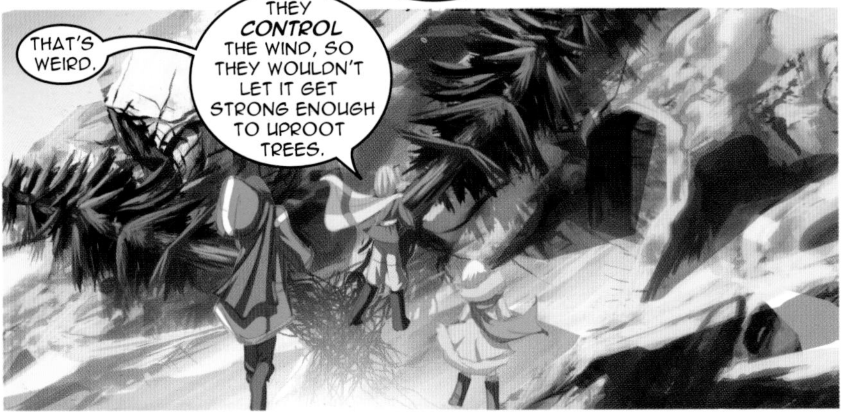
THAT'S WEIRD.
THEY *CONTROL* THE WIND, SO THEY WOULDN'T LET IT GET STRONG ENOUGH TO UPROOT TREES.

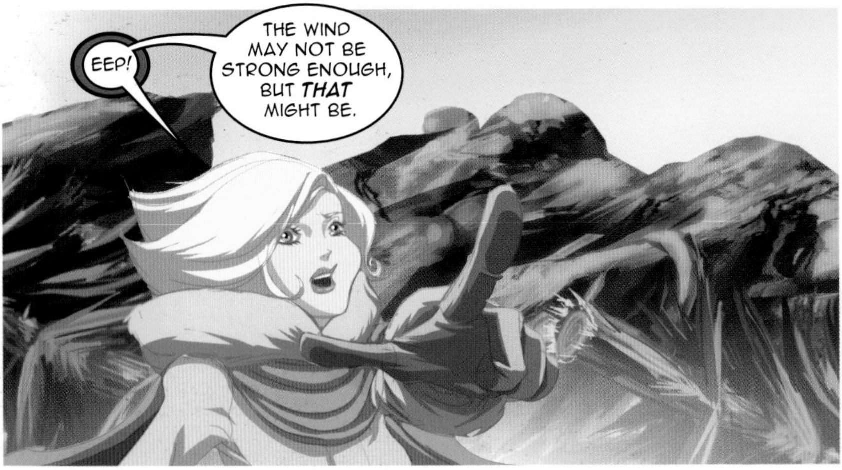
EEP!
THE WIND MAY NOT BE STRONG ENOUGH, BUT *THAT* MIGHT BE.

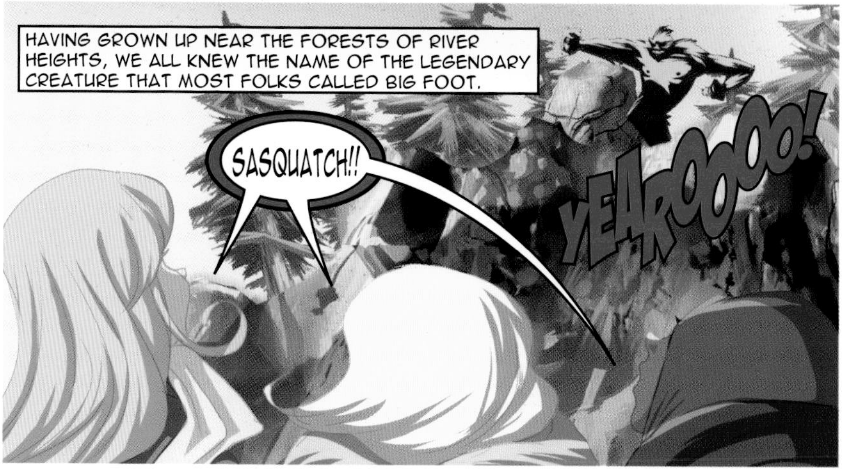
HAVING GROWN UP NEAR THE FORESTS OF RIVER HEIGHTS, WE ALL KNEW THE NAME OF THE LEGENDARY CREATURE THAT MOST FOLKS CALLED BIG FOOT.
SASQUATCH!!
YEAROOOO!

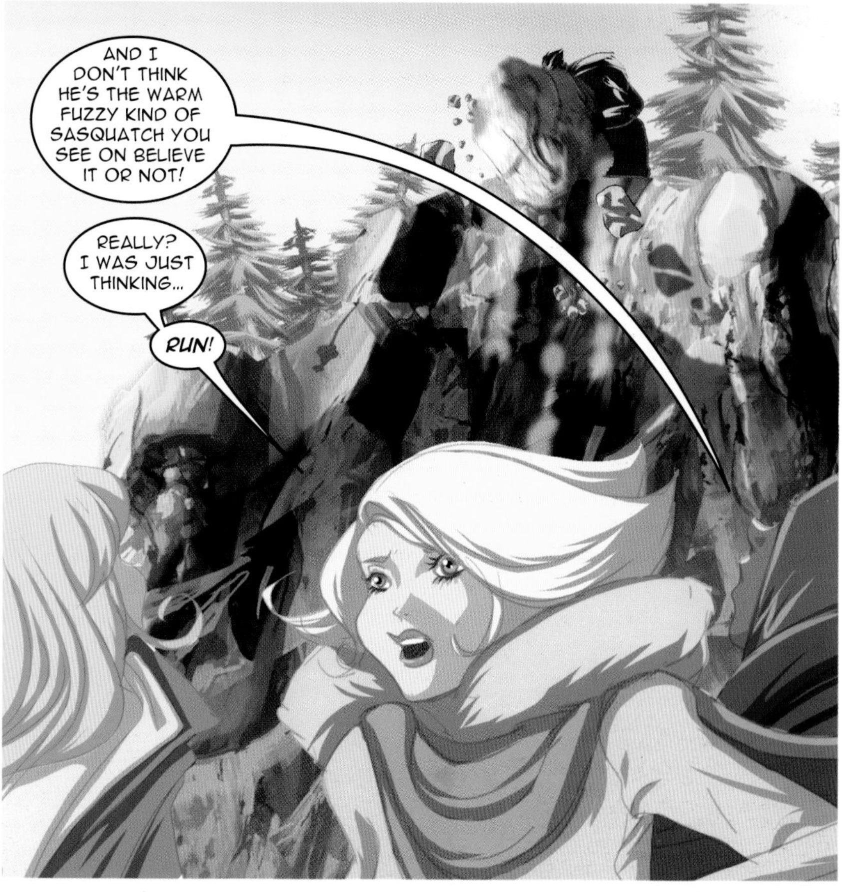
AND I DON'T THINK HE'S THE WARM FUZZY KIND OF SASQUATCH YOU SEE ON BELIEVE IT OR NOT!
REALLY? I WAS JUST THINKING...
RUN!

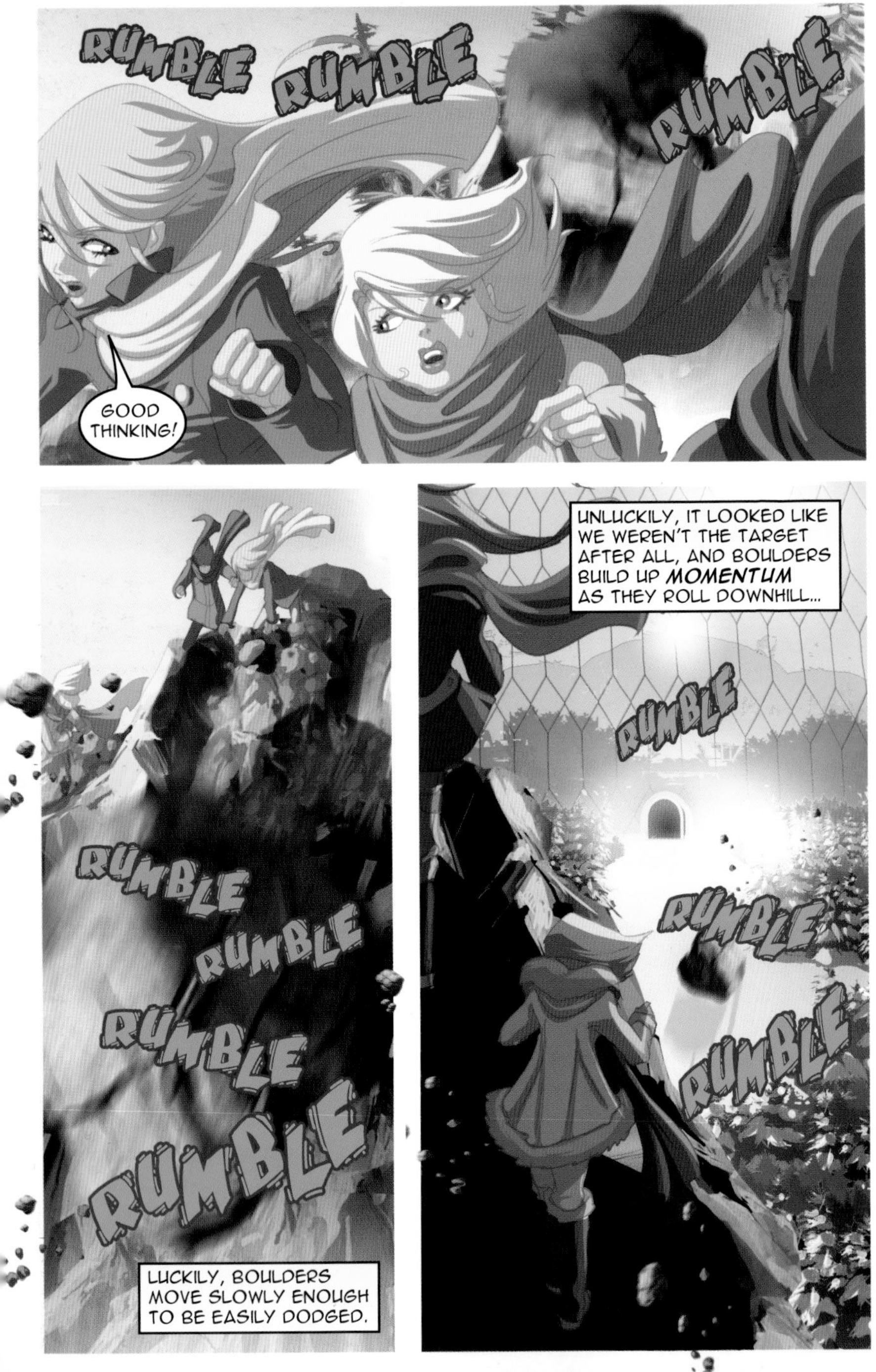
RUMBLE
RUMBLE
RUMBLE
GOOD THINKING!
RUMBLE
RUMBLE
RUMBLE
RUMBLE
LUCKILY, BOULDERS MOVE SLOWLY ENOUGH TO BE EASILY DODGED.
UNLUCKILY, IT LOOKED LIKE WE WEREN'T THE TARGET AFTER ALL, AND BOULDERS BUILD UP *MOMENTUM* AS THEY ROLL DOWNHILL...
RUMBLE
RUMBLE
RUMBLE

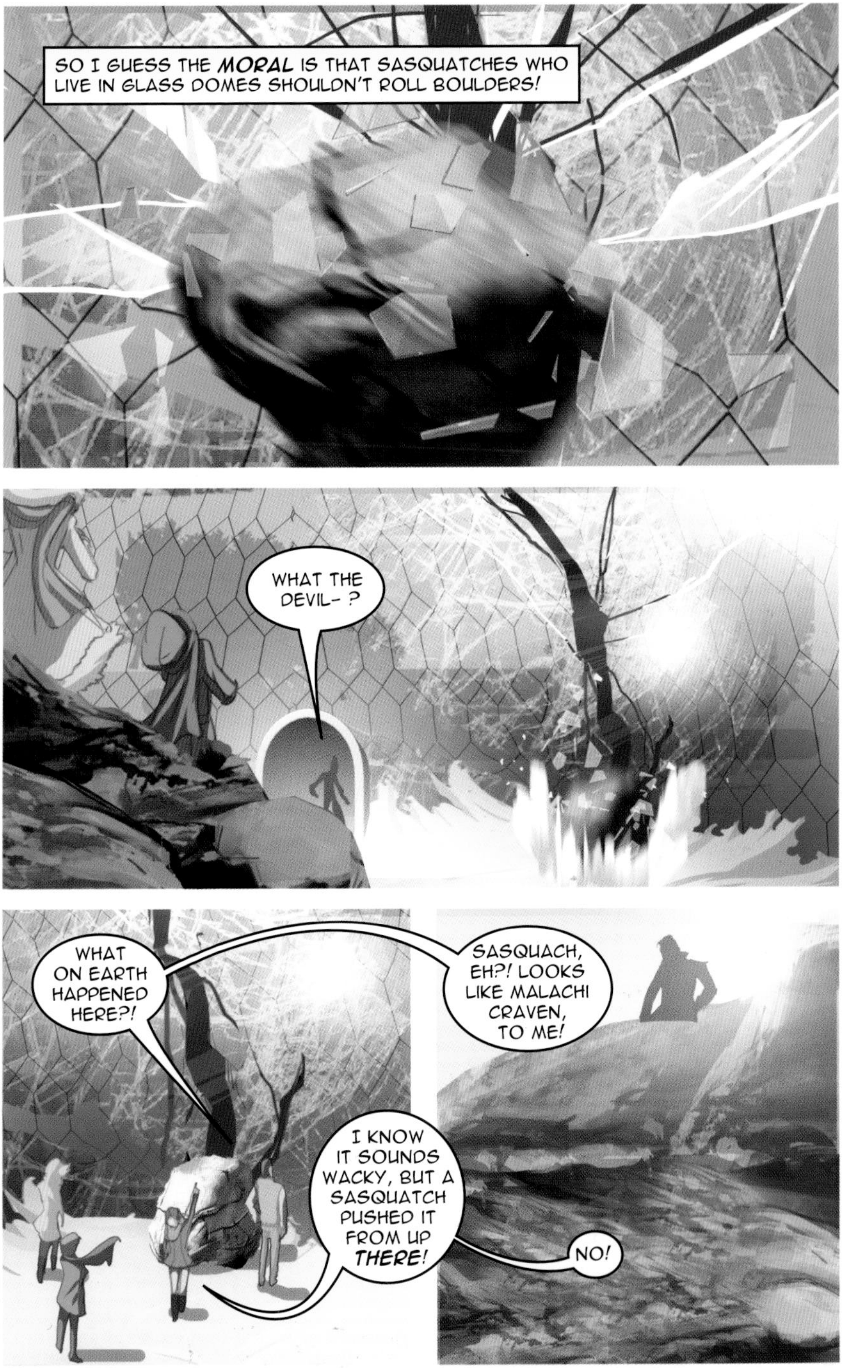
SO I GUESS THE *MORAL* IS THAT SASQUATCHES WHO LIVE IN GLASS DOMES SHOULDN'T ROLL BOULDERS!
WHAT THE DEVIL- ?
WHAT ON EARTH HAPPENED HERE?!
I KNOW IT SOUNDS WACKY, BUT A SASQUATCH PUSHED IT FROM UP *THERE*!
SASQUACH, EH?! LOOKS LIKE MALACHI CRAVEN, TO ME!
NO!

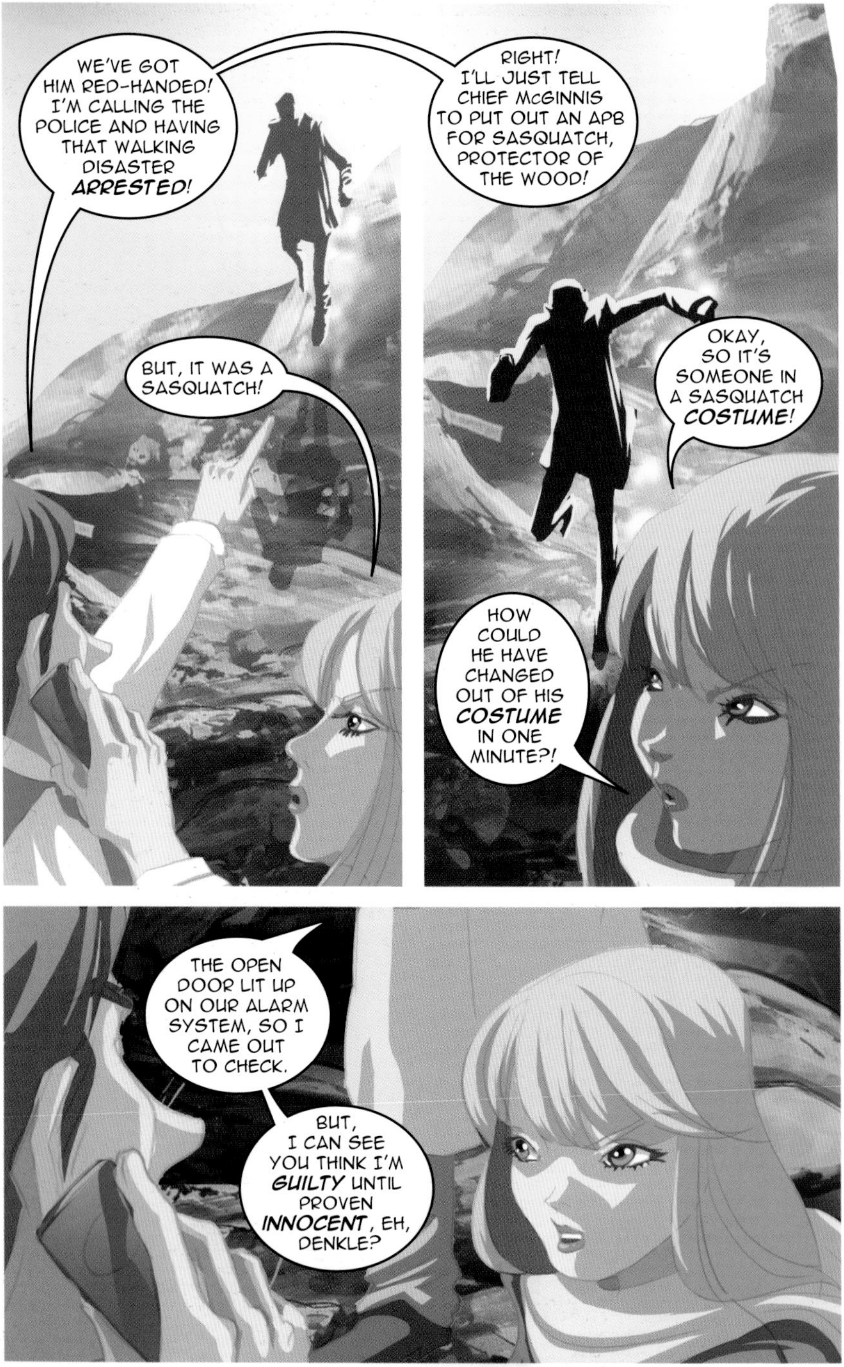
WE'VE GOT HIM RED-HANDED! I'M CALLING THE POLICE AND HAVING THAT WALKING DISASTER *ARRESTED*!
RIGHT! I'LL JUST TELL CHIEF McGINNIS TO PUT OUT AN APB FOR SASQUATCH, PROTECTOR OF THE WOOD!
BUT, IT WAS A SASQUATCH!
OKAY, SO IT'S SOMEONE IN A SASQUATCH *COSTUME*!
HOW COULD HE HAVE CHANGED OUT OF HIS *COSTUME* IN ONE MINUTE?!
THE OPEN DOOR LIT UP ON OUR ALARM SYSTEM, SO I CAME OUT TO CHECK.
BUT, I CAN SEE YOU THINK I'M *GUILTY* UNTIL PROVEN *INNOCENT*, EH, DENKLE?

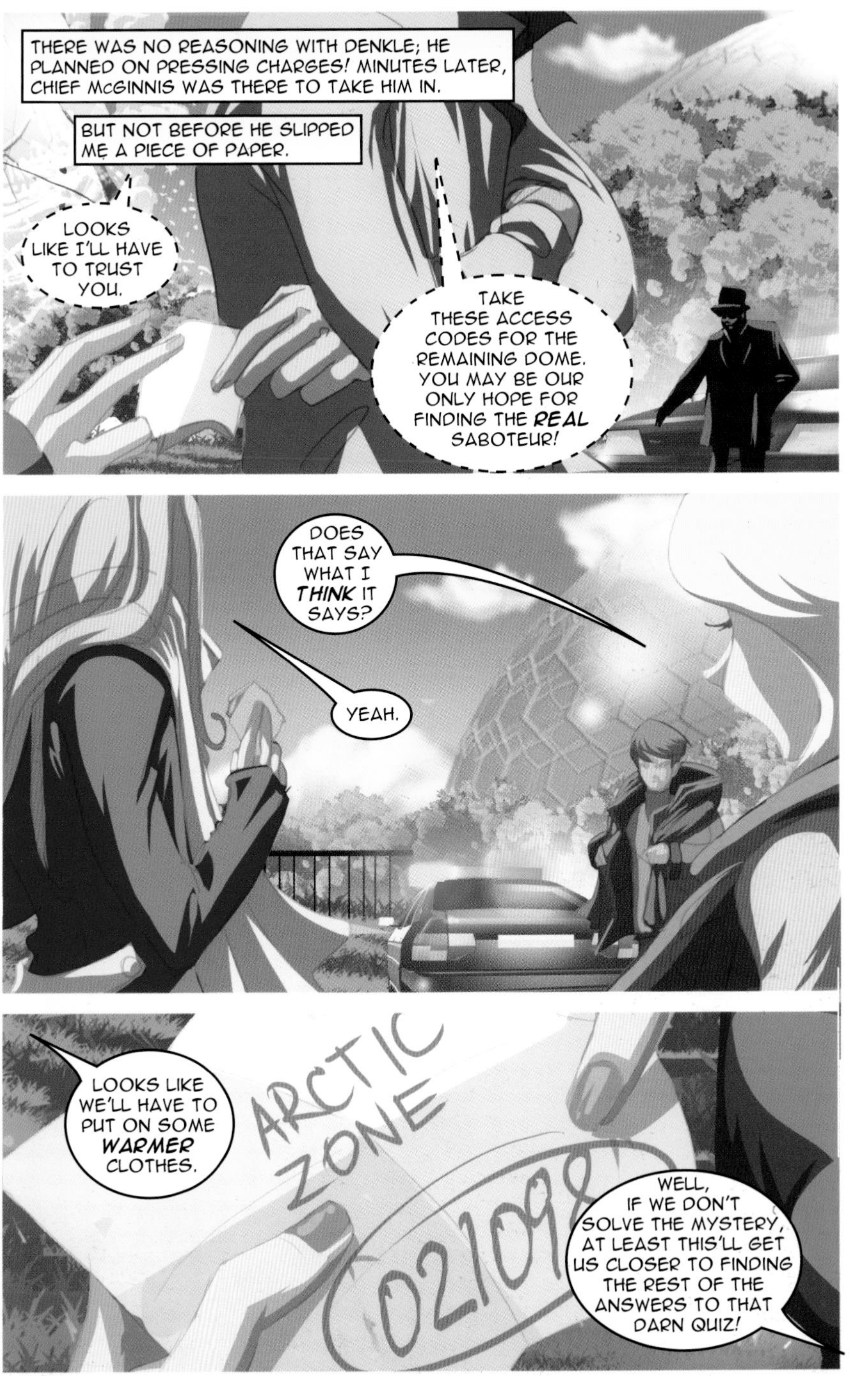
THERE WAS NO REASONING WITH DENKLE; HE PLANNED ON PRESSING CHARGES! MINUTES LATER, CHIEF McGINNIS WAS THERE TO TAKE HIM IN.
BUT NOT BEFORE HE SLIPPED ME A PIECE OF PAPER.
LOOKS LIKE I'LL HAVE TO TRUST YOU.
TAKE THESE ACCESS CODES FOR THE REMAINING DOME. YOU MAY BE OUR ONLY HOPE FOR FINDING THE REAL SABOTEUR!
DOES THAT SAY WHAT I THINK IT SAYS?
YEAH.
LOOKS LIKE WE'LL HAVE TO PUT ON SOME WARMER CLOTHES.
ARCTIC ZONE
021098
WELL, IF WE DON'T SOLVE THE MYSTERY, AT LEAST THIS'LL GET US CLOSER TO FINDING THE REST OF THE ANSWERS TO THAT DARN QUIZ!

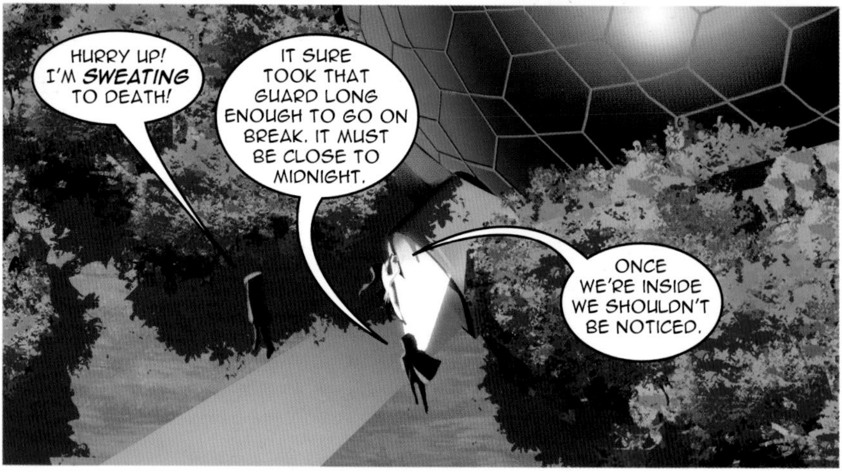
HURRY UP! I'M SWEATING TO DEATH!
IT SURE TOOK THAT GUARD LONG ENOUGH TO GO ON BREAK. IT MUST BE CLOSE TO MIDNIGHT.
ONCE WE'RE INSIDE WE SHOULDN'T BE NOTICED.

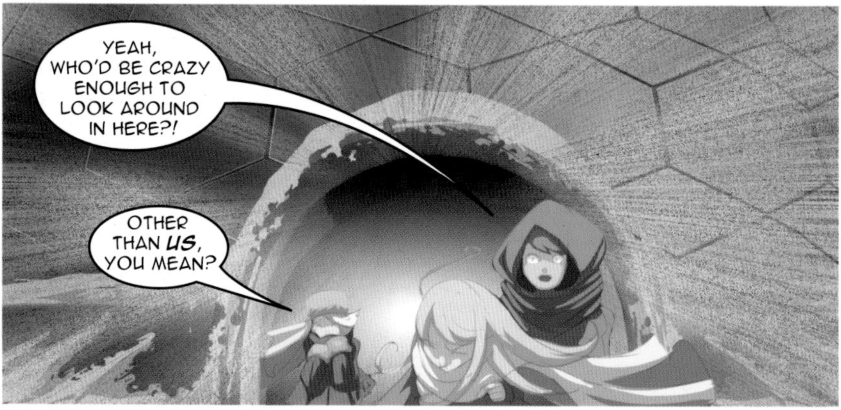
YEAH, WHO'D BE CRAZY ENOUGH TO LOOK AROUND IN HERE?!
OTHER THAN US, YOU MEAN?

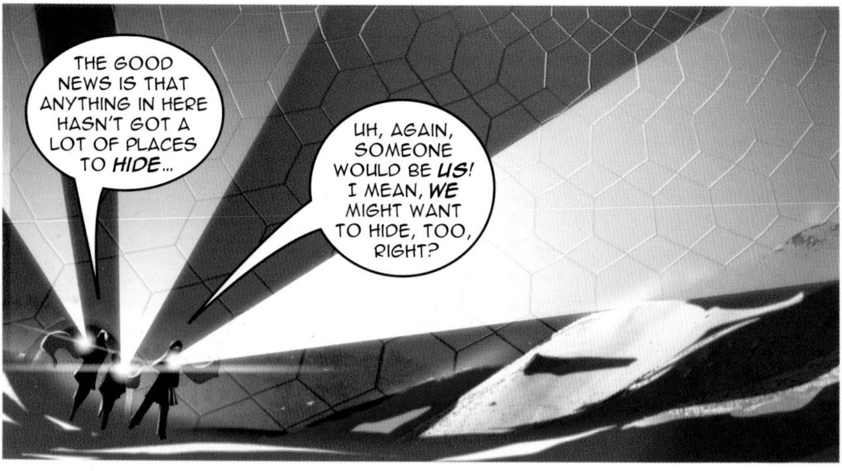
THE GOOD NEWS IS THAT ANYTHING IN HERE HASN'T GOT A LOT OF PLACES TO HIDE...
UH, AGAIN, SOMEONE WOULD BE US! I MEAN, WE MIGHT WANT TO HIDE, TOO, RIGHT?

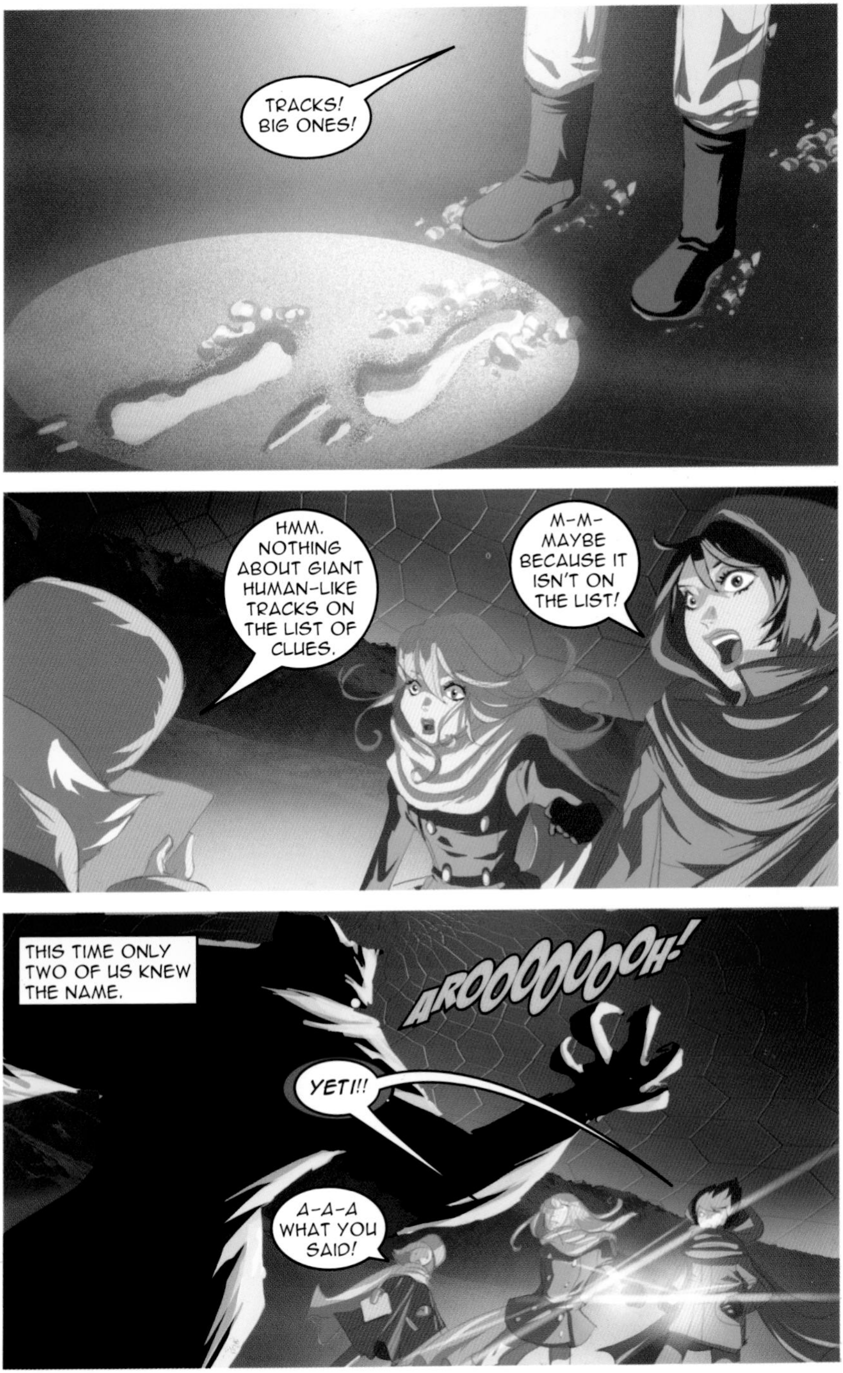
TRACKS! BIG ONES!
HMM. NOTHING ABOUT GIANT HUMAN-LIKE TRACKS ON THE LIST OF CLUES.
M-M-MAYBE BECAUSE IT ISN'T ON THE LIST!
THIS TIME ONLY TWO OF US KNEW THE NAME.
AROOOOOOOOH!
YETI!!
A-A-A WHAT YOU SAID!

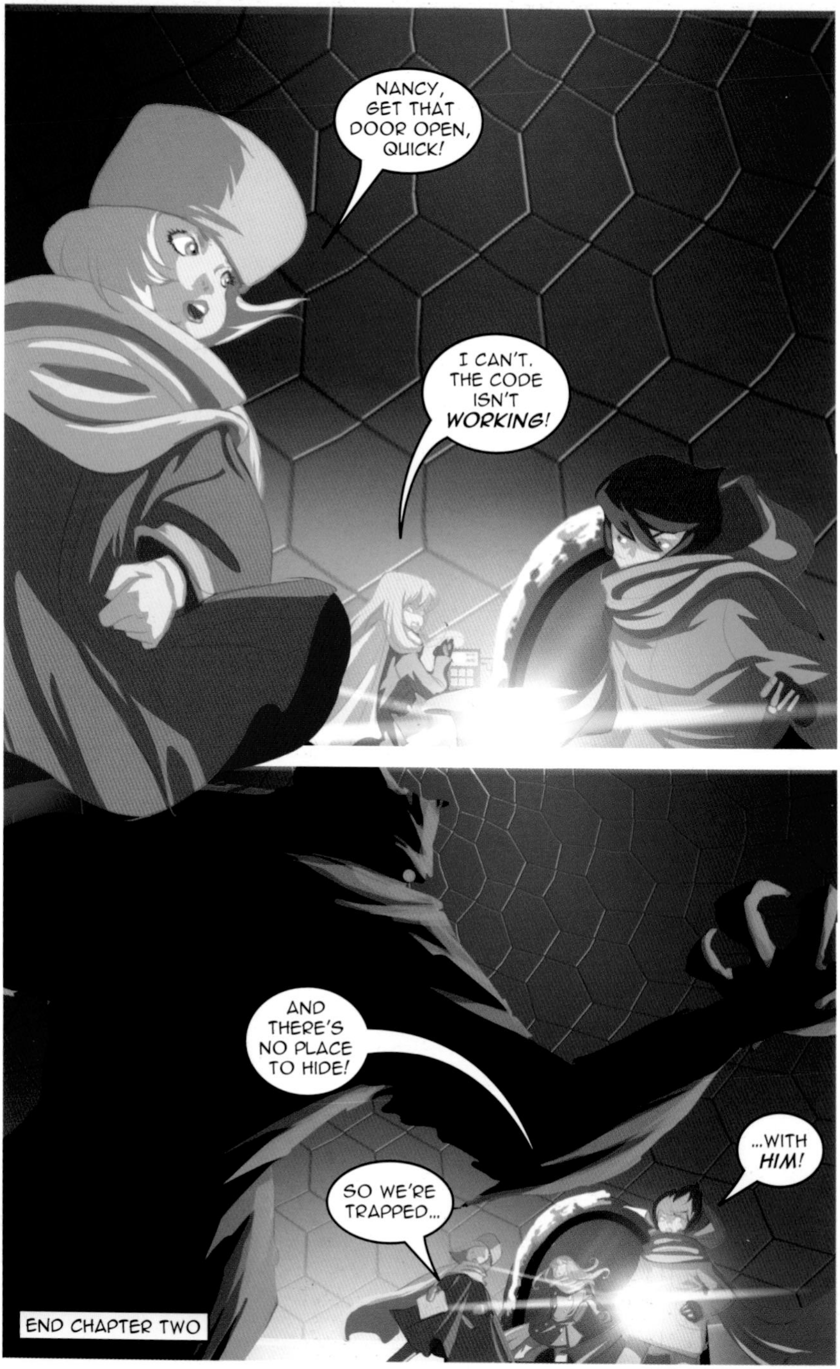
NANCY, GET THAT DOOR OPEN, QUICK!
I CAN'T. THE CODE ISN'T WORKING!
AND THERE'S NO PLACE TO HIDE!
SO WE'RE TRAPPED...
...WITH HIM!
END CHAPTER TWO

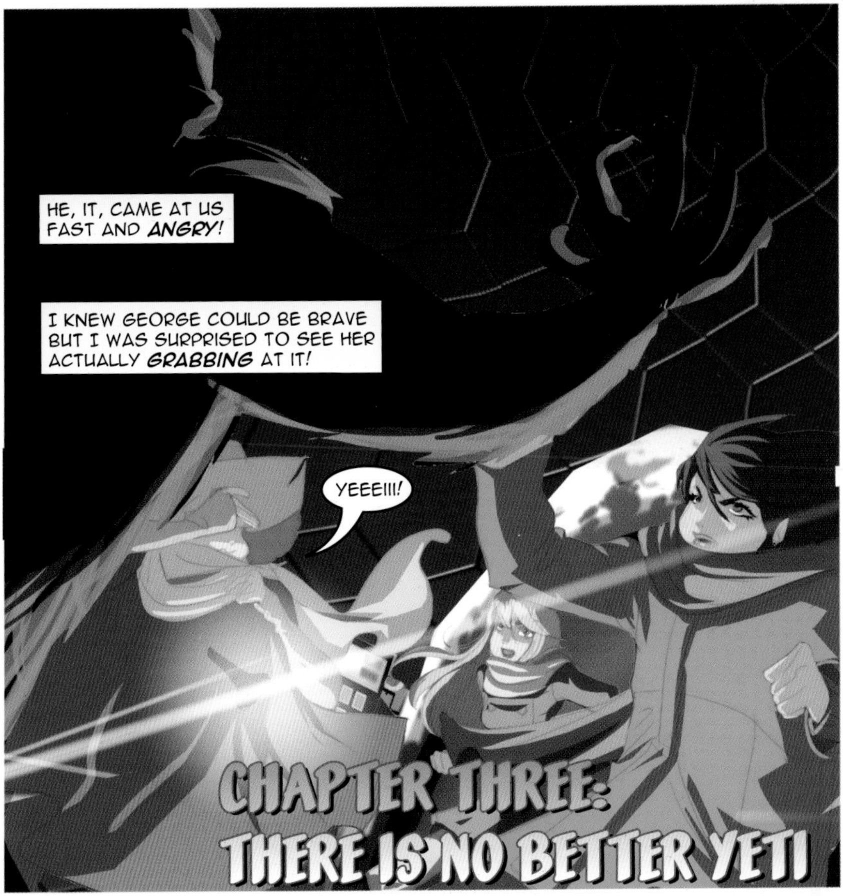
HE, IT, CAME AT US FAST AND *ANGRY*!
I KNEW GEORGE COULD BE BRAVE BUT I WAS SURPRISED TO SEE HER ACTUALLY *GRABBING* AT IT!
YEEEIII!
CHAPTER THREE:
THERE IS NO BETTER YETI

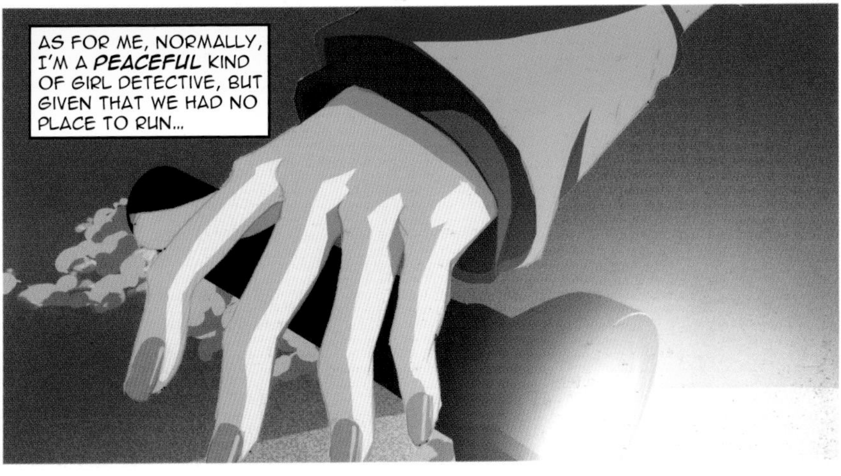
AS FOR ME, NORMALLY, I'M A *PEACEFUL* KIND OF GIRL DETECTIVE, BUT GIVEN THAT WE HAD NO PLACE TO RUN...

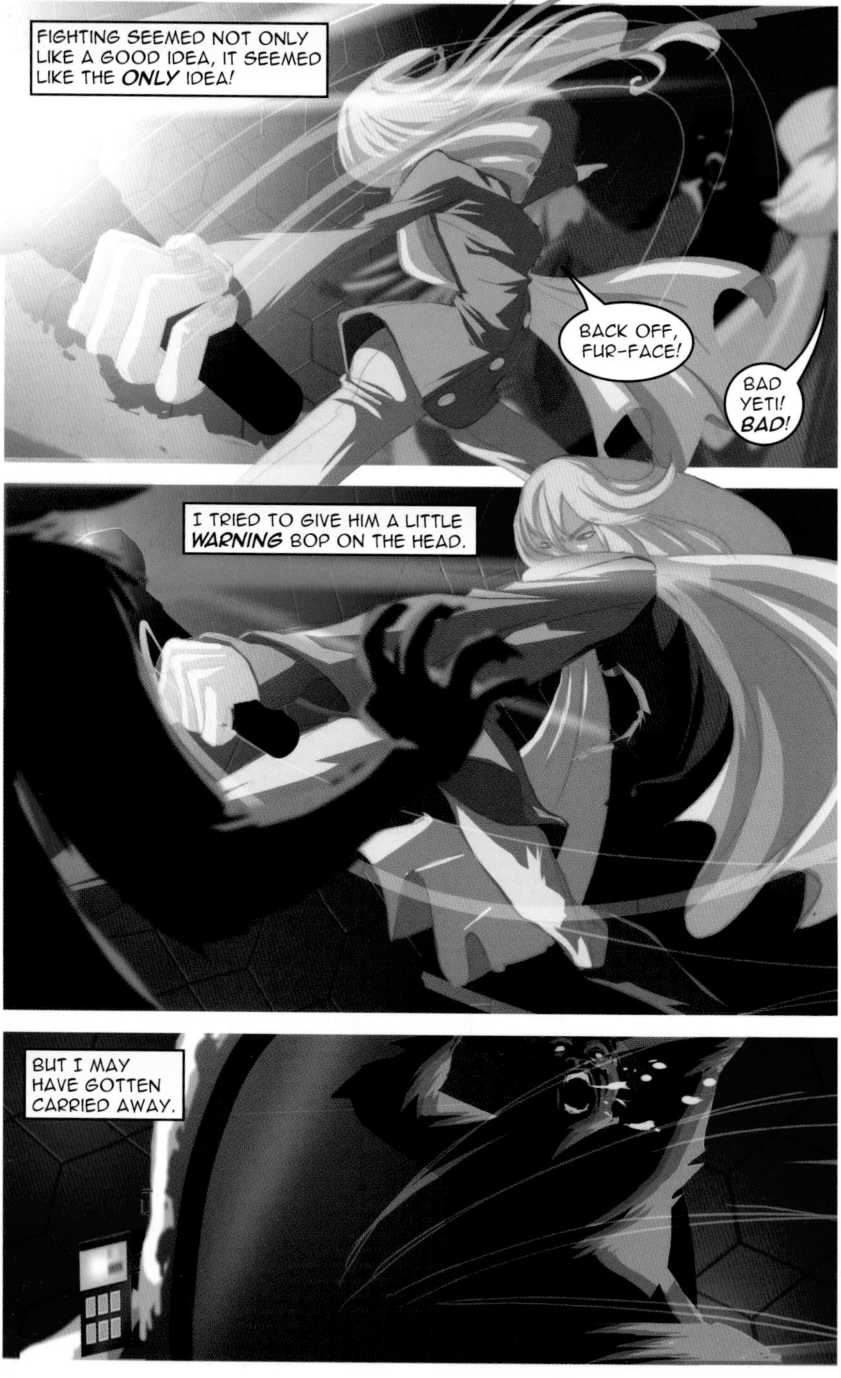
FIGHTING SEEMED NOT ONLY LIKE A GOOD IDEA, IT SEEMED LIKE THE ONLY IDEA!
BACK OFF, FUR-FACE!
BAD YETI! BAD!
I TRIED TO GIVE HIM A LITTLE WARNING BOP ON THE HEAD.
BUT I MAY HAVE GOTTEN CARRIED AWAY.

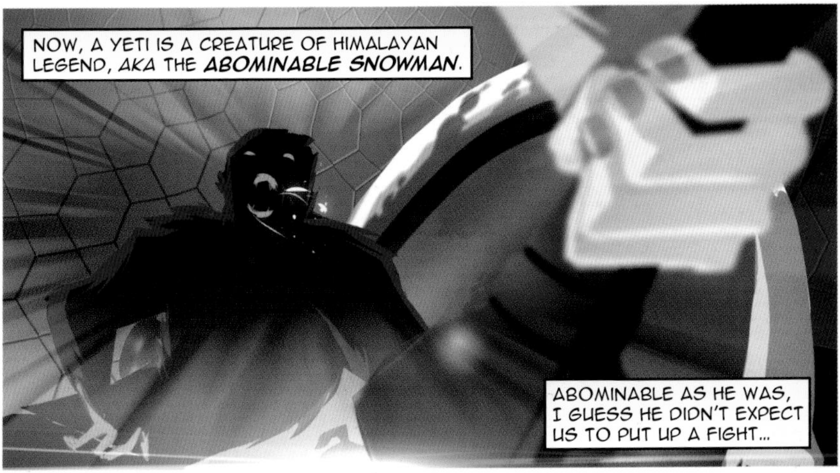
NOW, A YETI IS A CREATURE OF HIMALAYAN LEGEND, AKA THE ABOMINABLE SNOWMAN.
ABOMINABLE AS HE WAS, I GUESS HE DIDN'T EXPECT US TO PUT UP A FIGHT...

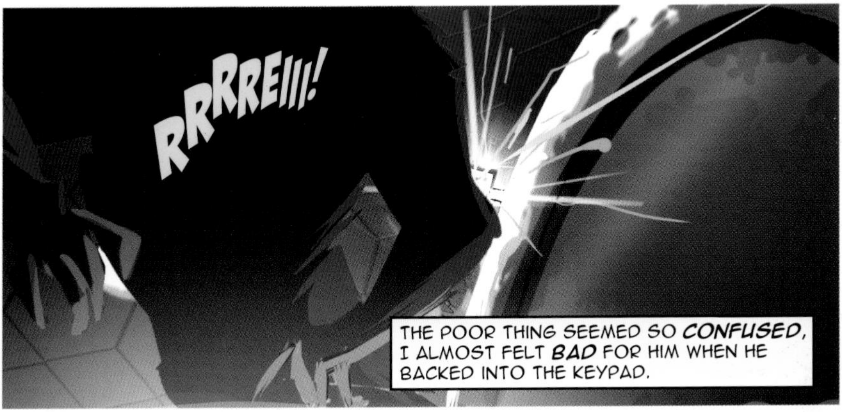
RRRREIIII!
THE POOR THING SEEMED SO CONFUSED, I ALMOST FELT BAD FOR HIM WHEN HE BACKED INTO THE KEYPAD.

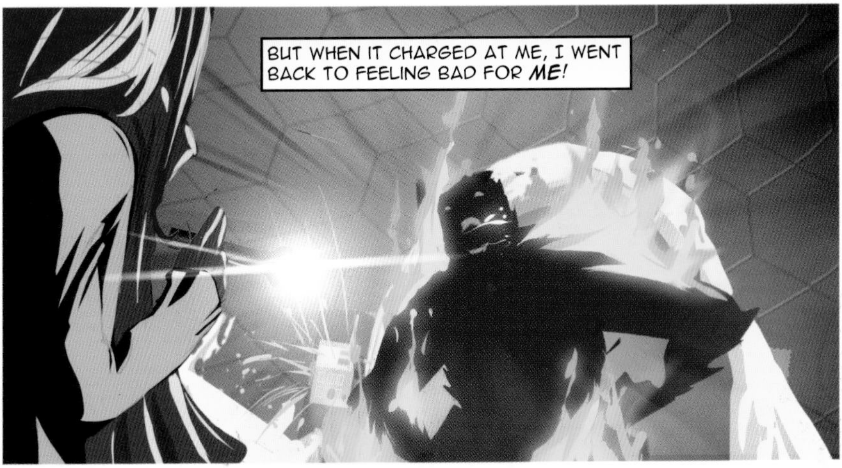
BUT WHEN IT CHARGED AT ME, I WENT BACK TO FEELING BAD FOR ME!

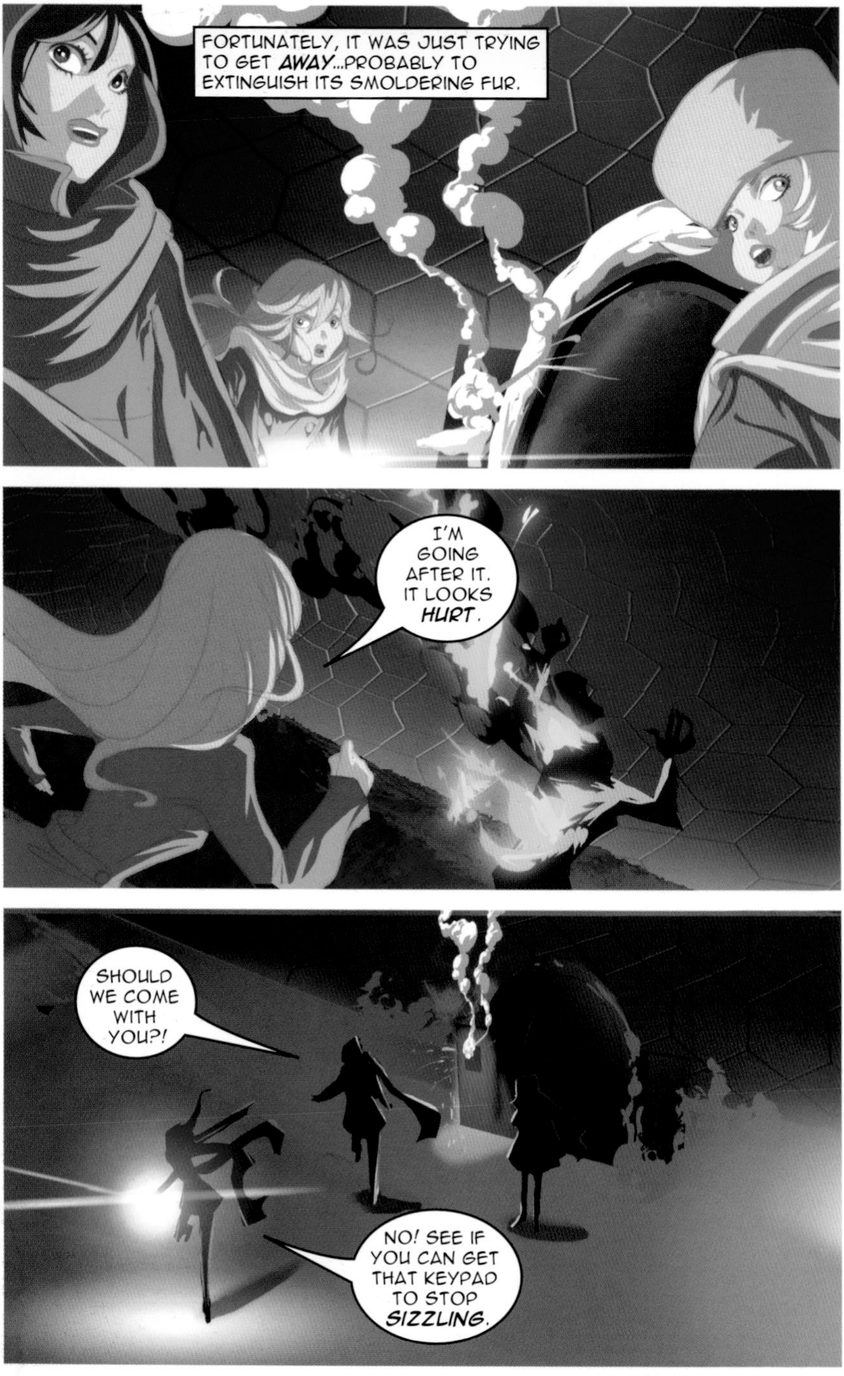
FORTUNATELY, IT WAS JUST TRYING TO GET AWAY...PROBABLY TO EXTINGUISH ITS SMOLDERING FUR.
I'M GOING AFTER IT. IT LOOKS HURT.
SHOULD WE COME WITH YOU?!
NO! SEE IF YOU CAN GET THAT KEYPAD TO STOP SIZZLING.

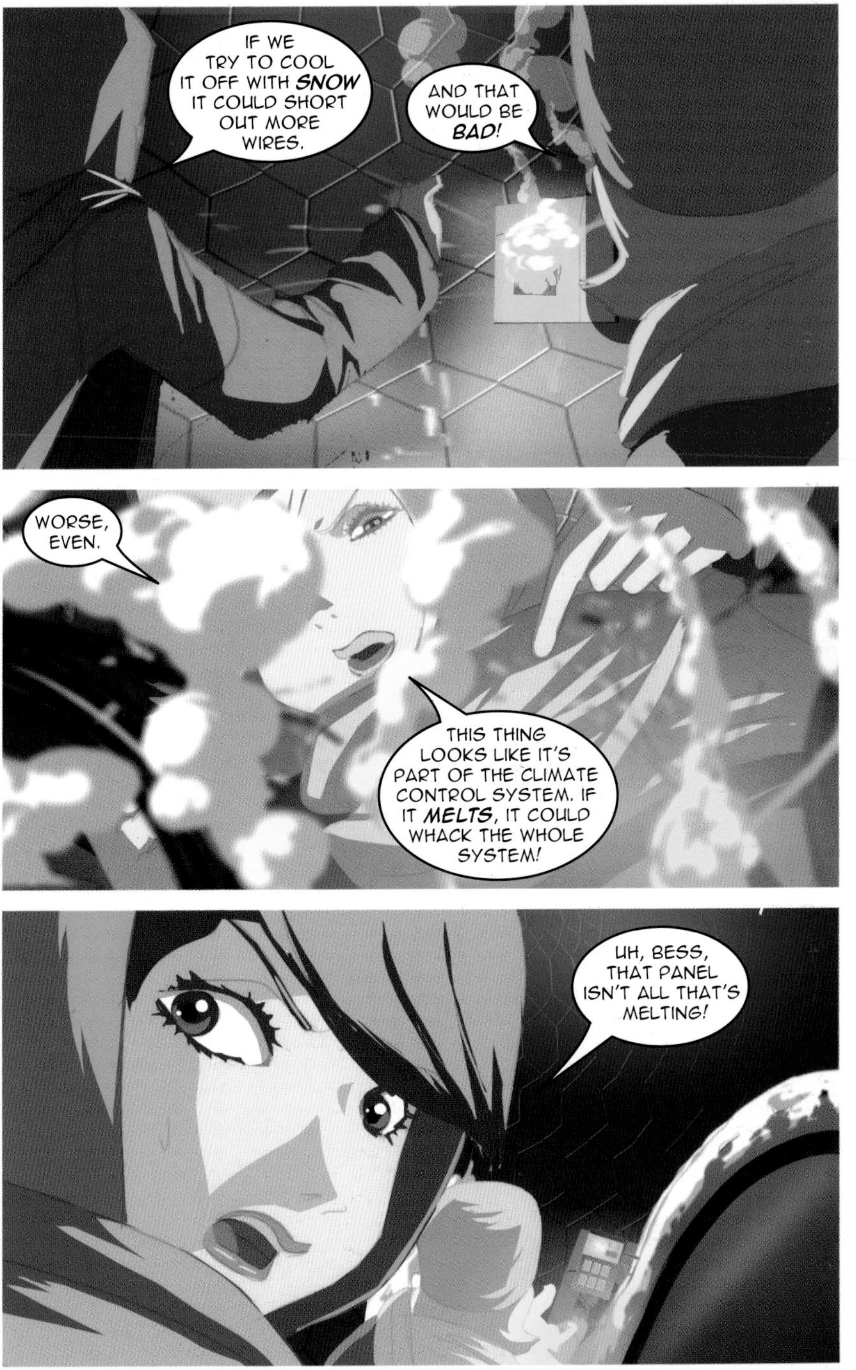
IF WE TRY TO COOL IT OFF WITH SNOW IT COULD SHORT OUT MORE WIRES.
AND THAT WOULD BE BAD!
WORSE, EVEN.
THIS THING LOOKS LIKE IT'S PART OF THE CLIMATE CONTROL SYSTEM. IF IT MELTS, IT COULD WHACK THE WHOLE SYSTEM!
UH, BESS, THAT PANEL ISN'T ALL THAT'S MELTING!

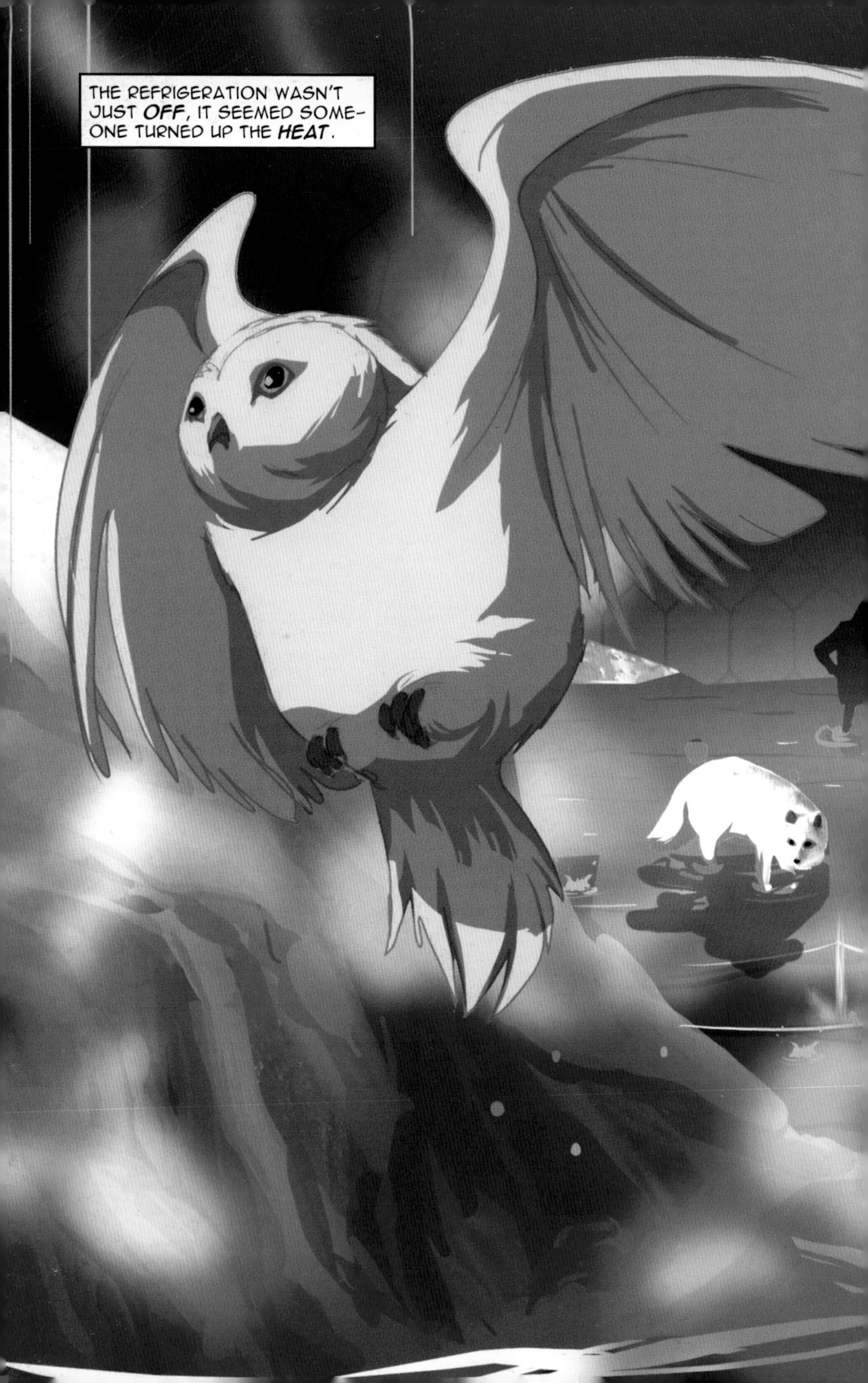
THE REFRIGERATION WASN'T JUST *OFF*, IT SEEMED SOME-ONE TURNED UP THE *HEAT*.

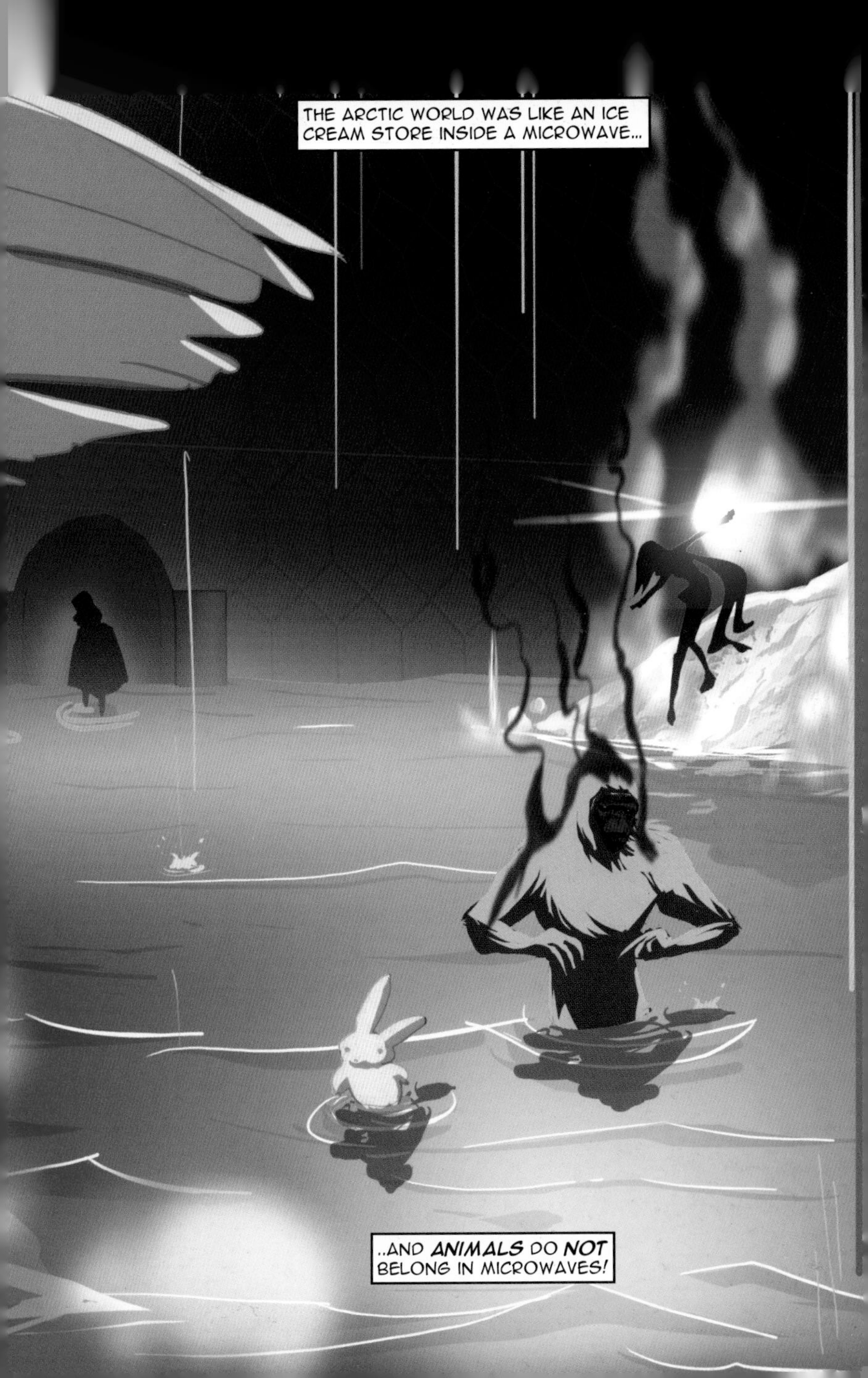
THE ARCTIC WORLD WAS LIKE AN ICE CREAM STORE INSIDE A MICROWAVE...
..AND ANIMALS DO NOT BELONG IN MICROWAVES!

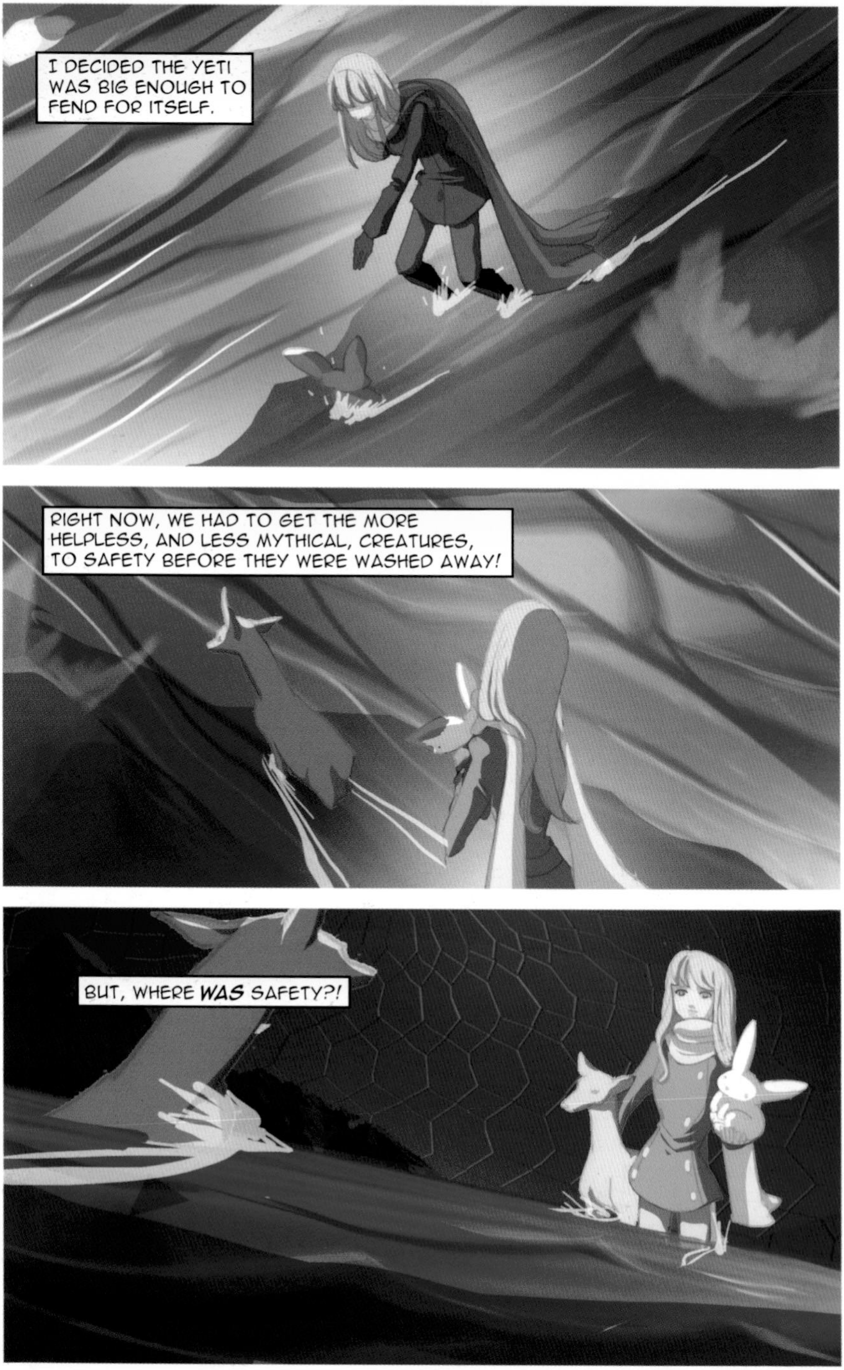
I DECIDED THE YETI WAS BIG ENOUGH TO FEND FOR ITSELF.
RIGHT NOW, WE HAD TO GET THE MORE HELPLESS, AND LESS MYTHICAL, CREATURES, TO SAFETY BEFORE THEY WERE WASHED AWAY!
BUT, WHERE ***WAS*** SAFETY?!

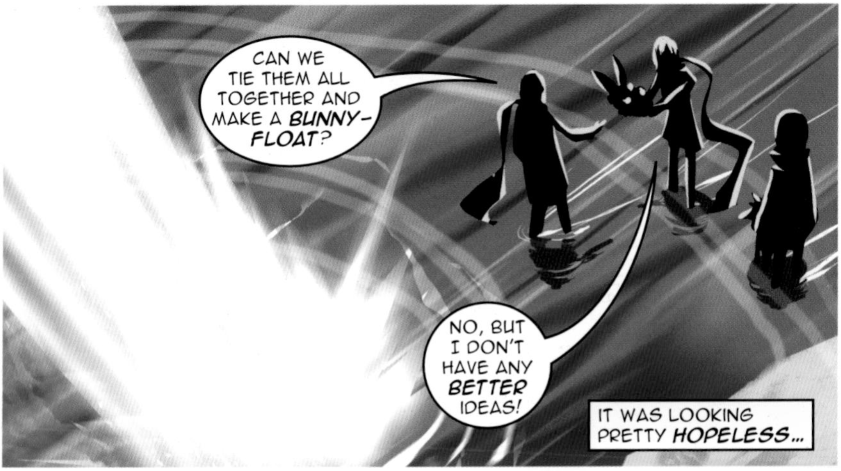
CAN WE TIE THEM ALL TOGETHER AND MAKE A BUNNY-FLOAT?
NO, BUT I DON'T HAVE ANY BETTER IDEAS!
IT WAS LOOKING PRETTY HOPELESS...

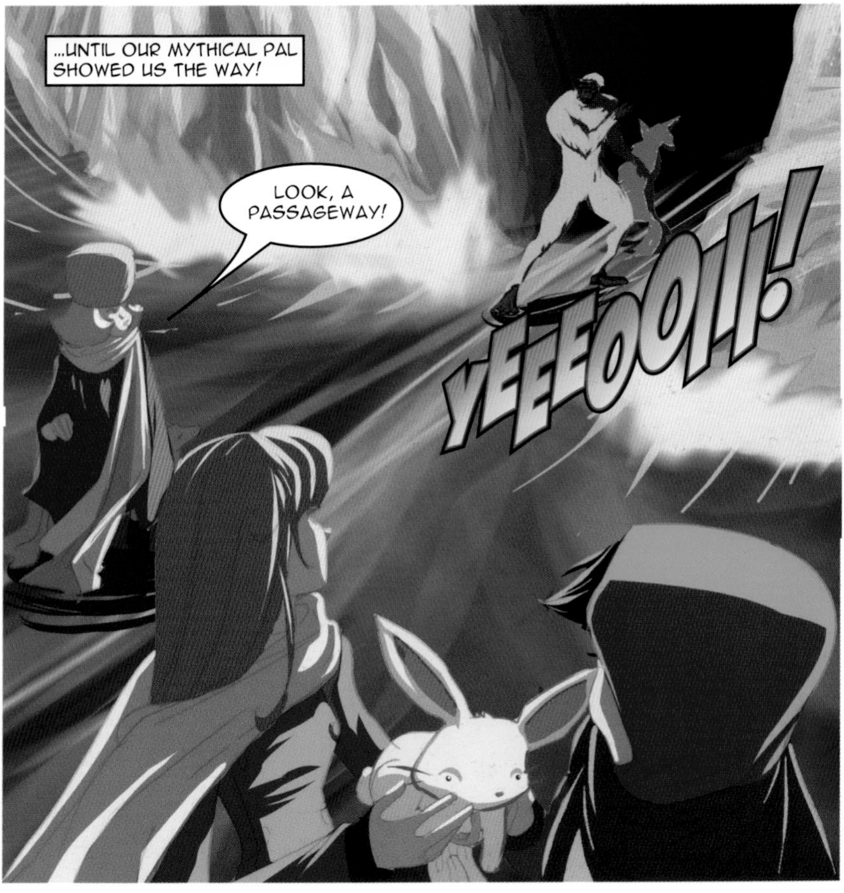
...UNTIL OUR MYTHICAL PAL SHOWED US THE WAY!
LOOK, A PASSAGEWAY!
YEEEOOH!

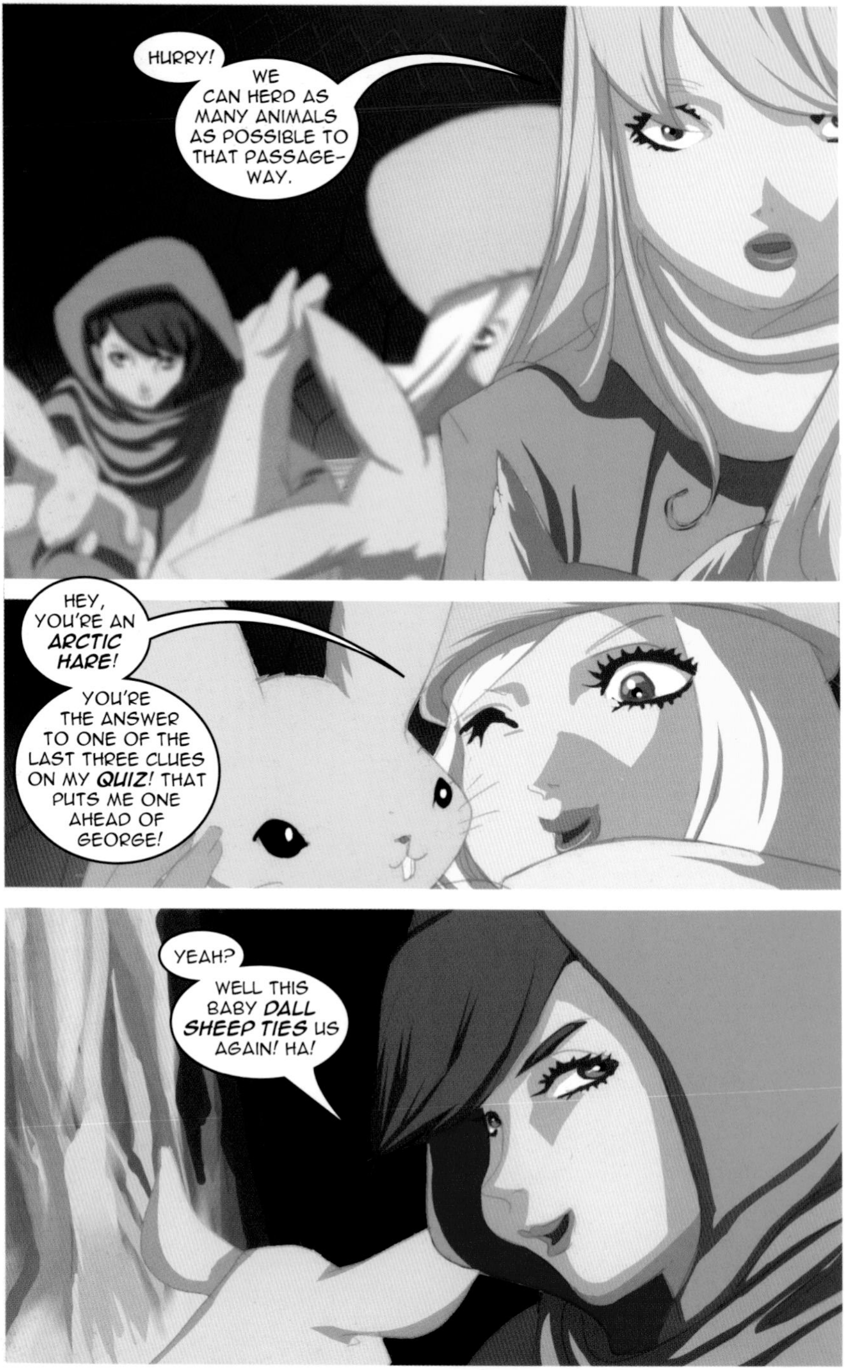
HURRY!
WE CAN HERD AS MANY ANIMALS AS POSSIBLE TO THAT PASSAGE-WAY.
HEY, YOU'RE AN *ARCTIC HARE*!
YOU'RE THE ANSWER TO ONE OF THE LAST THREE CLUES ON MY *QUIZ*! THAT PUTS ME ONE AHEAD OF GEORGE!
YEAH?
WELL THIS BABY *DALL SHEEP TIES* US AGAIN! HA!

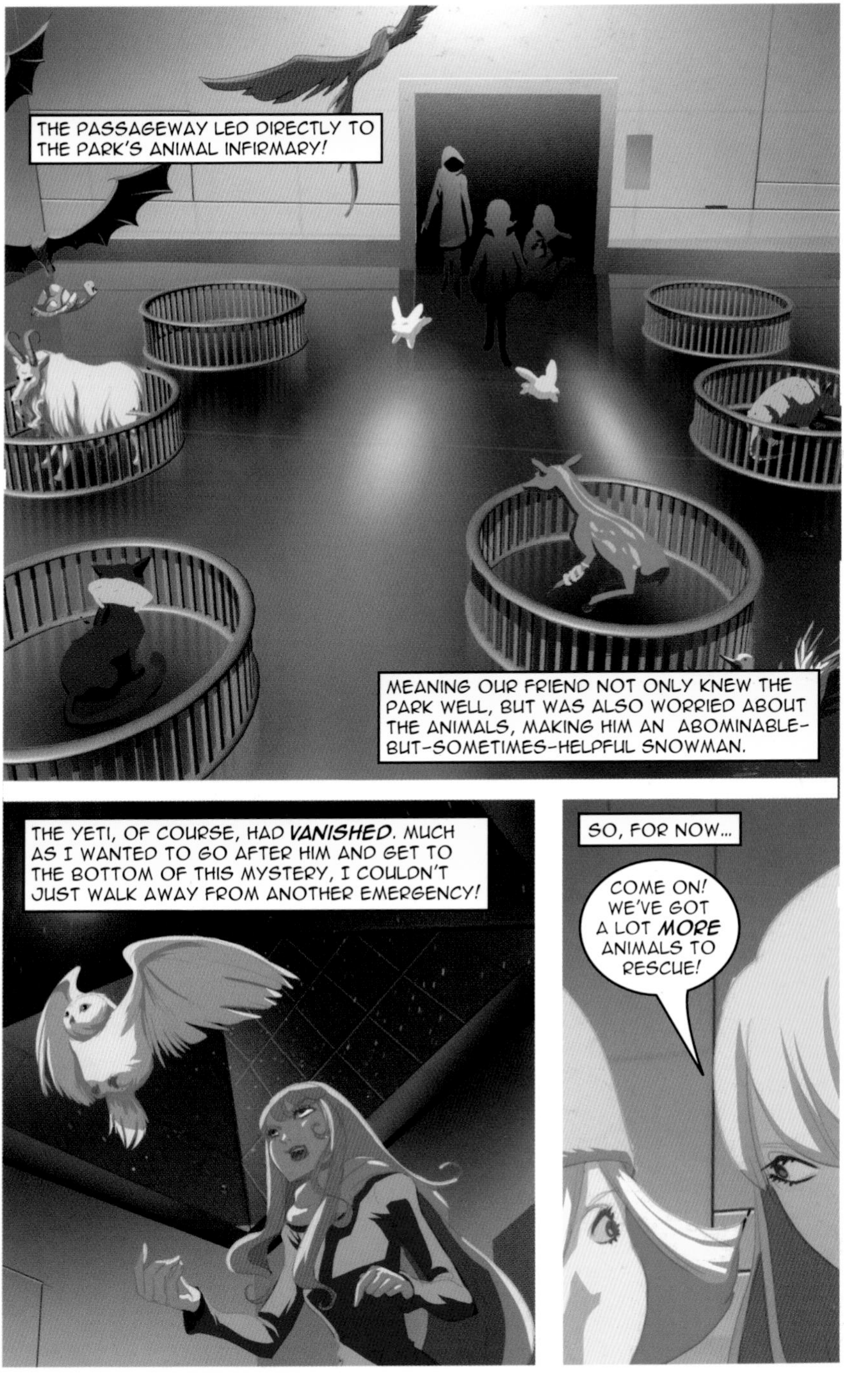
THE PASSAGEWAY LED DIRECTLY TO THE PARK'S ANIMAL INFIRMARY!
MEANING OUR FRIEND NOT ONLY KNEW THE PARK WELL, BUT WAS ALSO WORRIED ABOUT THE ANIMALS, MAKING HIM AN ABOMINABLE-BUT-SOMETIMES-HELPFUL SNOWMAN.
THE YETI, OF COURSE, HAD *VANISHED*. MUCH AS I WANTED TO GO AFTER HIM AND GET TO THE BOTTOM OF THIS MYSTERY, I COULDN'T JUST WALK AWAY FROM ANOTHER EMERGENCY!
SO, FOR NOW...
COME ON! WE'VE GOT A LOT *MORE* ANIMALS TO RESCUE!

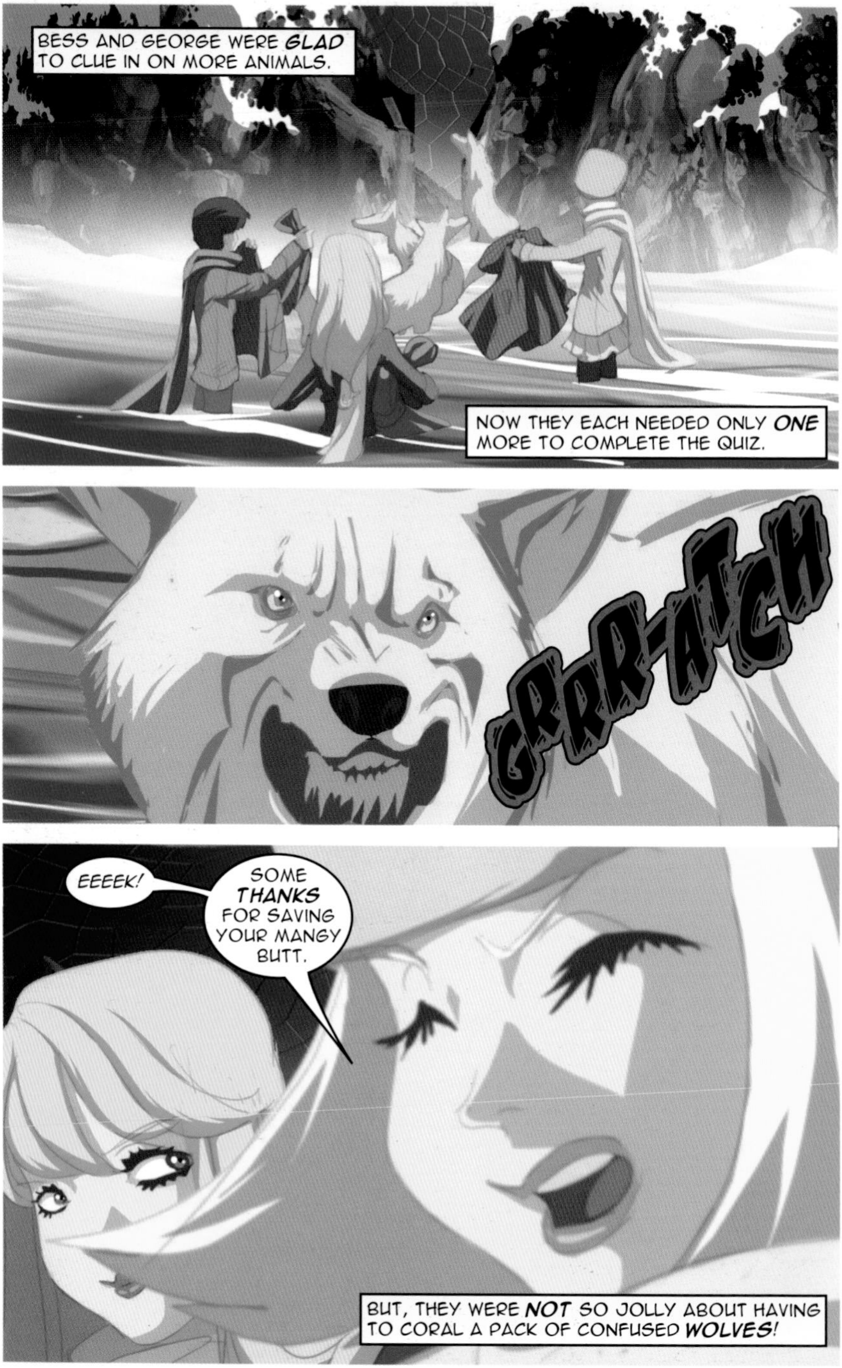
BESS AND GEORGE WERE *GLAD* TO CLUE IN ON MORE ANIMALS.
NOW THEY EACH NEEDED ONLY *ONE* MORE TO COMPLETE THE QUIZ.
GRRR-ATCH
EEEEK!
SOME *THANKS* FOR SAVING YOUR MANGY BUTT.
BUT, THEY WERE *NOT* SO JOLLY ABOUT HAVING TO CORAL A PACK OF CONFUSED *WOLVES*!

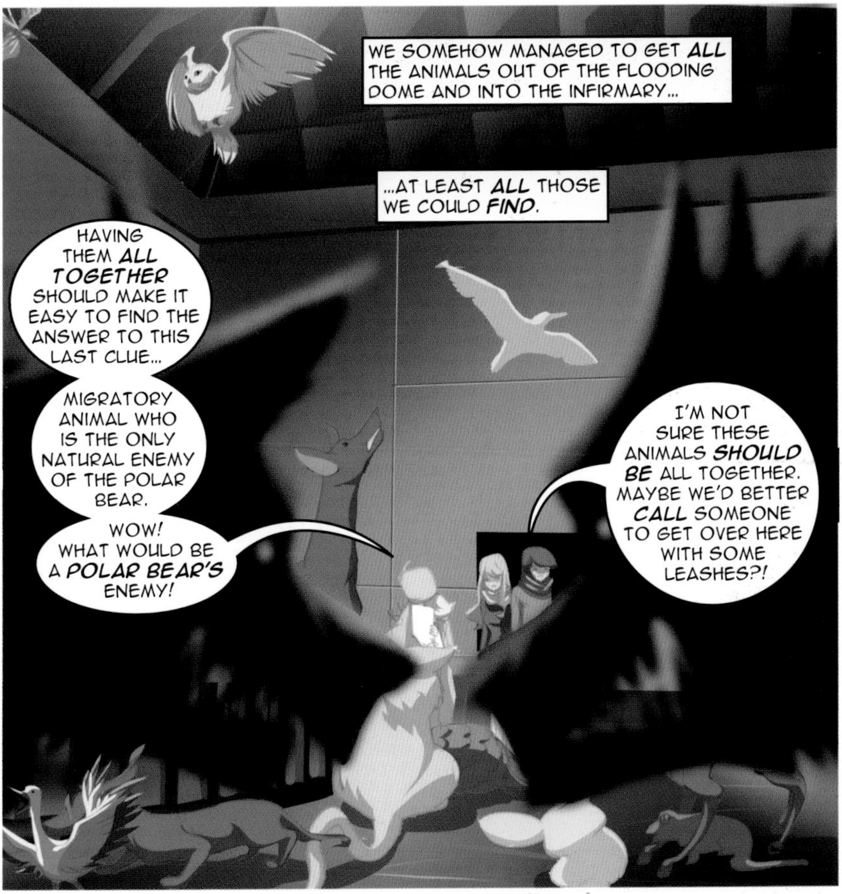
WE SOMEHOW MANAGED TO GET ALL THE ANIMALS OUT OF THE FLOODING DOME AND INTO THE INFIRMARY...
...AT LEAST ALL THOSE WE COULD FIND.
HAVING THEM ALL TOGETHER SHOULD MAKE IT EASY TO FIND THE ANSWER TO THIS LAST CLUE...
MIGRATORY ANIMAL WHO IS THE ONLY NATURAL ENEMY OF THE POLAR BEAR.
WOW! WHAT WOULD BE A POLAR BEAR'S ENEMY!
I'M NOT SURE THESE ANIMALS SHOULD BE ALL TOGETHER. MAYBE WE'D BETTER CALL SOMEONE TO GET OVER HERE WITH SOME LEASHES?!

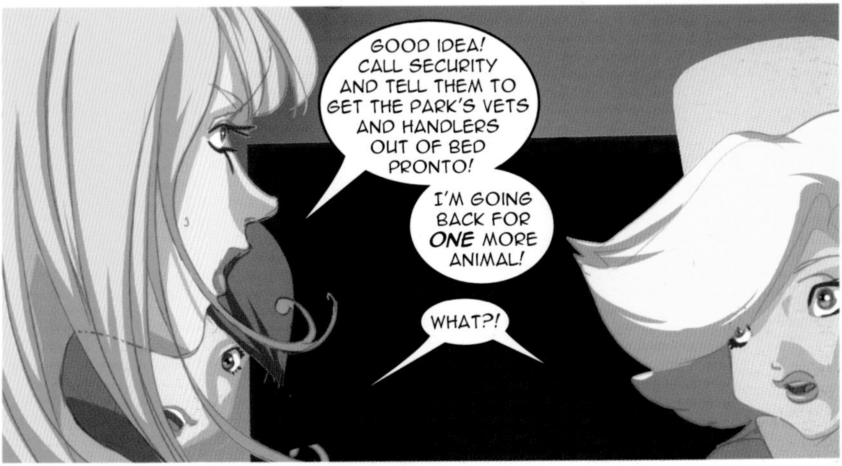
GOOD IDEA! CALL SECURITY AND TELL THEM TO GET THE PARK'S VETS AND HANDLERS OUT OF BED PRONTO!
I'M GOING BACK FOR ONE MORE ANIMAL!
WHAT?!

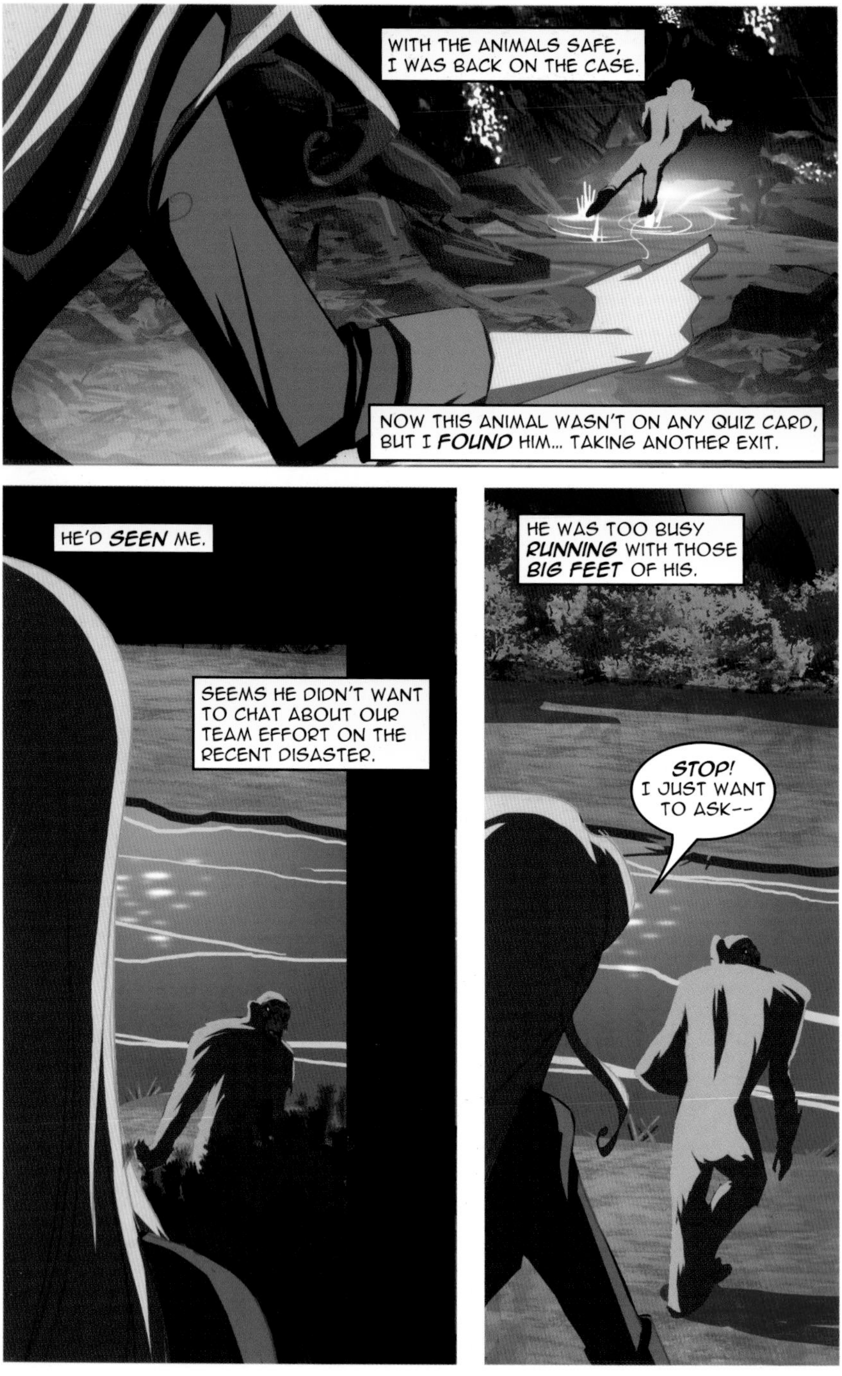
WITH THE ANIMALS SAFE, I WAS BACK ON THE CASE.
NOW THIS ANIMAL WASN'T ON ANY QUIZ CARD, BUT I *FOUND* HIM... TAKING ANOTHER EXIT.
HE'D *SEEN* ME.
SEEMS HE DIDN'T WANT TO CHAT ABOUT OUR TEAM EFFORT ON THE RECENT DISASTER.
HE WAS TOO BUSY *RUNNING* WITH THOSE *BIG FEET* OF HIS.
STOP! I JUST WANT TO ASK--

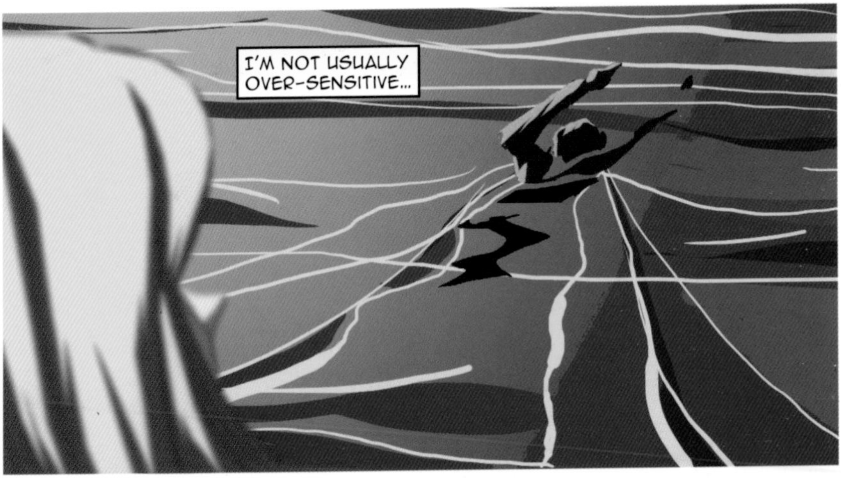
I'M NOT USUALLY OVER-SENSITIVE...

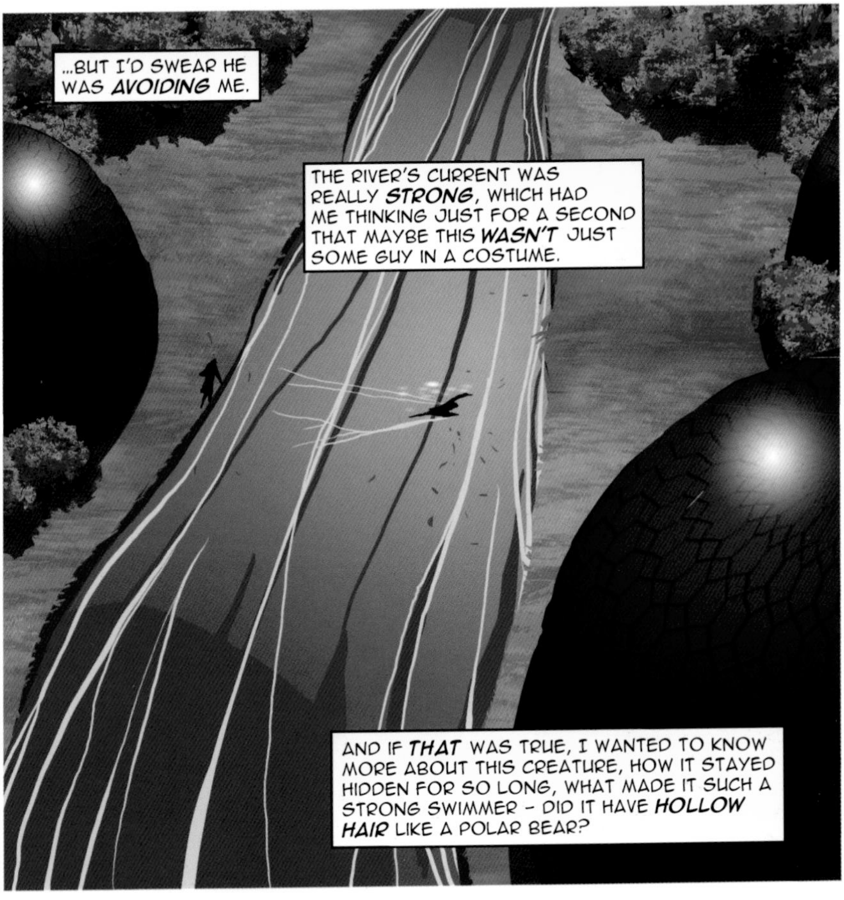
...BUT I'D SWEAR HE WAS AVOIDING ME.
THE RIVER'S CURRENT WAS REALLY STRONG, WHICH HAD ME THINKING JUST FOR A SECOND THAT MAYBE THIS WASN'T JUST SOME GUY IN A COSTUME.
AND IF THAT WAS TRUE, I WANTED TO KNOW MORE ABOUT THIS CREATURE, HOW IT STAYED HIDDEN FOR SO LONG, WHAT MADE IT SUCH A STRONG SWIMMER - DID IT HAVE HOLLOW HAIR LIKE A POLAR BEAR?

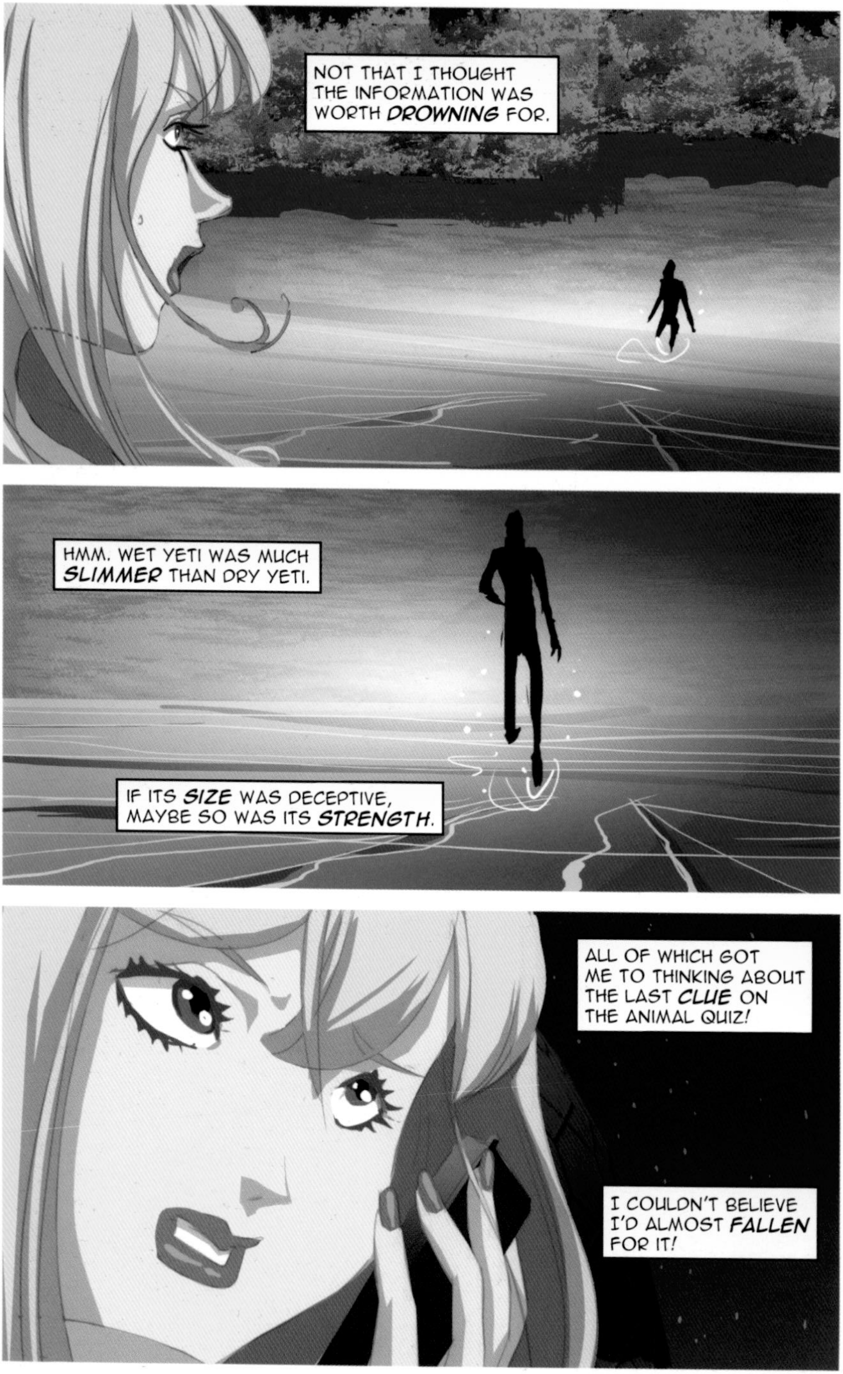
NOT THAT I THOUGHT THE INFORMATION WAS WORTH DROWNING FOR.
HMM. WET YETI WAS MUCH SLIMMER THAN DRY YETI.
IF ITS SIZE WAS DECEPTIVE, MAYBE SO WAS ITS STRENGTH.
ALL OF WHICH GOT ME TO THINKING ABOUT THE LAST CLUE ON THE ANIMAL QUIZ!
I COULDN'T BELIEVE I'D ALMOST FALLEN FOR IT!

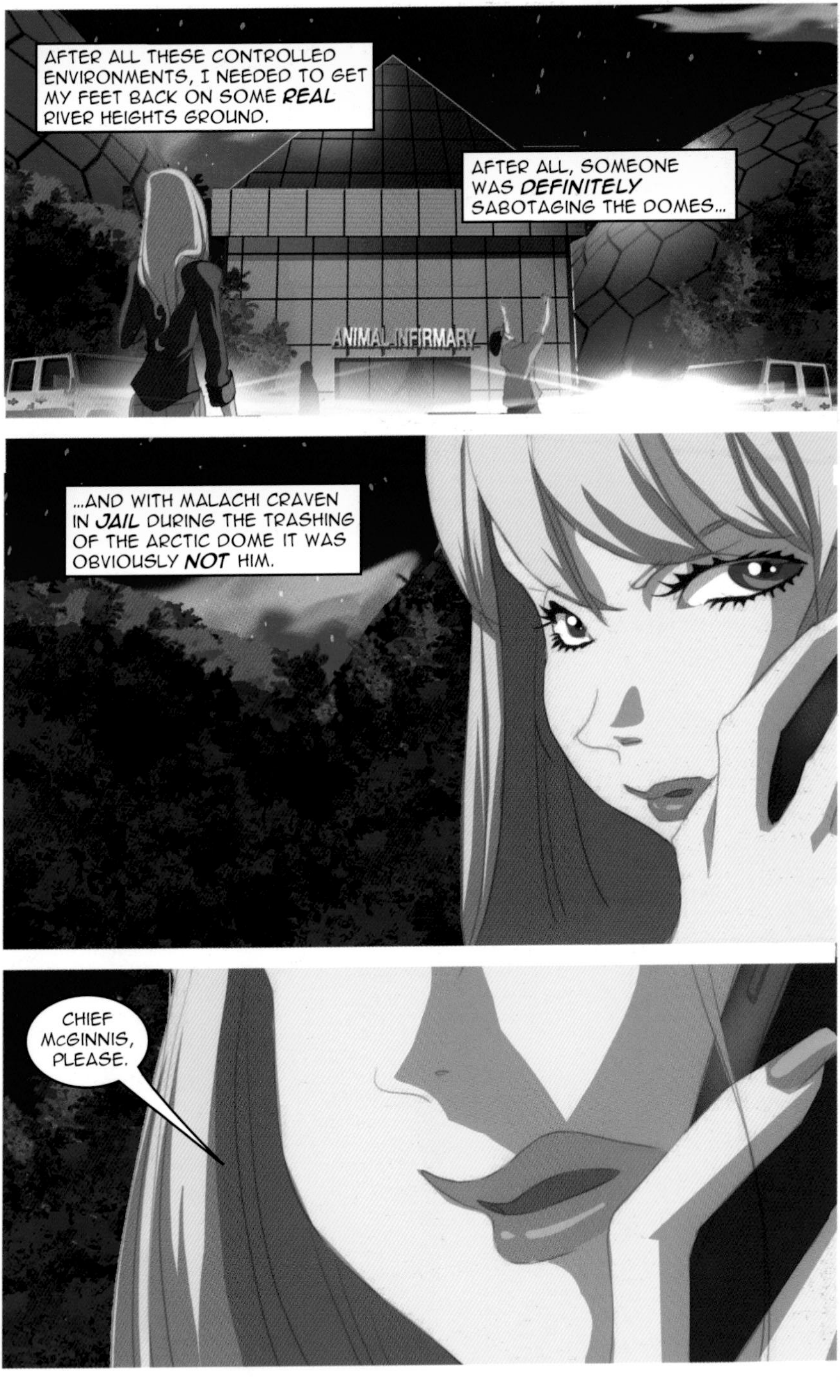
AFTER ALL THESE CONTROLLED ENVIRONMENTS, I NEEDED TO GET MY FEET BACK ON SOME REAL RIVER HEIGHTS GROUND.
AFTER ALL, SOMEONE WAS DEFINITELY SABOTAGING THE DOMES...
ANIMAL INFIRMARY
...AND WITH MALACHI CRAVEN IN JAIL DURING THE TRASHING OF THE ARCTIC DOME IT WAS OBVIOUSLY NOT HIM.
CHIEF McGINNIS, PLEASE.

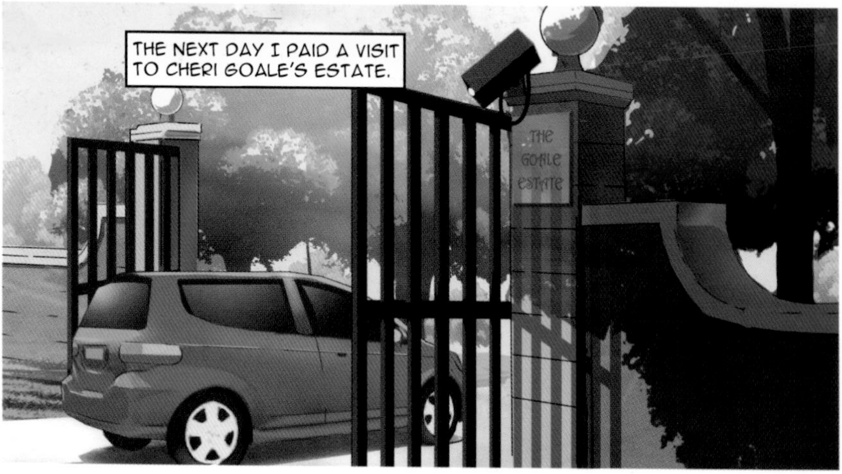
THE NEXT DAY I PAID A VISIT TO CHERI GOALE'S ESTATE.
THE GOALE ESTATE

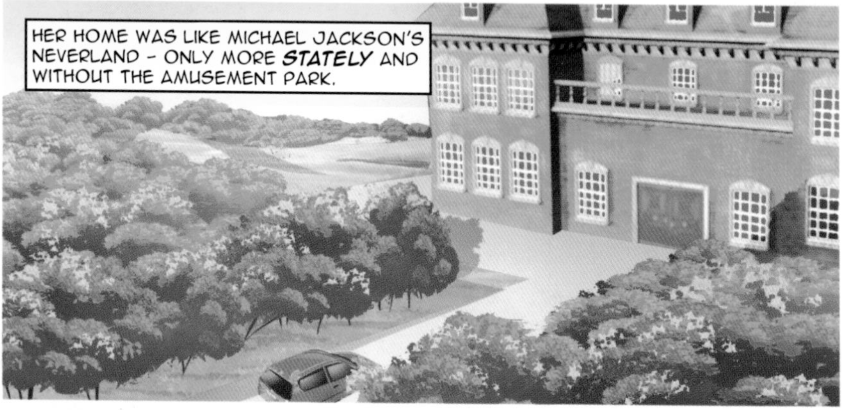
HER HOME WAS LIKE MICHAEL JACKSON'S NEVERLAND - ONLY MORE STATELY AND WITHOUT THE AMUSEMENT PARK.

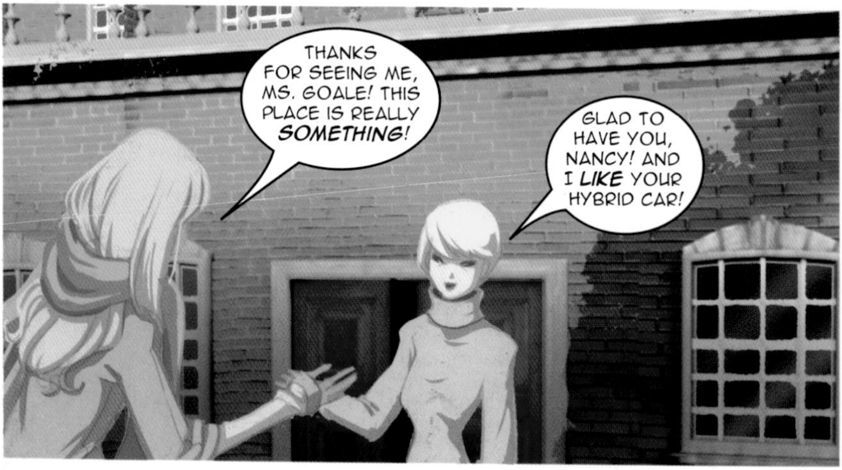
THANKS FOR SEEING ME, MS. GOALE! THIS PLACE IS REALLY SOMETHING!
GLAD TO HAVE YOU, NANCY! AND I LIKE YOUR HYBRID CAR!

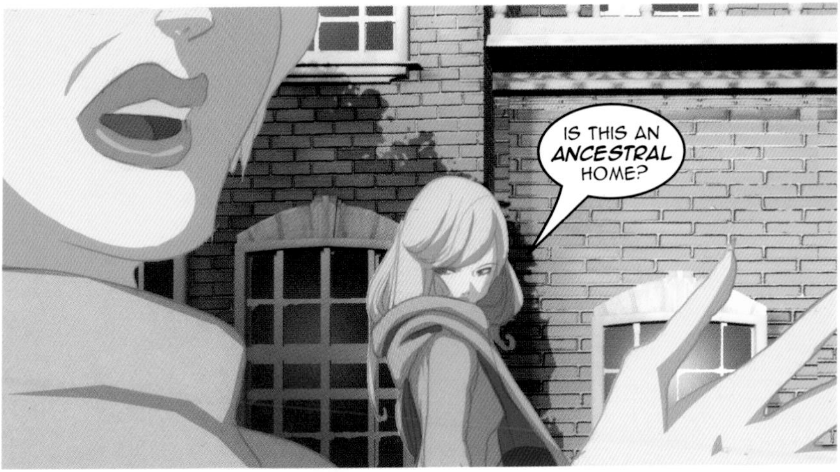
IS THIS AN ANCESTRAL HOME?

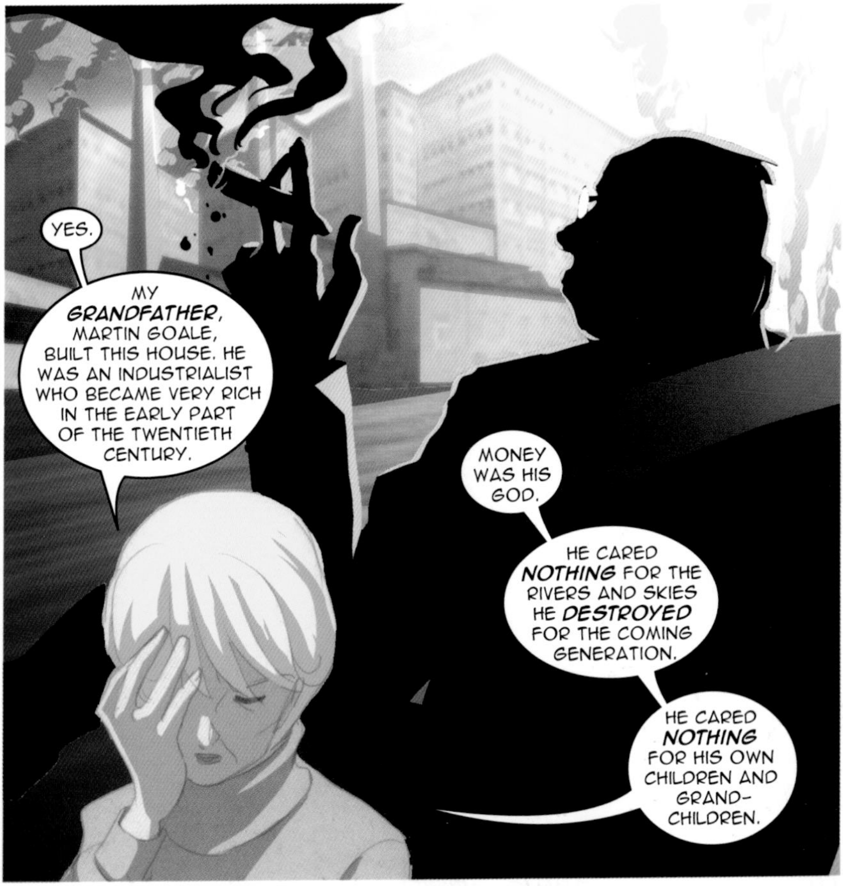
YES.
MY GRANDFATHER, MARTIN GOALE, BUILT THIS HOUSE. HE WAS AN INDUSTRIALIST WHO BECAME VERY RICH IN THE EARLY PART OF THE TWENTIETH CENTURY.
MONEY WAS HIS GOD.
HE CARED NOTHING FOR THE RIVERS AND SKIES HE DESTROYED FOR THE COMING GENERATION.
HE CARED NOTHING FOR HIS OWN CHILDREN AND GRAND-CHILDREN.

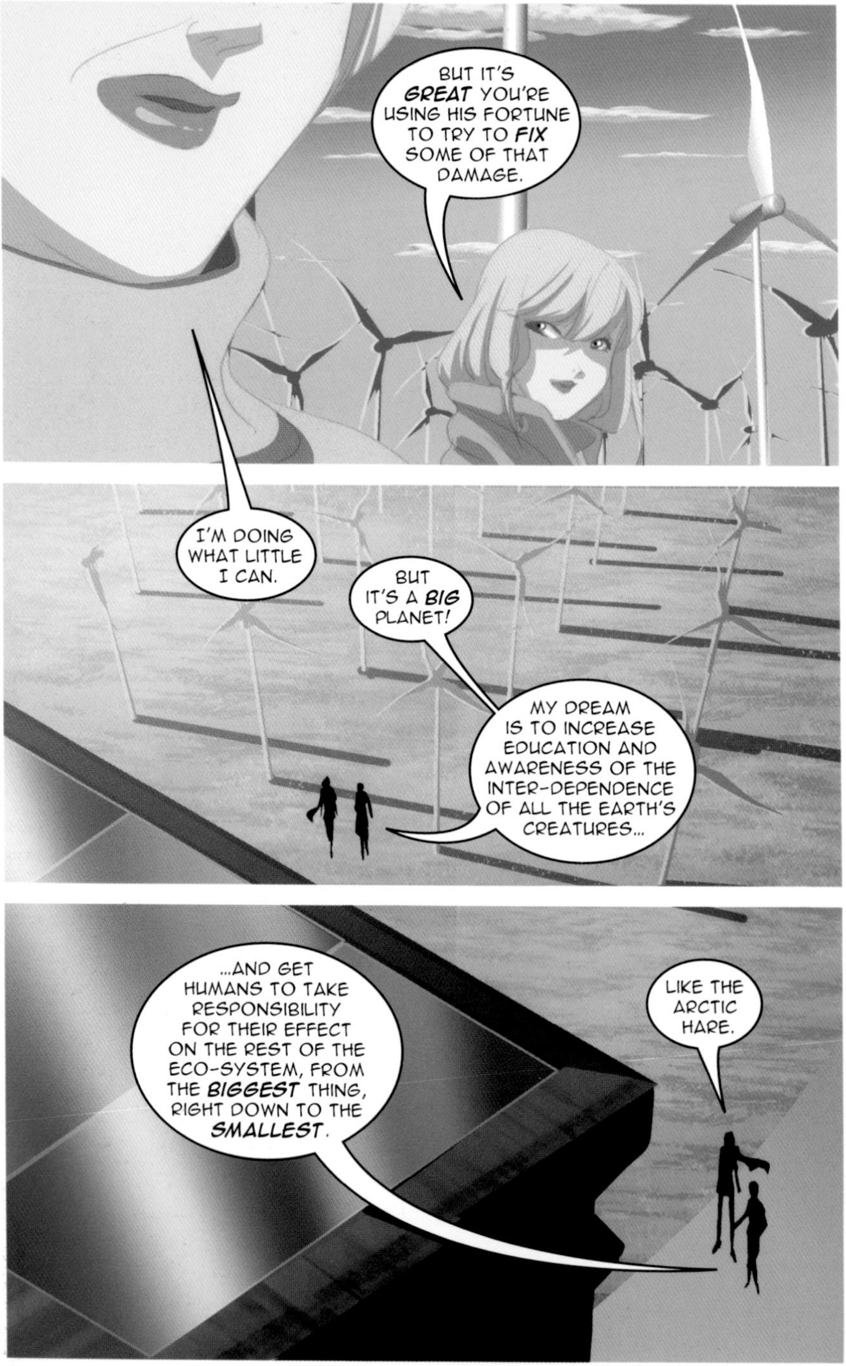
BUT IT'S GREAT YOU'RE USING HIS FORTUNE TO TRY TO FIX SOME OF THAT DAMAGE.
I'M DOING WHAT LITTLE I CAN.
BUT IT'S A BIG PLANET!
MY DREAM IS TO INCREASE EDUCATION AND AWARENESS OF THE INTER-DEPENDENCE OF ALL THE EARTH'S CREATURES...
...AND GET HUMANS TO TAKE RESPONSIBILITY FOR THEIR EFFECT ON THE REST OF THE ECO-SYSTEM, FROM THE BIGGEST THING, RIGHT DOWN TO THE SMALLEST.
LIKE THE ARCTIC HARE.

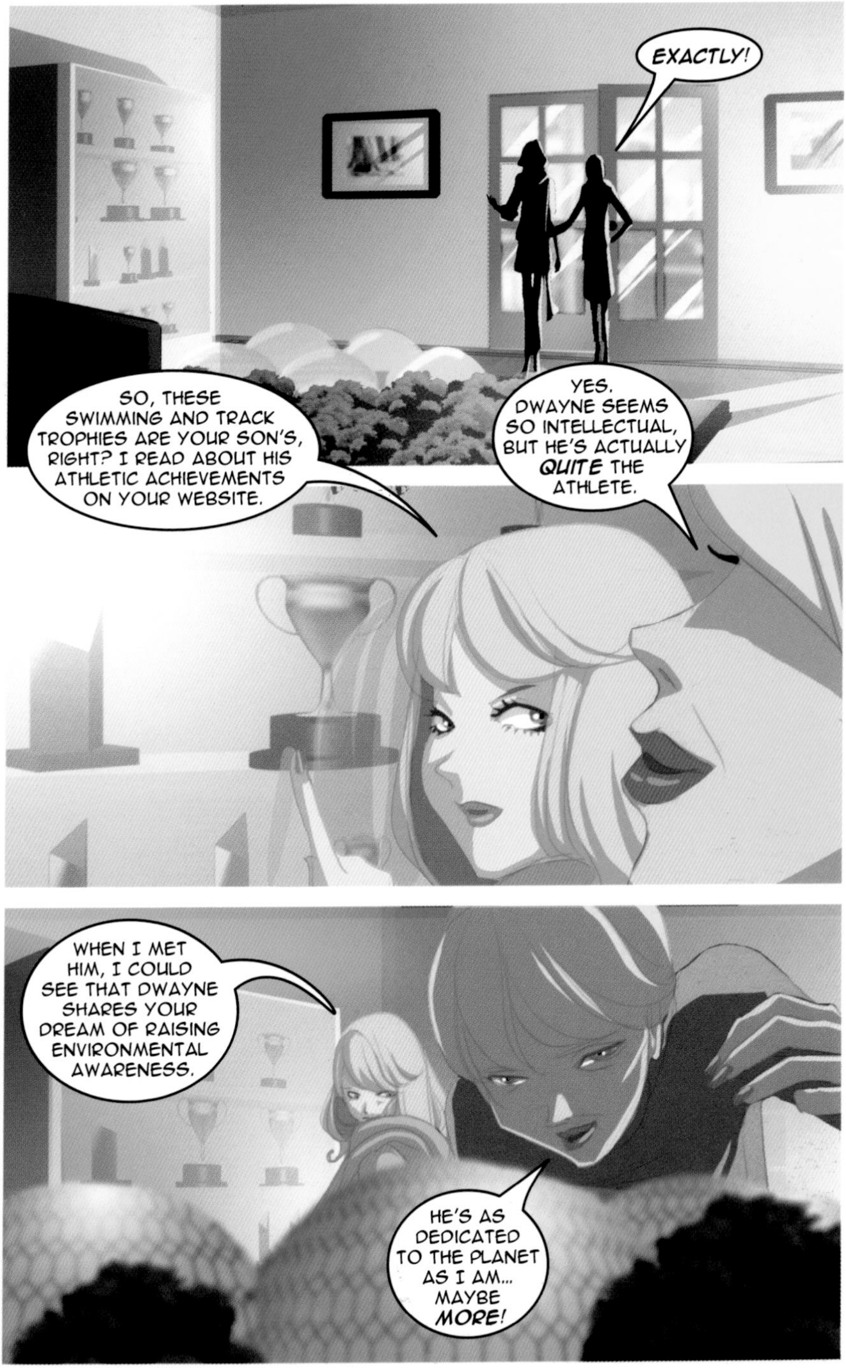
EXACTLY!
SO, THESE SWIMMING AND TRACK TROPHIES ARE YOUR SON'S, RIGHT? I READ ABOUT HIS ATHLETIC ACHIEVEMENTS ON YOUR WEBSITE.
YES. DWAYNE SEEMS SO INTELLECTUAL, BUT HE'S ACTUALLY QUITE THE ATHLETE.
WHEN I MET HIM, I COULD SEE THAT DWAYNE SHARES YOUR DREAM OF RAISING ENVIRONMENTAL AWARENESS.
HE'S AS DEDICATED TO THE PLANET AS I AM... MAYBE MORE!

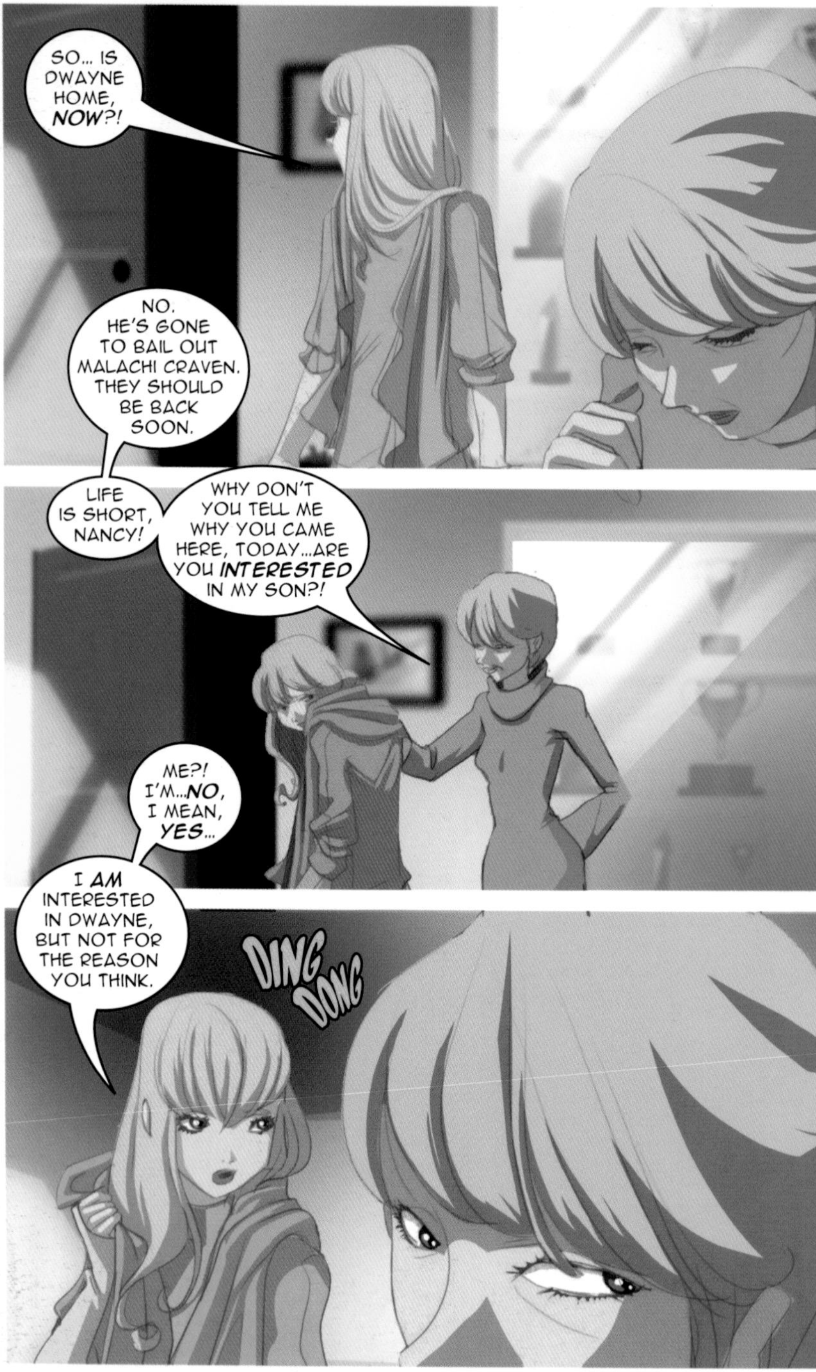
SO... IS DWAYNE HOME, NOW?!
NO. HE'S GONE TO BAIL OUT MALACHI CRAVEN. THEY SHOULD BE BACK SOON.
LIFE IS SHORT, NANCY!
WHY DON'T YOU TELL ME WHY YOU CAME HERE, TODAY...ARE YOU INTERESTED IN MY SON?!
ME?! I'M...NO, I MEAN, YES...
I AM INTERESTED IN DWAYNE, BUT NOT FOR THE REASON YOU THINK.
DING DONG

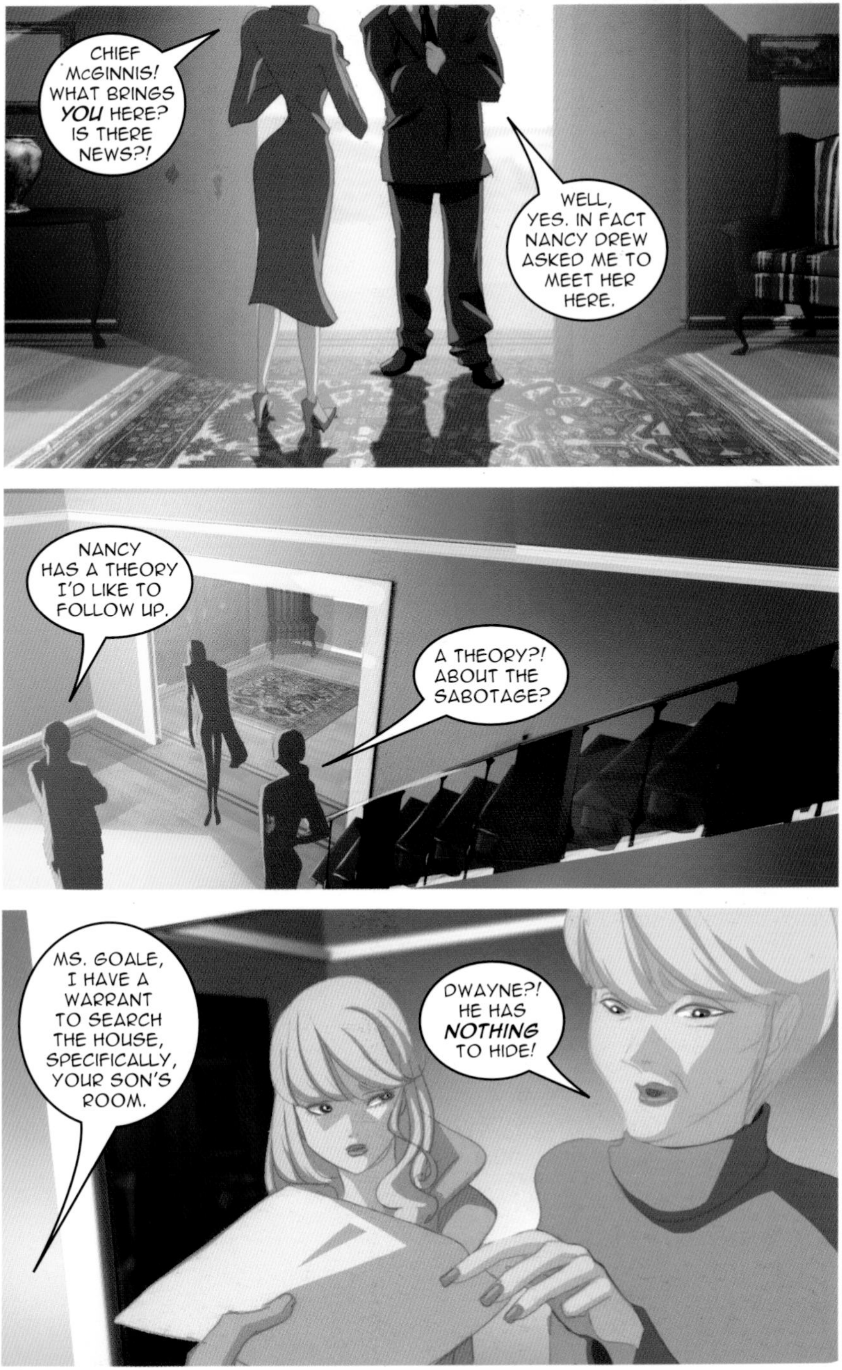
CHIEF McGINNIS! WHAT BRINGS *YOU* HERE? IS THERE NEWS?!
WELL, YES. IN FACT NANCY DREW ASKED ME TO MEET HER HERE.
NANCY HAS A THEORY I'D LIKE TO FOLLOW UP.
A THEORY?! ABOUT THE SABOTAGE?
MS. GOALE, I HAVE A WARRANT TO SEARCH THE HOUSE, SPECIFICALLY, YOUR SON'S ROOM.
DWAYNE?! HE HAS *NOTHING* TO HIDE!

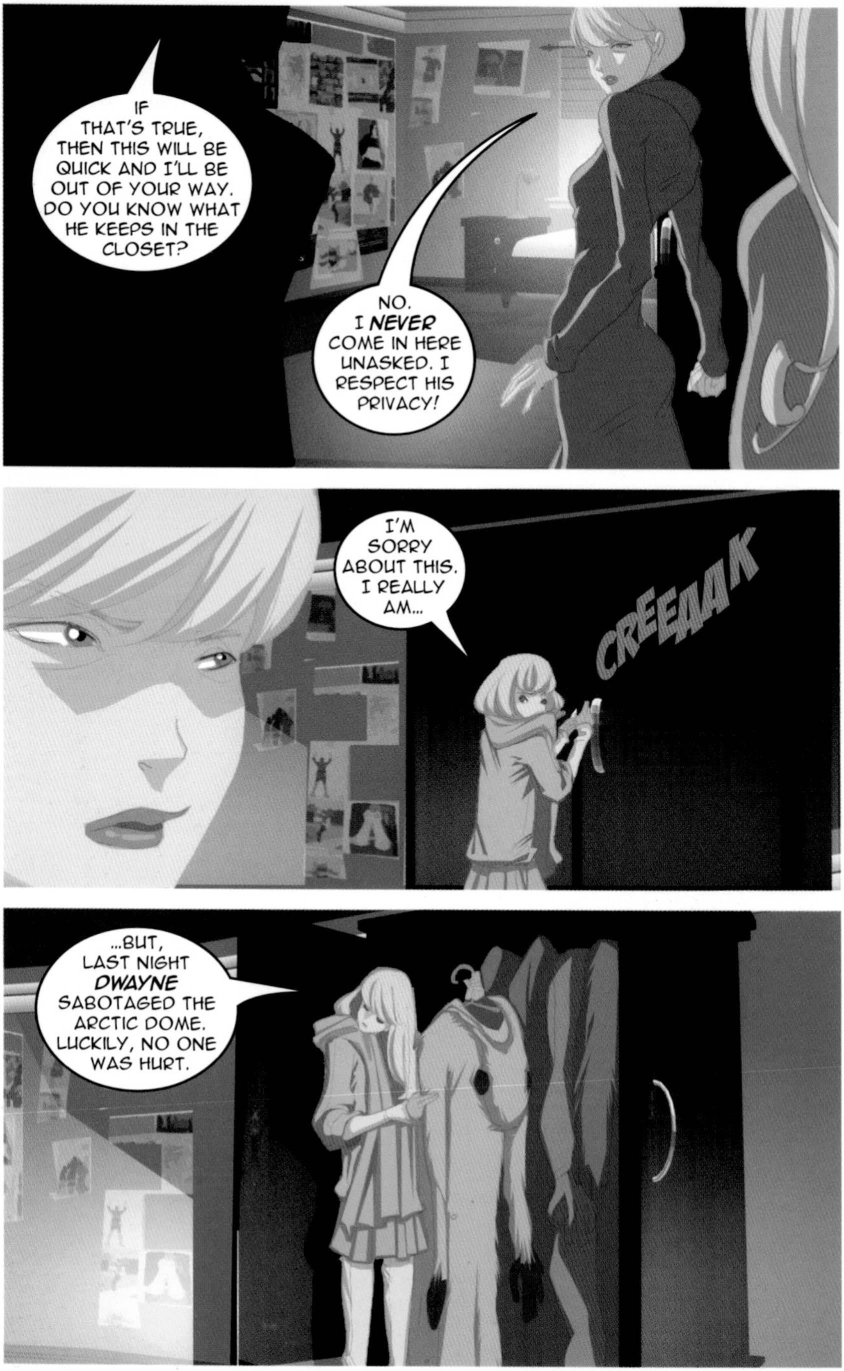
IF THAT'S TRUE, THEN THIS WILL BE QUICK AND I'LL BE OUT OF YOUR WAY. DO YOU KNOW WHAT HE KEEPS IN THE CLOSET?
NO. I *NEVER* COME IN HERE UNASKED. I RESPECT HIS PRIVACY!
I'M SORRY ABOUT THIS. I REALLY AM...
CREEAAK
...BUT, LAST NIGHT *DWAYNE* SABOTAGED THE ARCTIC DOME. LUCKILY, NO ONE WAS HURT.

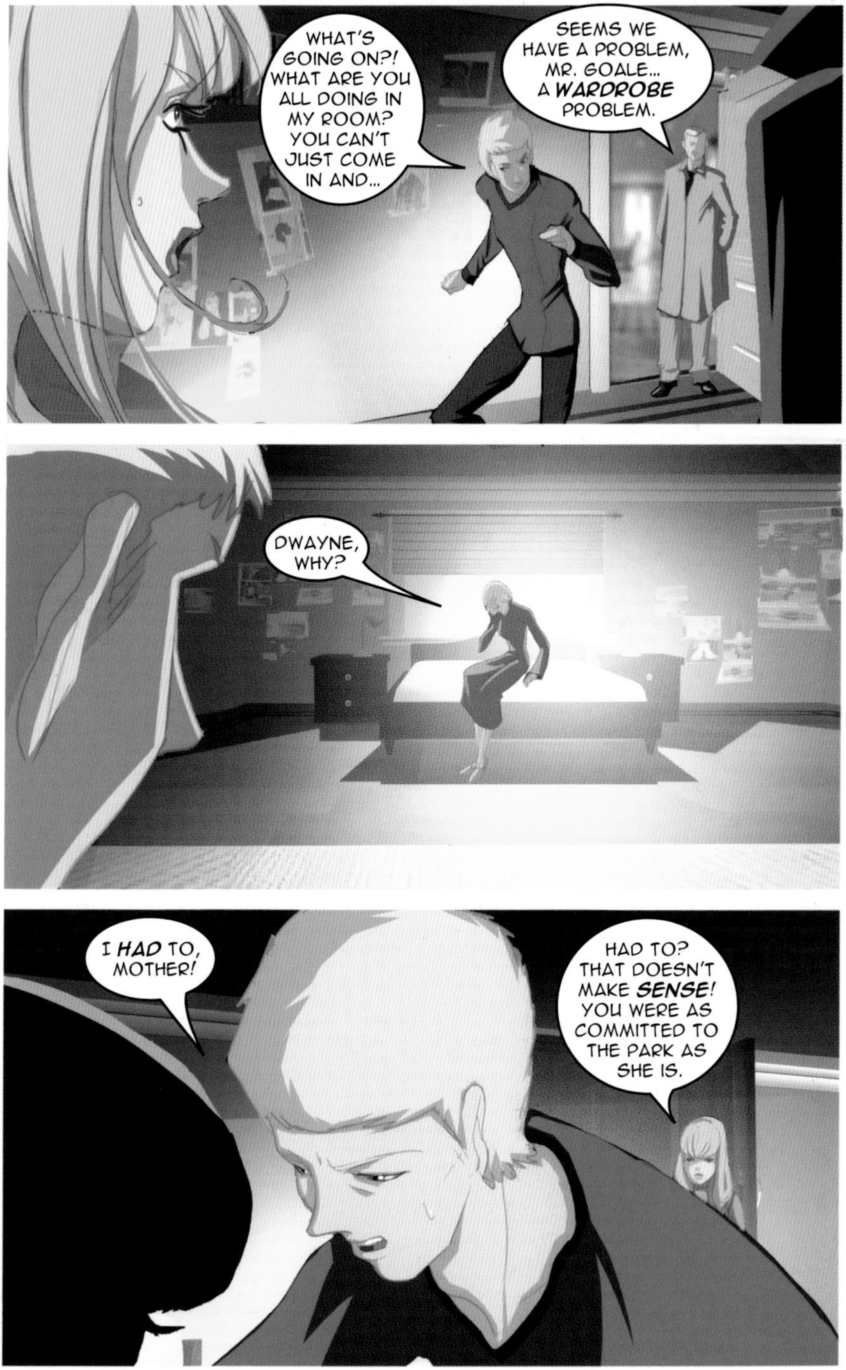
WHAT'S GOING ON?! WHAT ARE YOU ALL DOING IN MY ROOM? YOU CAN'T JUST COME IN AND...
SEEMS WE HAVE A PROBLEM, MR. GOALE... A WARDROBE PROBLEM.
DWAYNE, WHY?
I HAD TO, MOTHER!
HAD TO? THAT DOESN'T MAKE SENSE! YOU WERE AS COMMITTED TO THE PARK AS SHE IS.

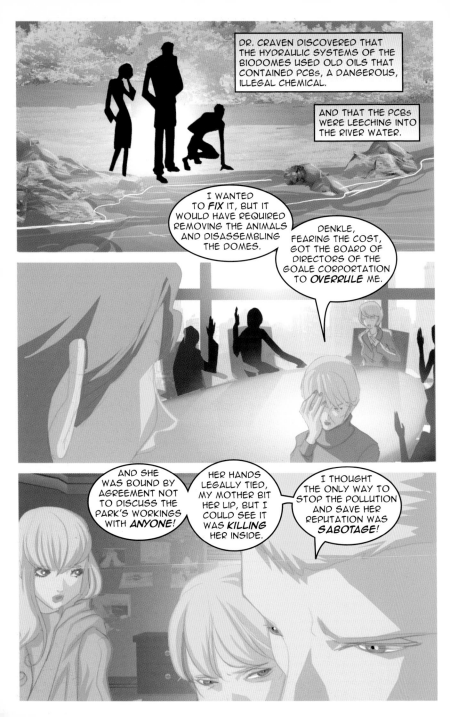

DR. CRAVEN DISCOVERED THAT THE HYDRAULIC SYSTEMS OF THE BIODOMES USED OLD OILS THAT CONTAINED PCBs, A DANGEROUS, ILLEGAL CHEMICAL.

AND THAT THE PCBs WERE LEECHING INTO THE RIVER WATER.

I WANTED TO *FIX* IT, BUT IT WOULD HAVE REQUIRED REMOVING THE ANIMALS AND DISASSEMBLING THE DOMES.

DENKLE, FEARING THE COST, GOT THE BOARD OF DIRECTORS OF THE GOALE CORPORTATION TO *OVERRULE* ME.

AND SHE WAS BOUND BY AGREEMENT NOT TO DISCUSS THE PARK'S WORKINGS WITH *ANYONE!*

HER HANDS LEGALLY TIED, MY MOTHER BIT HER LIP, BUT I COULD SEE IT WAS *KILLING* HER INSIDE.

I THOUGHT THE ONLY WAY TO STOP THE POLLUTION AND SAVE HER REPUTATION WAS *SABOTAGE!*

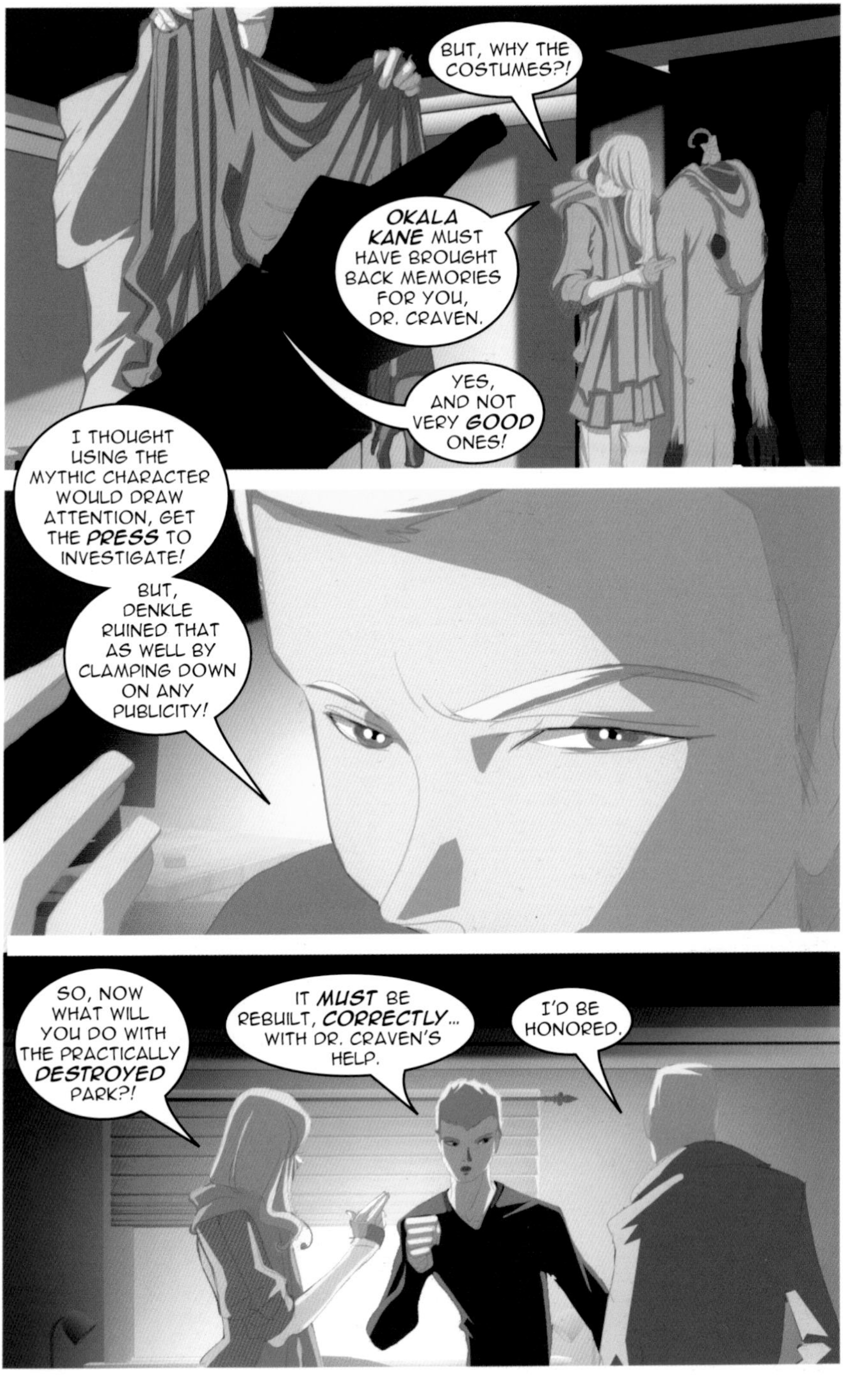
BUT, WHY THE COSTUMES?!
OKALA KANE MUST HAVE BROUGHT BACK MEMORIES FOR YOU, DR. CRAVEN.
YES, AND NOT VERY GOOD ONES!
I THOUGHT USING THE MYTHIC CHARACTER WOULD DRAW ATTENTION, GET THE PRESS TO INVESTIGATE!
BUT, DENKLE RUINED THAT AS WELL BY CLAMPING DOWN ON ANY PUBLICITY!
SO, NOW WHAT WILL YOU DO WITH THE PRACTICALLY DESTROYED PARK?!
IT MUST BE REBUILT, CORRECTLY... WITH DR. CRAVEN'S HELP.
I'D BE HONORED.

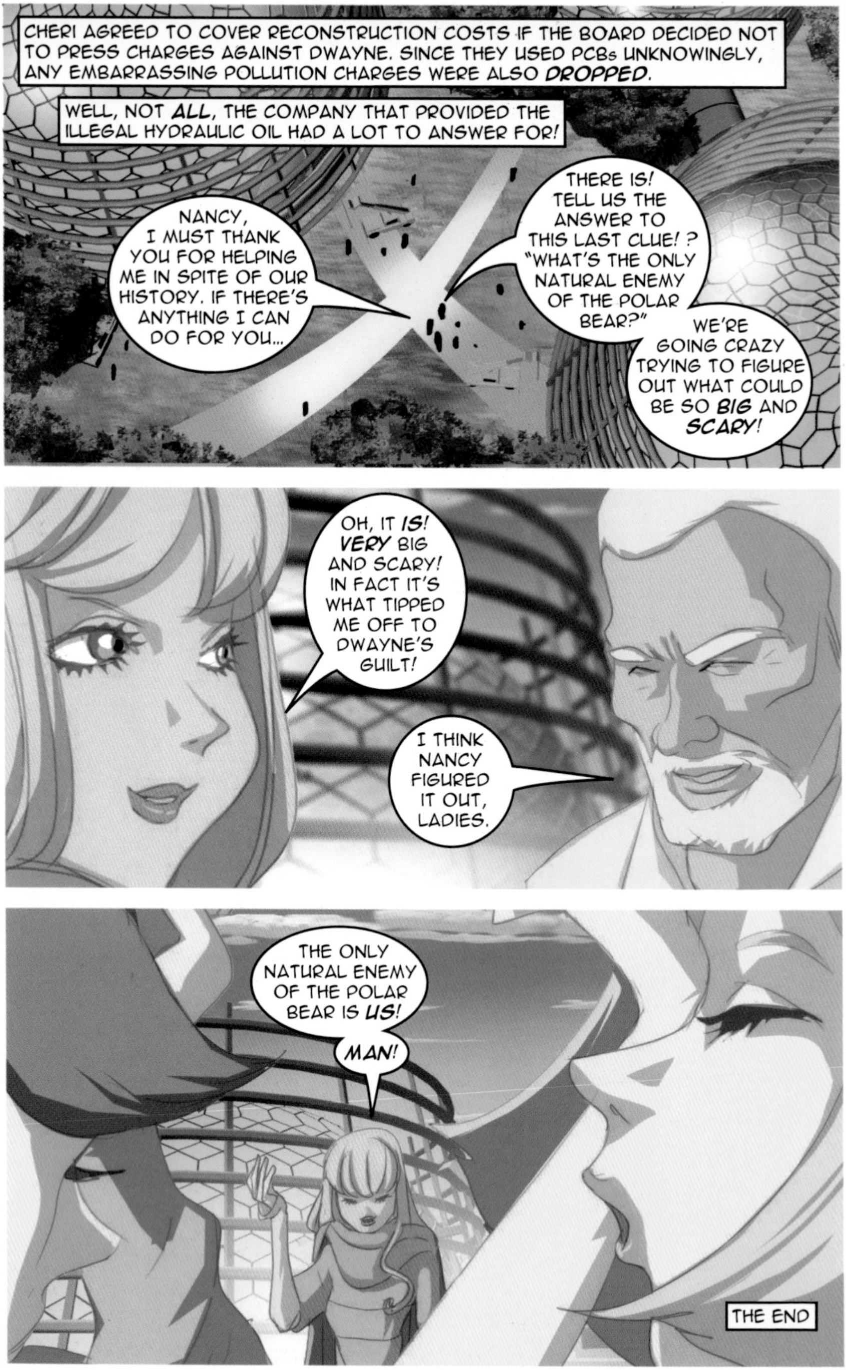
CHERI AGREED TO COVER RECONSTRUCTION COSTS IF THE BOARD DECIDED NOT TO PRESS CHARGES AGAINST DWAYNE. SINCE THEY USED PCBs UNKNOWINGLY, ANY EMBARRASSING POLLUTION CHARGES WERE ALSO *DROPPED*.
WELL, NOT *ALL*, THE COMPANY THAT PROVIDED THE ILLEGAL HYDRAULIC OIL HAD A LOT TO ANSWER FOR!
NANCY, I MUST THANK YOU FOR HELPING ME IN SPITE OF OUR HISTORY. IF THERE'S ANYTHING I CAN DO FOR YOU...
THERE IS! TELL US THE ANSWER TO THIS LAST CLUE! ? "WHAT'S THE ONLY NATURAL ENEMY OF THE POLAR BEAR?"
WE'RE GOING CRAZY TRYING TO FIGURE OUT WHAT COULD BE SO *BIG* AND *SCARY*!
OH, IT *IS*! *VERY* BIG AND SCARY! IN FACT IT'S WHAT TIPPED ME OFF TO DWAYNE'S GUILT!
I THINK NANCY FIGURED IT OUT, LADIES.
THE ONLY NATURAL ENEMY OF THE POLAR BEAR IS *US*!
MAN!
THE END

Back when Nancy Drew and her friend Kalpana were trying to escape from the bad guys in Nancy Drew graphic novel #4 "The Girl Who Wasn't There," they chose to get into a wooden box. It wasn't one of the Girl Detective's better ideas – they got bounced around pretty bad before getting re-captured.

What is a good idea, however, is collecting the first four volumes of Nancy Drew's Papercutz graphic novels in a box. It's such a good idea, that the first four Hardy Boys Papercutz graphic novels are also being collected in a boxed set. If you just started reading either series, these boxed sets are a great way to catch up on the early volumes at a great price. It's also a cool way to store your Nancy Drew and Hardy Boys graphic novels on your bookshelf.

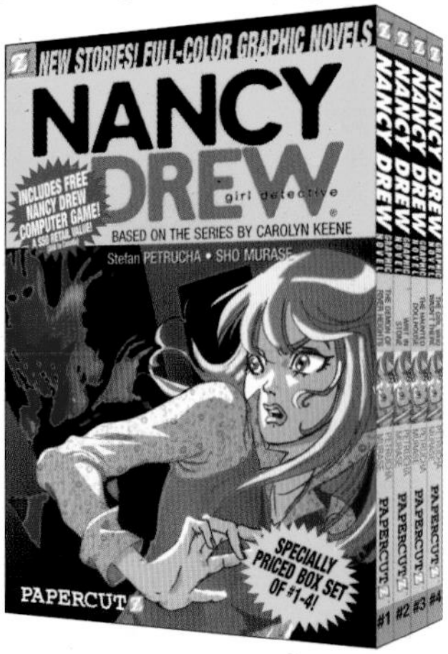
NEW STORIES! FULL-COLOR GRAPHIC NOVELS
NANCY DREW
girl detective
INCLUDES FREE NANCY DREW COMPUTER GAME!
BASED ON THE SERIES BY CAROLYN KEENE
Stefan PETRUCHA • SHO MURASE
SPECIALLY PRICED BOX SET OF #1-4!
PAPERCUTZ

As a super special bonus, every Nancy Drew boxed set also features the Her Interactive Nancy Drew PC game "The Haunted Carousel." The game itself is sold separately for about $20.00, but comes free with the Nancy Drew boxed set. This has got to be one of the best deals ever! And since the Boxed Set also features Nancy Drew graphic novel #4, you get to see how Nancy and Kalpana finally do escape the bad guys!

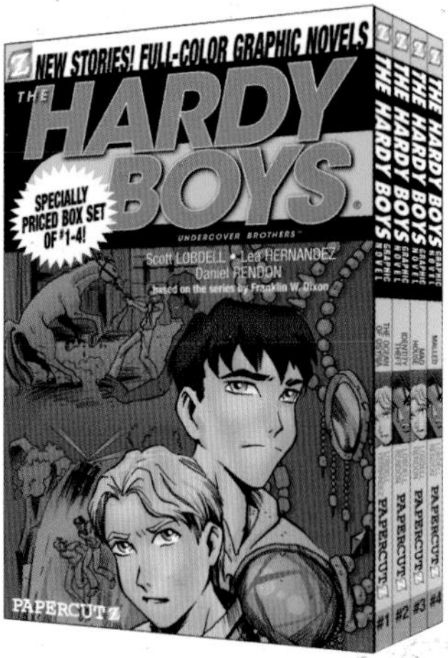
NEW STORIES! FULL-COLOR GRAPHIC NOVELS
THE HARDY BOYS
SPECIALLY PRICED BOX SET OF #1-4!
UNDERCOVER BROTHERS
Scott LOBDELL • Lea HERNANDEZ
Daniel RENDON
PAPERCUTZ

Even if you already have these great graphic novels, the Nancy Drew and The Hardy Boys Boxed Sets make a great holiday or birthday present for friends or family.

If you can't find these great Papercutz Boxed Sets at your favorite bookstores, or at Target or Sam's Clubs, just ask your favorite bookstore to order it for you. They'll be happy to do it.

TWO FOR THE BOOKS...

Everyone at Papercutz is still bustin' with pride that our very first Nancy Drew graphic novel, "The Demon of River Heights" won the 2006 Ben Franklin Award for Best Graphic Novel of the year. So you can just imagine how we felt when we saw The New Book of Knowledge 2006 Annual and it featured an article about the 75th Anniversary of Nancy Drew. The Young People's Book of the Year highlights events from 2005, and right there on page 259 is the beautiful cover of Nancy Drew graphic novel # 1 drawn by Sho Murase. The article is very well-written, giving a fact-filled history of everyone's favorite Girl Detective.

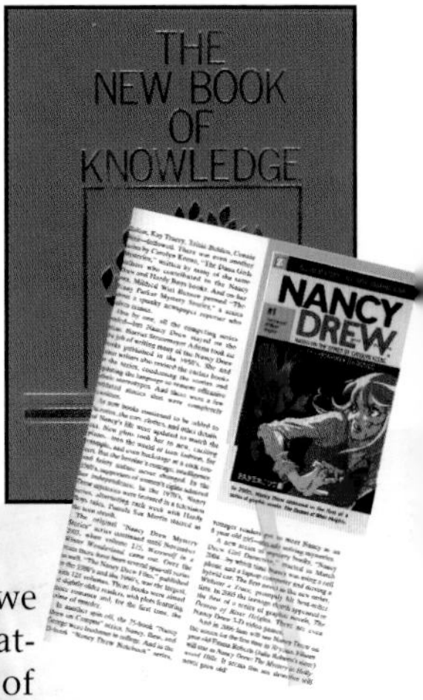
THE NEW BOOK OF KNOWLEDGE
NANCY DREW

For all of us at Papercutz, the publication of our first graphic novels was a major event. After all, we were launching our company as well. We're flattered that the editors of The New Book of Knowledge included the Nancy Drew graphic novel amongst all the amazing events of 2005. We're proud to be a small part of pop culture phenomenon that is Nancy Drew.

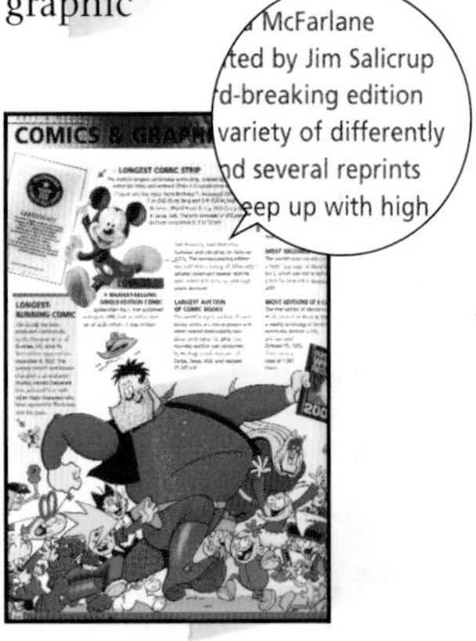

And if all of that wasn't enough to give us all swelled heads, you should've seen our Editor-in-Chief Jim Salicrup when Papercutz letterer Mark Lerer showed him the 2007 Guinness Book of World Records. Turns out that Spider-Man #1, the comic written and drawn by Todd McFarlane that Jim launched back when he was an editor at Marvel Comics is cited as the biggest-selling single-edition issue of comic ever published. While Jim is thrilled by the recognition, he vows to break that record at Papercutz. And at the rate things have been going for the graphic novel publisher for tweens, that may not be such an impossible goal!

Announcing a
NANCY DREW
Adventure so

BIG

IT *TAKES* **3** *GRAPHIC NOVELS*
TO *TELL THE ENTIRE STORY!*

THE HIGH MILES MYSTERY

*Has Nancy Drew solved the energy crisis? This all-new story begins
when she sets out to find a long-lost engine able to get 200 miles
per gallons. There's just one problem – the engine is haunted.*

Special Advance Preview of NANCY DREW # 9 – "Ghost In The Machinery"

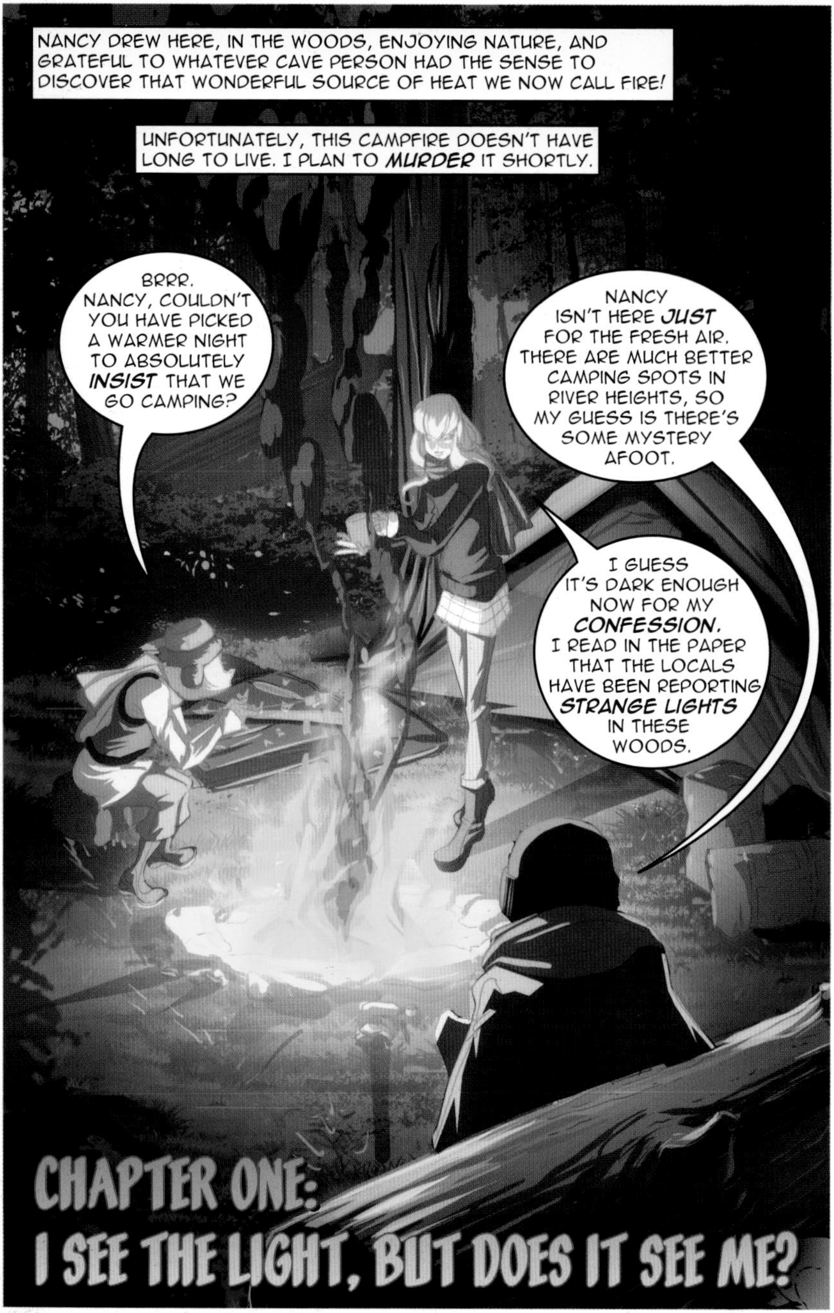
NANCY DREW HERE, IN THE WOODS, ENJOYING NATURE, AND GRATEFUL TO WHATEVER CAVE PERSON HAD THE SENSE TO DISCOVER THAT WONDERFUL SOURCE OF HEAT WE NOW CALL FIRE!
UNFORTUNATELY, THIS CAMPFIRE DOESN'T HAVE LONG TO LIVE. I PLAN TO MURDER IT SHORTLY.
BRRR. NANCY, COULDN'T YOU HAVE PICKED A WARMER NIGHT TO ABSOLUTELY INSIST THAT WE GO CAMPING?
NANCY ISN'T HERE JUST FOR THE FRESH AIR. THERE ARE MUCH BETTER CAMPING SPOTS IN RIVER HEIGHTS, SO MY GUESS IS THERE'S SOME MYSTERY AFOOT.
I GUESS IT'S DARK ENOUGH NOW FOR MY CONFESSION. I READ IN THE PAPER THAT THE LOCALS HAVE BEEN REPORTING STRANGE LIGHTS IN THESE WOODS.
CHAPTER ONE:
I SEE THE LIGHT, BUT DOES IT SEE ME?

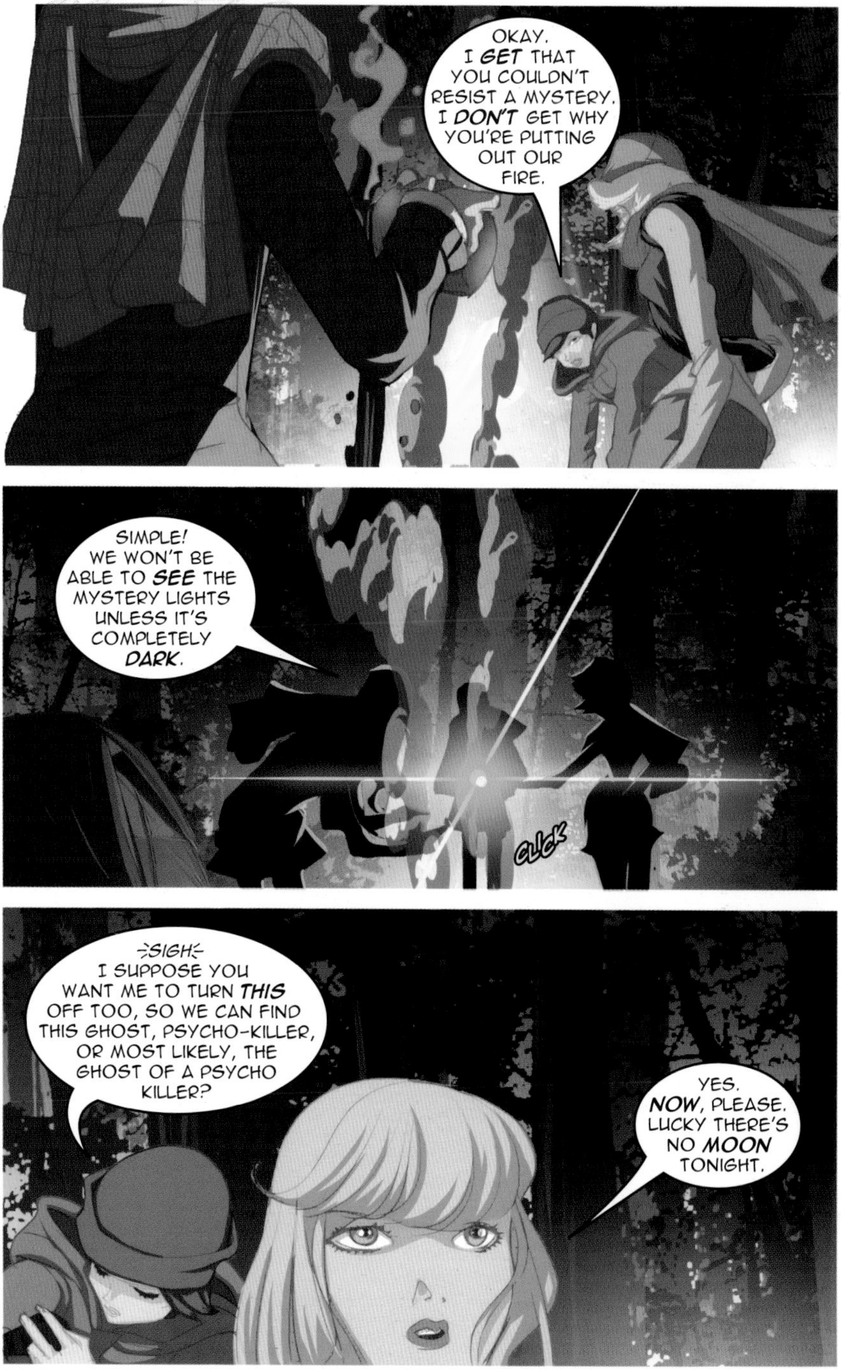
OKAY. I GET THAT YOU COULDN'T RESIST A MYSTERY. I DON'T GET WHY YOU'RE PUTTING OUT OUR FIRE.
SIMPLE! WE WON'T BE ABLE TO SEE THE MYSTERY LIGHTS UNLESS IT'S COMPLETELY DARK.
CLICK
-SIGH- I SUPPOSE YOU WANT ME TO TURN THIS OFF TOO, SO WE CAN FIND THIS GHOST, PSYCHO-KILLER, OR MOST LIKELY, THE GHOST OF A PSYCHO KILLER?
YES. NOW, PLEASE. LUCKY THERE'S NO MOON TONIGHT.

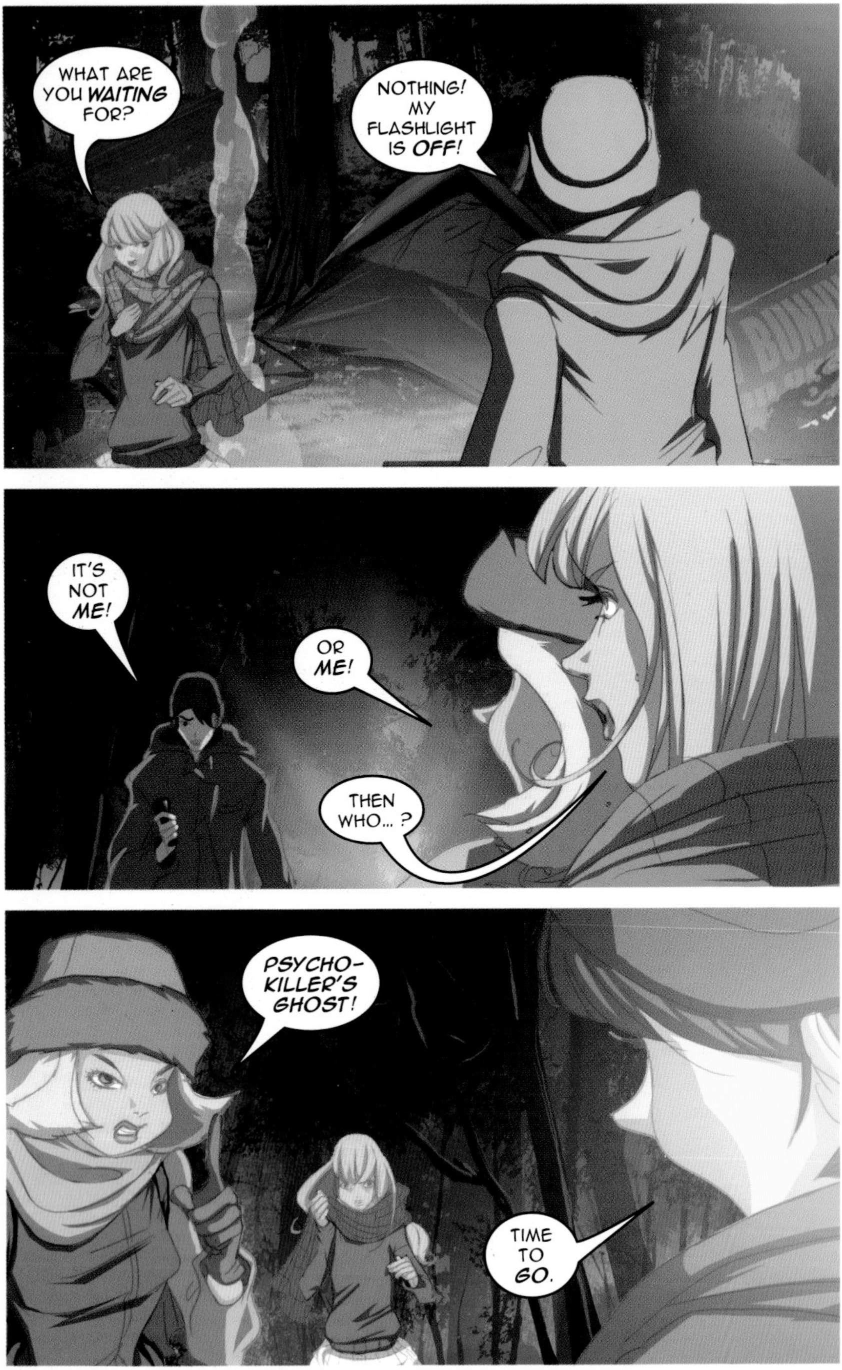
WHAT ARE YOU *WAITING* FOR?
NOTHING! MY FLASHLIGHT IS *OFF*!
IT'S NOT *ME*!
OR *ME*!
THEN WHO... ?
PSYCHO-KILLER'S GHOST!
TIME TO *GO*.

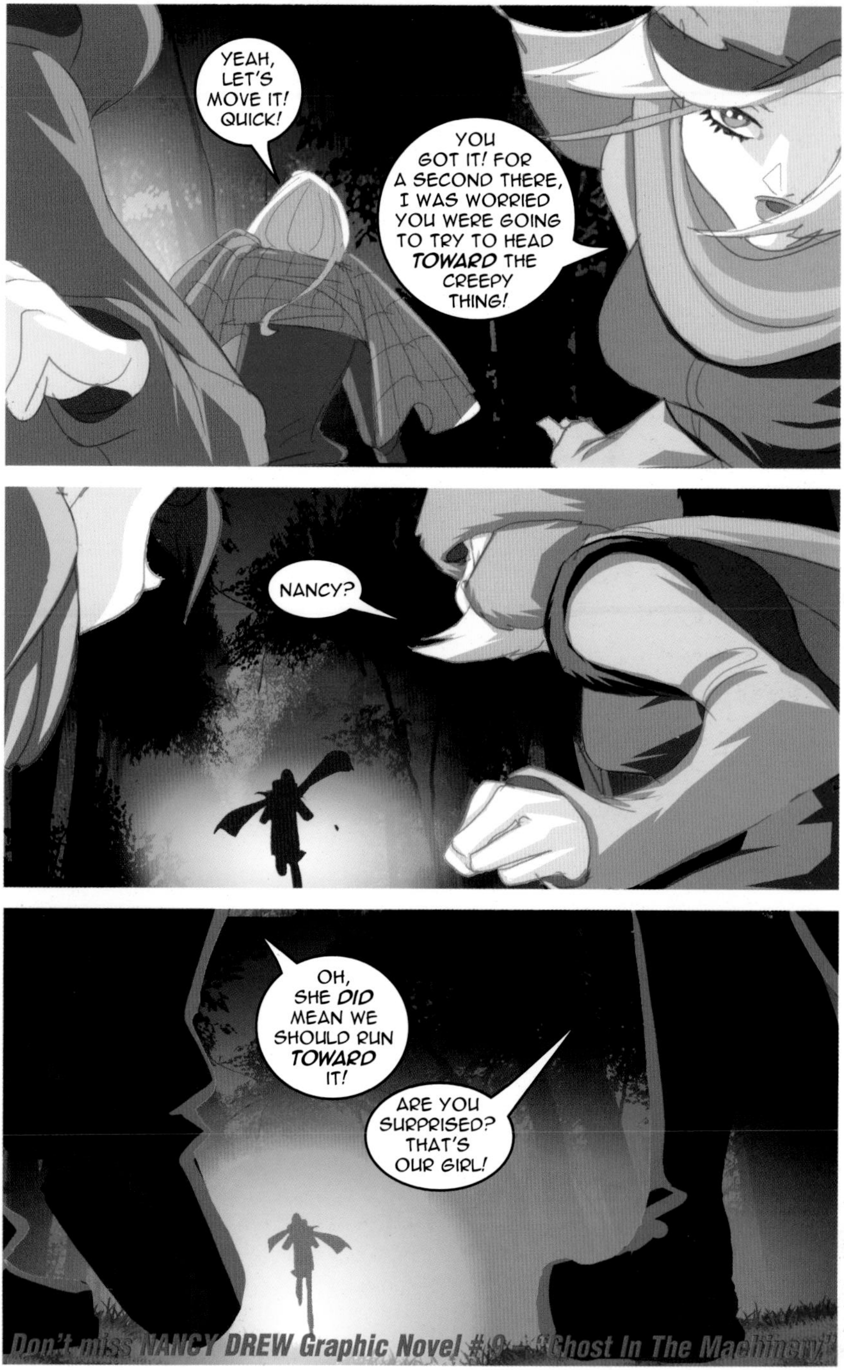
YEAH, LET'S MOVE IT! QUICK!
YOU GOT IT! FOR A SECOND THERE, I WAS WORRIED YOU WERE GOING TO TRY TO HEAD *TOWARD* THE CREEPY THING!
NANCY?
OH, SHE *DID* MEAN WE SHOULD RUN *TOWARD* IT!
ARE YOU SURPRISED? THAT'S OUR GIRL!
Don't miss NANCY DREW Graphic Novel #9 - "Ghost In The Machinery"

Go Undercover in Paris
as Nancy Drew® in
Danger by Design

You, as Nancy Drew, are in Paris to work undercover for a prestigious fashion designer. Minette is all the rage in the fashion world, but strange threats and unwelcome guests are causing her to unravel. It's up to you to stitch the clues together and unmask the mystery in this PC adventure game.

dare to play™

FOR MYSTERY FANS
10 to Adult

Nancy Drew PC Adventure Game #14
Order online at www.HerInteractive.com
or call 1-800-461-8787. Also in stores!
Compatible with WINDOWS® 98/2000/Me/XP/Vista

Created by

Copyright © 2008 Her Interactive, Inc. HER INTERACTIVE, the HER INTERACTIVE logo and DARE TO PLAY are trademarks of Her Interactive, Inc. NANCY DREW is a registered trademark of Simon & Schuster, Inc. Licensed by permission of Simon & Schuster, Inc.

THE HARDY BOYS

A NEW GRAPHIC NOVEL EVERY 3 MONTHS!

#1 "The Ocean of Osyria",
ISBN 1-59707-001-7
#2 "Identity Theft," ISBN 1-59707-003-3
#3 "Mad House," ISBN 1-59707-010-6
#4 "Malled," ISBN 1-59707-014-9
#5 "Sea You, Sea Me!",
ISBN 1-59707-022-X
NEW! Hyde & Shriek
Joe and Frank are enlisted as undercover protection for a visiting dignitary's daughter attending a party at a horror-themed restaurant. An assassin lurks...
ISBN 1-59707-028-9
Each: 5x7 1/2, 96pp., full color paperback: $7.95,
Also available in hardcover!
$12.95 each.
Vol. 1: ISBN 1-59707-005-X
Vol. 2: ISBN 1-59707-007-6
Vol. 3: ISBN 1-59707-011-4
Vol. 4: ISBN 1-59707-015-7
Vol. 5: ISBN 1-59707-023-8
Vol. 6: ISBN 1-59707-029-7

ZORRO®

#1 "Scars!," ISBN 1-59707-016-5
#2 "Drownings!," ISBN 1-59707-018-1
#3 "Vultures," ISBN 1-59707-020-3
Each: 5x7 1/2, 96pp., full color paperback: $7.95
Also available in hardcover!
$12.95 each.
Vol. 1: ISBN 1-59707-017-3
Vol. 2: ISBN 1-59707-019-X
Vol. 3: ISBN 1-59707-021-1

The Hardy Boys: Undercover Brothers™ Simon & Schuster

©2006 Zorro Productions, Inc. All Rights Reserved. ZORRO®.

PAPERCUTZ™

At your store or order at Papercutz, 40 Exchange Pl., Ste. 1308, New York, NY 10005, 1-800-886-1223 (M-F 9-6 EST)

MC, VISA, AMEX accepted, add $3 P&H for 1st item, $1 each additional. Distributed by Holtzbrinck

www.papercutz.com

Eye a mystery . . .

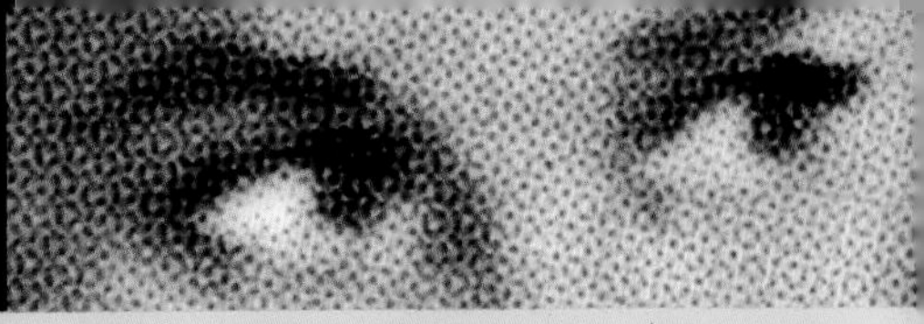

Read NANCY DREW

girl detective™

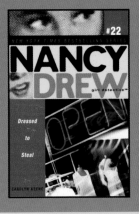

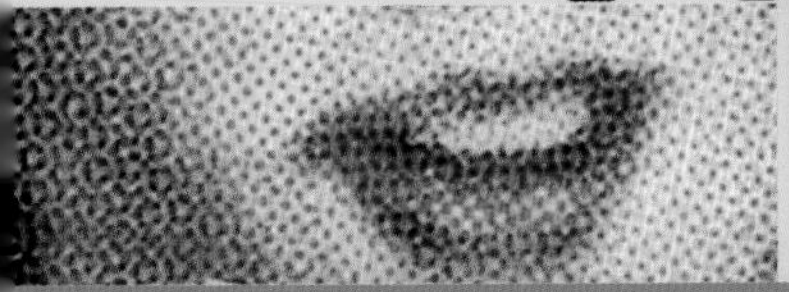

#22

Dressed to Steal
New in February 2007

Hot young designer Alicia Adams is opening a boutique in her hometown of River Heights, and the press isall over the event. Opening day turns out to be more popular than expected—a surging crowd leads to the store window being smashed! Alicia's most expensive dress is destroyed, and her whole store is vandalized. Nancy may not be a fashion expert, but this is one case she's ready to size up!

Have you solved all of Nancy's latest cases?

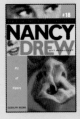

Pit of Vipers

The Orchid Thief

Getting Burned

Close Encounters

Coming in April!

Troubled Waters

Visit www.SimonSaysSleuth.com for more Nancy Drew books.

WATCH OUT FOR PAPERCUTZ™
The publisher of graphic novels created just for YOU!

Hi, Papercutz people! It's me Jim Salicrup, the luckiest graphic novel editor in the world! Every day I get to work with the best writers, artists, letterers, and colorists to create comics for the best fans in the world – YOU!

As you may've noticed, we've added these Papercutz back-pages — at no extra cost – to all of our ongoing graphic novel series. It's our way of keeping you up-to-date with all the excitement happening at Papercutz.

For example, we've got a great interview with Hardy Boys writer Scott Lobdell, an update on the new Nancy Drew movie, reports on Papercutz on Campus and in The New Book of Knowledge, and even a look at the very first Hardy Boys comicbook!

In fact, we're covering so much that we don't have any room left to tell you what's up in the world of Totally Spies! You'll just have to check www.papercutz.com or www.totallyspies.com for latest news regarding Alex, Sam, and Clover.

And don't forget – we always want to hear from you! Tell us what you think of our stories, our artwork, our characters, or anything at all regarding our graphic novels! Email me at salicrup@papercutz.com or send your comments to Papercutz, 40 Exchange Place, Ste. 1308, New York, NY 10005. Our goal is to create the kind of graphic novels that you want – so tell us how we're doing!
Thanks,

JIM

Totally Spies! is a trademark of Marathon Animation ©2006 Marathon-Mystery Animation Inc. All rights resesrrved. Caricature drawn by Steve Brodner at The 2005 MoCCA Art Fest.

PAPERCUTZ™
ON CAMPUS

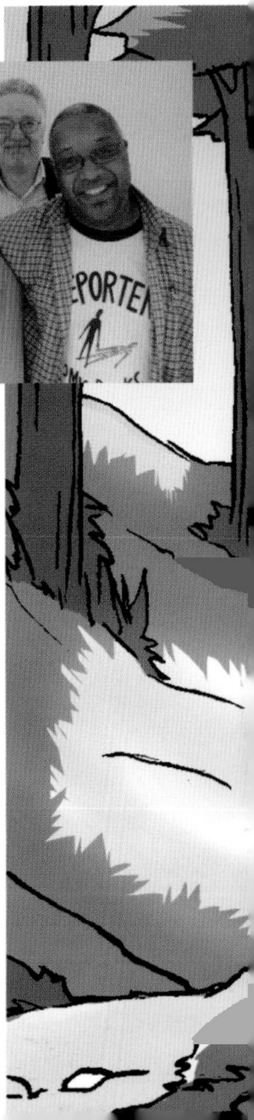

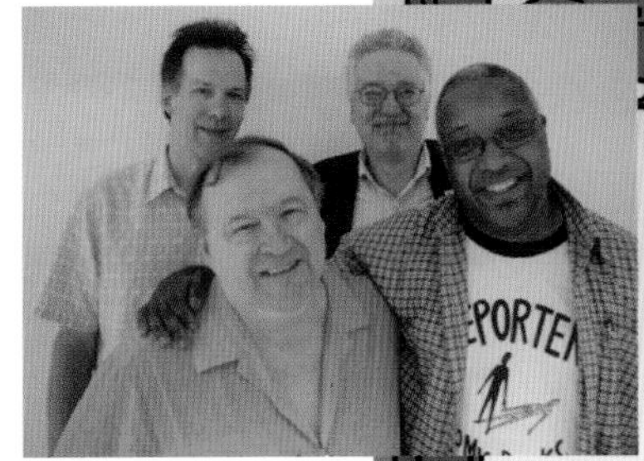

This may be hard to believe, but once upon a time comics were actually looked down upon by certain ill-informed individuals. We're delighted to report that those dark days are far behind us. These days comics and graphic novels are now strongly embraced by the academic community. Recently Papercutz Editor-in-Chief Jim Salicrup and Zorro writer Don McGregor were invited to join Pete Friedrich, editor of Roadstrips: A Graphic Journey Across America, on a panel hosted by Publishers Weekly Senior News Editor, Calvin Reid, all about graphic novels at the Columbia School of Journalism. The panel was presented before the one hundred students enrolled in the publishing course, which included graphic novels. The highly attentive audience had lots of great questions during the Q&A segment, and moderator Calvin Reid did an amazing job of keeping our long-winded Editor-in-Chief from going off on too many tangents. Don McGregor, whose Sabre graphic novel was one of the first to be offered to the American comics market directly in 1978, spoke enthusiastically, in his inimitable manner, about his experiences in the comics world. Jim Salicrup shared some of his experiences working with Don, especially how they approached taking the classic Zorro character and adapting it into the Papercutz graphic novel style. That style is to create the best possible graphic novels for audiences of all ages. In Zorro graphic novels #1-3, Don along with artist Sidney Lima does just that. Both Jim and Don had a great time talking to the students, and signing copies of Zorro graphic novel #1, "Scars!" But when it was all over, Jim had to restrain himself from saying, "Class dismissed!"

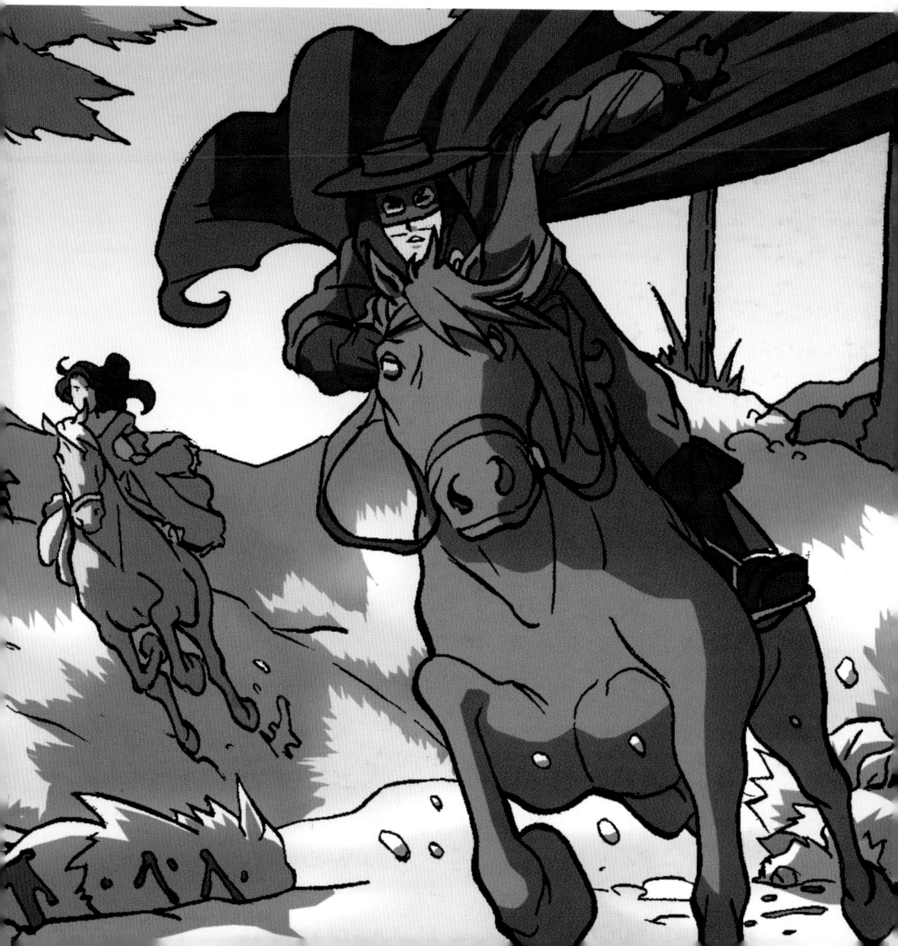

The Write Stuff

The Write Stuff

When Papercutz decided to publish the adventures of The Hardy Boys in all-new graphic novels, we never imagined we'd be able to land superstar writer Scott Lobdell, famed for his best-selling run on Marvel's The Uncanny X-Men, but somehow we did! We're thankful that Scott recently took time out of his busy movie and comics writing to answer a few questions for this interview…

The Hardy Boys ®Simon & Schuster

Papercutz: Tell us, Scott, where are you from?
Scott: I come from a small town in upstate New York where I was raised with six brothers and sisters —quite a different experience from Joe and Frank's upbringing! I will tell you one thing, though, when you live in such a large family there isn't a lot of room for privacy so you come to appreciate your secrets because they are yours. Now, here I am, all these years later, writing the adventures of two of the world's most famous secret-busters.

Papercutz: How did you become a writer?
Scott: Years and years of rejection letters from magazines, comics, book publishers... but I kept trying. And maybe more importantly, I kept listening to the criticism and instructions from friends, family, and editors. I think, too often, beginning writers want only praise for their efforts and it is difficult to hear suggestions, or to hear that something is unclear or confusing in early drafts. I think by listening I was able to challenge myself to be a better writer. I used to say of comics "Either they are going to give up or I am! And I'm not!"

Papercutz: Did you read all the original Hardy Boys books by Franklin W. Dixon? Which is your favorite?
Scott: That is like asking me to pick out my favorite ice cream — or favorite snowflake! Every book is its own experience!

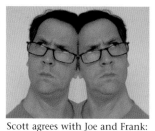

Papercutz: How would you describe the Hardy Boys?

Scott agrees with Joe and Frank: when solving crimes, two heads are better than one!

Scott: There have been a lot of famous detectives over the years, each interesting in their own way. But

what I think is so compelling about Joe and Frank is their relationship. In some families there are brothers who haven't spoken for years — but here are the Hardy Boys who not only share their every adventure, but need to trust each other along every step of every case. They enjoy being together and they've always got each other's back. The only thing cooler than having a cool brother is being one.

Papercutz: Where do you get your ideas?
Scott: Specifically, my Hardy Boys ideas seem to come from the headlines. The *Ocean of Osyria* and *Identity Theft* were both based on an all too real world problems. I often think, "If Joe and Frank lived in the here and now, what kind of problems would they be called on to solve as undercover brothers?"... And then I start writing.

The Hardy Boys in Comics!

Did you know that the all-new Hardy Boys graphic novels from Papercutz are not the first time Joe and Frank Hardy appeared in comics? It's actually the third series of Hardy Boys comics. We've done a little detective work ourselves and have come up with a bit of background information on the historic, very first series of Hardy Boys comics.

Way back in the 1940s and 1950s, one of the biggest comicbook publishers was Dell Comics. Known for their snappy motto, "Dell Comics are Good Comics," one of their top titles was called Four Color Comics, a reference to the four basic colors used in printing comicbooks. Surprisingly, the "Four Color Comics" title wasn't on most of its covers. According to the Official Overstreet Comic Book Price Guide, Dell published two series of Four Color Comics, the first lasting just 25 issues, and the second running for a record-breaking 1,354 issues. Yet it only was called Four Color Comics on #19 – 25 of the first series and on #1-99 and 101 of the second. Each issue featured a popular TV, movie, or comic strip character, and it was the name of the featured character that was displayed as the title on the covers. One issue could feature a western adventure based on the Gunsmoke TV series, another could adapt a John Wayne movie such as The Searchers, and yet another could spotlight comic-strip star, Mandrake, the Magician. In 1956, Four Color Comics #760 featured Walt Disney's The Hardy Boys.

"*Walt Disney's* The Hardy Boys"? That's correct. Back in 1955, the daily Disney TV series, The Mickey Mouse Club, featured a live-action four-part Hardy Boys adventure, "The Mystery of the Applegate Treasure" based on the classic Franklin W. Dixon series. The serial starred Tim Considine as Frank Hardy, Tommy Kirk as Joe Hardy, Russ Conway as Fenton Hardy, Carol Ann Campbell as Iola Morton, and Sarah Selby as Aunt Gertrude. Each episode was just fifteen minutes long, but it must've packed quite a punch. Just a couple of years later, the same cast were reunited for a fifteen-part Hardy Boys serial for The Mickey Mouse Club called "The Mystery of the Ghost Farm." The episodes have recently been released on DVD as part of the Walt Disney Treasures series.

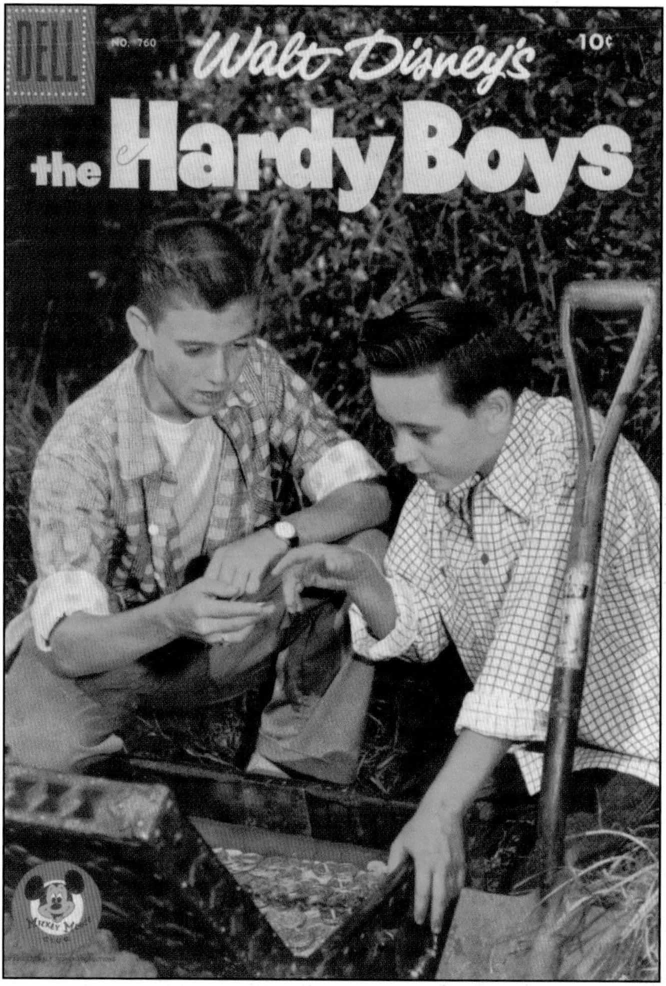
DELL
NO. 760
Walt Disney's
10¢
the Hardy Boys

The Hardy Boys ®Simon & Schuster

The very first Hardy Boys comicbook.

Papercutz Trivia Quiz

1) Who is the other Papercutz superstar who appeared on a Disney series in the 50s?
2) Which real-life Papercutz person appeared on Disney's The Mickey Mouse Club?
(Answers on next page)

Since Four Color Comics adapted so many Disney TV shows, it seemed only natural that they'd also include the TV version of The Hardy Boys. While the stars were just 15 and 14 years old at the time of their first Hardy Boys serial, and Tommy Kirk wasn't blond, the serial did capture the spirit of the classic books. The comic-book covers featured photos from the TV serial, and the interior artwork featured the actors' likenesses. The first comic nicely adapted "The Mystery of the Applegate Treasure," with suitably shadowy artwork providing the proper mysterious mood. Three more issues of Four Color Comics featured The Hardy Boys, #830 (August '57), #887 (January '58), and #964 (January '59). The Hardy Boys wouldn't appear in comics again until 1970 – but that's a story we'll save for the next installment of "The Hardy Boys in Comics!"

Walt Disney
TREASURES
THE HARDY BOYS
THE MICKEY MOUSE CLUB
FEATURES RARE MATERIAL

Hardy Boys DVD

NEW STORY! FULL-COLOR GRAPHIC NOVEL
THE HARDY BOYS
#8
BOARD TO DEATH
UNDERCOVER BROTHERS
Scott LOBDELL
Paulo HENRIQUE
PAPERCUTZ

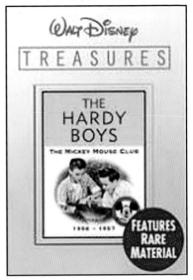

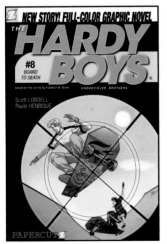

Available now!

Answers:

1)The star of three Papercutz graphic novels, Zorro. He was played by Guy Williams in the Disney TV series, which debuted September, 1957.

2)Papercutz Editor-in-Chief Jim Salicrup appeared on an episode of the 90's revival of The Mickey Mouse Club, which also featured Britney Spears, Christina Aguilera, K.C. Chasez, Keri Russell, Ryan Gosling, and Justin Timberlake.

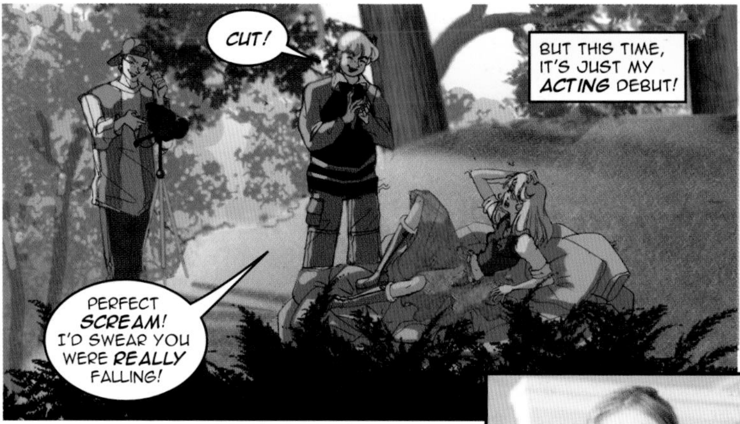
CUT!
BUT THIS TIME, IT'S JUST MY ACTING DEBUT!
PERFECT SCREAM! I'D SWEAR YOU WERE REALLY FALLING!

Nancy Drew®Simon & Schuster

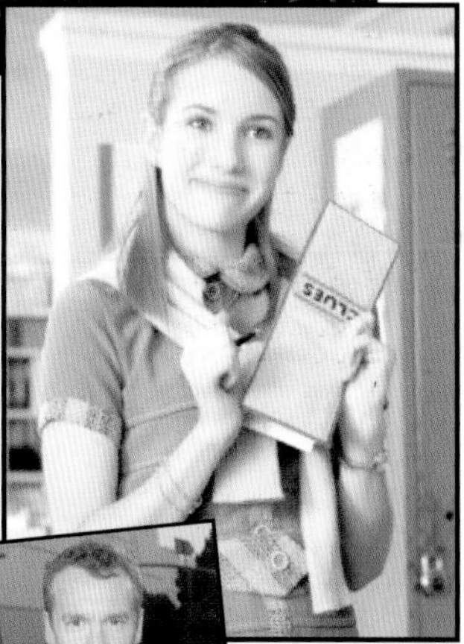

NANCY DREW MOVIE UPDATE – COMING SOONER!

Great news, Nancy Drew fans! The release of the all-new Nancy Drew movie Warner Bros. has been moved from August 2007 to June 2007! That's right, the movie we've all been waiting for will soon be at your local multiplex starting the 15th of June 2007, starring Emma Roberts, of Nickelodeon's hit show *Unfabulous*, as our favorite Girl Detective.

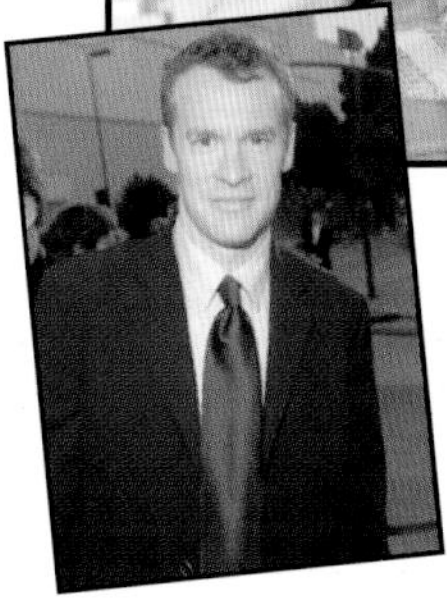

Time Magazine, commenting on a Emma's similarity to a certain major movie star said, "Jeepers, she looks familiar!" Noting that Emma "shares the broad, screen-ready smile of her Aunt Julia (yes, that Julia)." The New York Daily News reported that Emma thought making the film "was a lot of hard work" but that she "liked the way it turned out." In the movie she has to "unravel a Hollywood mystery. Probably the most challenging thing was there was a lot of running around and a lot of stunts." The movie also stars Tate Donovan, as Nancy's lawyer dad, Carson Drew.

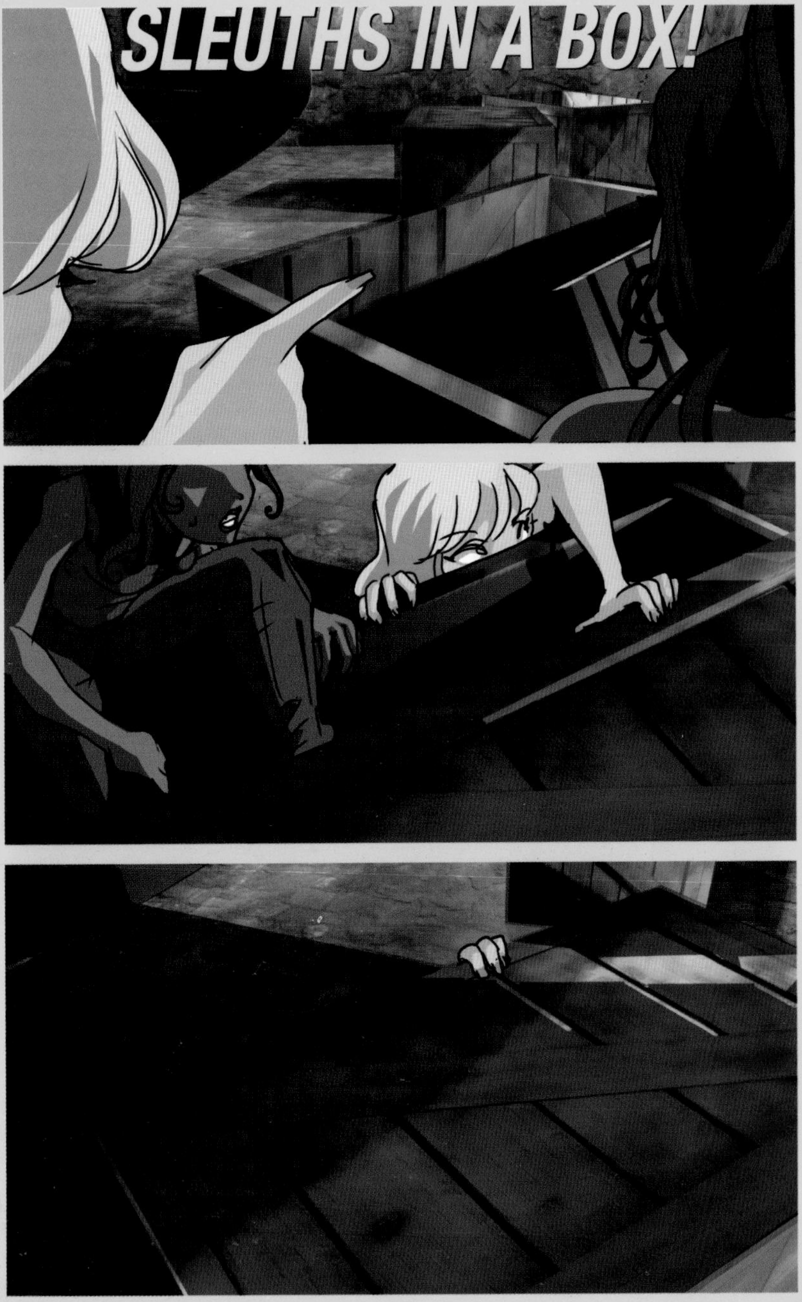
SLEUTHS IN A BOX!

Nancy Drew in a box.

...it's young Karol Wojtyla, the boy who would become Pope John Paul II.

It's just a small part of the special Papercutz graphic novel The Life of John Paul II ...*In Comics!* It's an epic true tale of a young Polish boy and his amazing life. Here's a review that we just have to share with you...

"Once in a lifetime, someone extraordinary rises from the sea of humanity to lead by example.

"Pope John Paul II, Karol Wojtyla, was that man for our century. The leader of the Catholic Church, he rose from war torn Poland amidst propaganda, from a life of athletics to answer the greater call. Karol Wojtyla (1920-2005) gave himself fully to the Church, his savior Jesus, and to the service of those around him.

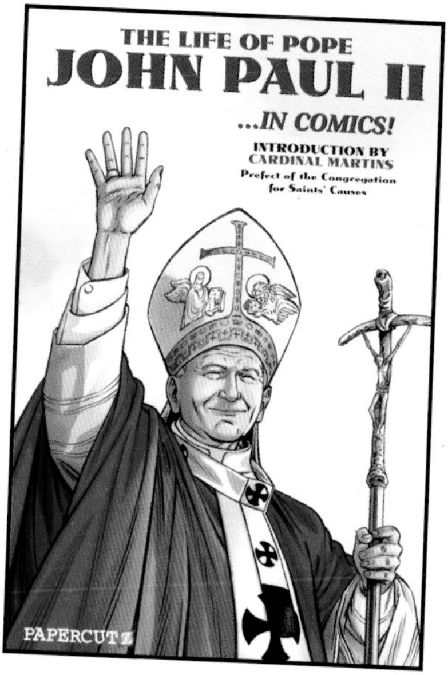
THE LIFE OF POPE
JOHN PAUL II
...IN COMICS!
INTRODUCTION BY
CARDINAL MARTINS
Prefect of the Congregation
for Saints' Causes
PAPERCUTZ

"Alessandro Mainardi and Werner Maresta and have combined their talents to tell the story of the Man who would be Pope, the man who reached out to the youth of the world, the man who reached out with an olive branch of ecumenism. The resulting 96 page graphic novel is outstanding. With such an active life, this could easily have been a thousand-pages long, but prayerfully chosen incidents portray the growth of young Karol from child, to actor, to priest, to bishop to Pope. Along the way, God's hand can be clearly seen in his life. As Pope, he traveled the world. As Pope, he reached out to any who hear. As Pope, he visited his native Poland to bring the gospel message and hope.

"The inspirational papacy he led is described from his own words and his faith and hope clearly shine through. I love the inclusion of scripture, and the thoughtful pacing of the story. Even after his passing, his influence will carry on.

"One of the many faith filled moments that captured me as I read this was the closing of his letters...OAMG, 'Omnium ad Maioram Dei Gloriam', all in the highest glory of God. I was filled with awe and a sense of admiration for Pope John Paul II.

"Through his example, the whole world was inspired. Just like you will be when you read this book.

"Look for this at your local bookstore or online at www.papercutz.com.

"I remain,

"A man of faith.

"Tim Lasiuta

"OAMG"

A PAPERCUTZ™ MINI-MYSTERY?

Can you identify the boy being shot at on this page?

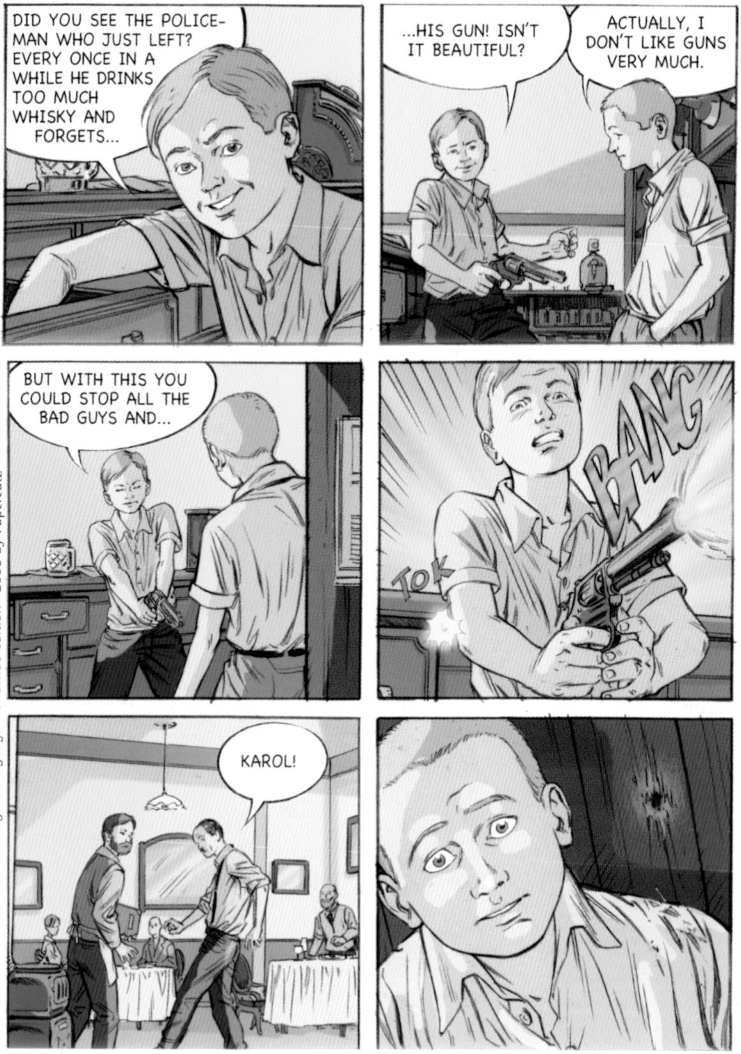

DID YOU SEE THE POLICEMAN WHO JUST LEFT? EVERY ONCE IN A WHILE HE DRINKS TOO MUCH WHISKY AND FORGETS...
...HIS GUN! ISN'T IT BEAUTIFUL?
ACTUALLY, I DON'T LIKE GUNS VERY MUCH.
BUT WITH THIS YOU COULD STOP ALL THE BAD GUYS AND...
BANG
TOK
KAROL!

Turn the page for the answer...